This book is exceptional. It is a great read well worth your time.
—*Book Referees*

Also by Bernard L. McFadden

Also by Bernice L. McFadden:

Gathering of Waters
Glorious
Nowhere Is a Place
Loving Donovan
The Warmest December
Sugar
Camilla's Roses
This Bitter Earth

The Book of Harlan

Bernice L. McFadden

JACARANDA

This edition first published in Great Britain 2021
Jacaranda Books Art Music Ltd
27 Old Gloucester Street,
London WC1N 3AX
www.jacarandabooksartmusic.co.uk

A CIP catalogue record for this book is available from the British
Library

ISBN: 9781913090807
eISBN: 9781909762442

Cover Design: Jeremy Hopes
Typeset by: Kamillah Brandes
Printed and bound by CPI Group (UK) Ltd, Croydon, CR0 4YY

For the Ancestors

I am the man, I suffered, I was there.
—Walt Whitman

Part I

Macon, Georgia

Chapter I

No matter what you may have heard about Macon, Georgia—the majestic magnolias, gracious antebellum homes, the bright stars it produced that went on to dazzle the world—if you were Emma Robinson, bubbling with teenage angst and lucid dreaming about silver-winged sparrows gliding over a perfumed ocean, well then, Macon felt less like the promised land and more like a noose.

Emma, the lone girl, the last child behind three brothers, was born on June 19. Juneteenth—one of the most revered days on the Negro calendar. Triply blessed with a straight nose, milky-brown complexion, and soft hair that would never have to endure the smoldering teeth of a hot comb.

Emma Robinson lived with her family in a mint-green and white L-shaped Victorian cottage located in the highfalutin colored section of Macon known as Pleasant Hill—a district peopled with doctors, lawyers, ministers, and teachers. Not a maid or ditch digger amongst them.

In her home, she had many pets: a brown mutt called Peter, a calico named Samantha, and Adam and Eve, a pair of lovebirds that lived in a cage so ornate, it resembled a crown.

The Robinson family traveled the city in a shiny black buggy, pulled by not one but two horses.

Emma should have been christened Riley because that's whose life she was living. Not only that, she was a natural-born pianist who took to the classics as easily as flame to paper. Emma could listen to a piece of music once and replicate it perfectly. She was so skilled that at the age of seven her minister father installed her as the lead organist in his church.

Reverend Tenant M. Robinson was a dark-skinned, rotund man whose spirited sermons at the Cotton Way Baptist Church attracted a large and dedicated following. On Sunday mornings, those parishioners who did not have the good sense to arrive early enough to claim a seat found themselves standing in the vestibule or shoulder to shoulder against a wall.

Emma's mother, Louisa Robinson, was a beautiful, soft-spoken woman who had come to God late in life, but now walked in his light with grace and humility.

On the outside, Emma didn't seem to want for anything, but let's be clear—she was starving on the inside. Not the coal-burning-belly type of hunger of the destitute, but the agonizing longing of a free spirit, caged.

Emma's best friend was Lucille Nelson, who'd been singing in the church choir for as long as Emma had been playing the organ. Their renditions of "Steal Away to Jesus," "Amazing Grace," and "Go Down Moses" rattled the wood-slated church and brought the congregation to their feet.

While they loved singing about the Lord, whenever the girls could escape their parents' watchful eyes, they headed down to the juke joint on Ocmulgee River. There, hidden in the tall grass, they spied on those shaking, shimmying sinners who raised glasses of gut liquor to the very music Emma's father vehemently railed against.

"The blues promotes the devil's glee," he growled from the pulpit, "encouraging infidelity and lawlessness!"

Sometimes, when Lucille was washing dishes and passing them off to her mother Minnie to dry, those sinful songs found their way onto her tongue.

Minnie would cock her head and ask, "Where'd you hear that from?"

And Lucille would just laugh, grab Minnie's soapy hands, and dance her around the kitchen.

Chapter 2

In 1915, when the girls were still just teenagers, Lucille went out for and won a bit part in a local musical. On opening night, she walked onto the stage of the Douglass Theatre, barely whispered her one line—"I see a rainbow"—and then belted out a song that brought the house down.

Leonard Harper, the founder of the Leonard Harper Minstrel Stock Company, happened to be there that night. By the time Lucille joined the other actors onstage for a final bow, Harper had already located her parents. When the curtain fell, the ink on the contract he had them sign was still damp.

Weeks later, Harper whisked Lucille off on a seven-month tour of the American South. When she returned home to Macon, the old year was dead, and Lucille was a brand-new woman.

When Emma heard that Lucille was back in town, she immediately rushed over to see her, sweeping into the parlor like a gale. But Emma lost all her bluster when her eyes collided with Lucille's rouged cheeks, shiny marcelled hair, and painted lips.

"Lu-Lucille?"

"Hey, Em." Lucille strolled toward her with newly unshackled hips swaying like the screen door of a whorehouse.

"Lucille?" Emma muttered again as she took a cautious backward step.

Lucille wrapped her arms around Emma's shoulders, smothering her in cinnamon-and-rose-scented perfume. "I missed you

16

so much."

"Me... me too," Emma stammered in response, as she broke the embrace. "You look different."

"Yeah, I guess." Lucille shrugged. "How you been?"

Emma couldn't stop staring. "Okay."

"That's good." Lucille sauntered over to the piano, sat down, and skipped her fingers over the black and white keys. "You still go down to the river on Saturday afternoons?"

"Nah. They closed that juke joint down."

Lucille's eyebrows arched. "Was that your daddy's doing?"

Now it was Emma's turn to shrug her shoulders.

"Oh, that's awful," Lucille huffed. "That place was the one good thing about this town."

The statement stabbed at Emma's heart. They were best friends so shouldn't she be the one good thing about this town?

Lucille scratched her cheek. "So you just gonna stand there gawking at me?"

"Oh, please," Emma smirked, "like you something to look at." She plopped down onto the bench beside Lucille. With her ponytail and plain cotton frock, Emma felt dull and dreary next to the shiny new Lucille. "I swear," she started out of nowhere, "if I have to listen to one more rag, I'm going to lose my mind."

Lucille chuckled. "Ragtime ain't so bad."

"It is when that's all there is."

"Yeah, I guess you're right."

Emma's fingers joined Lucille's, and together they tapped out a tune.

"Well, what are you waiting for?" Emma said coolly. "Tell me all about it."

Lucille happily shared about the hypnotic roll of the bus,

the mystery of falling asleep under a moon in one town and waking to the sun in another, and the thrill of standing before an audience of strangers shouting her name, begging her to sing just one more song.

She told Emma about Bill Hegamin, the man who wouldn't have given her the time of day had their paths converged in Macon. But luckily for her, their destinies collided in Jacksonville, Florida, when most of the old Lucille had flaked away along the highways and byways that crisscrossed the Southern states.

"Now," she concluded with a blushing smile, "he say he wanna give me all the time of day and night."

Emma nearly choked on the bile of jealousy rising in her throat.

Chapter 3

In 1916, Sam Elliott arrived in Macon on the heels of Lucille's triumphant return. Born and bred in Louisville, Kentucky; the color of a newly minted penny; lean and easy on the eyes with a mouthful of strong white teeth that never failed to startle a smile out of women and even some men—Sam was a carpenter by trade, quiet and inconspicuous. He could be in a room filled with people, and the next day, not one person could recall him having been there, which was why it took a minute before Emma even noticed him.

The first time Sam saw Emma Robinson he was sitting in the barbershop with his back to the glass-pane window, staring at his reflection in the wall of mirrors, trying to decide whether or not to get his shoes shined before the barber called him to the chair. Sam lowered his eyes, slipped his hand into the pocket of his coat, and thoughtfully fingered the loose coins inside.

When he looked up again, Emma's reflection appeared in the mirror, sheathed in yellow sunlight, glowing like an apparition.

"Pssst," Sam hissed at the barber.

"Yeah, boss?"

He tilted his chin at the reflection. "You see that girl?"

The barber's head swiveled from the mirror to the window and then back to Sam. "Yeah, I see her," he replied, and then added with a chuckle and a wink: "Wouldn't mind seeing more of her though."

Sam grimaced at the barber's off-color remark.

"You know that's the reverend's daughter, don't you?"

"Is it?" Sam replied.

"Yep. So you ain't got a chance in hell."

Sam thought about Emma for the rest of that Thursday, but by Friday afternoon his mind had moved on to more immediate concerns, like work and food and rent.

But just as quickly as Emma was crowded out of Sam's memory, she was thrust back in when she passed him in the street on Saturday morning and then again the following Tuesday. The encounters continued with increased frequency until Sam became convinced that God was trying to tell him something, which was funny in and of itself because Sam wasn't quite sure if he even believed in the Almighty.

That aside, Sam had become undeniably smitten with the pretty Emma Robinson and decided that he'd better develop a personal relationship with God if he wanted to get acquainted with her. So the following Sunday, Sam walked into the Cotton Way Baptist Church smack in the middle of Reverend Robinson's fiery sermon.

An usher planted herself squarely in Sam's path and aimed her white-gloved index finger at a space along the wall.

"I see a free seat up front," Sam whispered.

The grim-faced usher shook her head and again pointed at the wall.

Sam didn't budge. He and the old woman glared at one another until Sam feigned submission. When the usher dropped her guard, he faked left and then right, swiftly maneuvered around the woman, and trotted noisily up the center aisle. He had to climb over a mother and her three small children to get to the vacant seat. In the process, his heel came down on the woman's big toe and she cried out, "Lawd, Jesus!"

Sam apologized profusely, but the woman's godliness had sailed out the window. She swatted his arm with her fan and called him a fool under her breath.

When the service was over, the hoodwinked usher cornered Sam in the pew and gave him a good tongue-lashing. By the time she was done, the reverend and his family were standing on the church steps shaking hands and exchanging pleasantries with the parishioners.

Sam thought of joining the line of congregants, but decided against it. The time didn't seem quite right, and besides, the barber's discouraging words had rattled his confidence. Sam would have to repair it before he moved forward.

That night, unable to sleep, Sam went down to the Ocmulgee. The river had teeth, so he hung back amongst the saplings, a safe enough distance between him and the alligators trolling the riverbanks for food. Overhead, a family of bats swooped and screeched in the milky glow of the quarter moon; the blanket of leaves on the ground crackled with foraging insects and snakes.

He stood for hours pondering the murky waters. In time, his mother's words echoed in his mind: *Son, if you take your problems to the water, she will solve them for you.*

His mother had never told a lie. Within minutes, Sam felt able.

Chapter 4

The following Sunday, Sam marched confidently into the church and took a seat in the pew directly behind Emma's mother and brothers. When the reverend directed the congregation to greet their church family, Louisa's eyebrows climbed at Sam's strong grip and too-wide grin.

After service, he went to stand beneath a flourishing hickory tree as Emma and her parents said their Sunday farewells.

When Emma started down the church steps, leaving her family behind, he straightened his back and walked boldly toward her.

"Good morning to you, Miss Emma."

Emma blushed. "And to you, Mr. ... um."

"Sam. Sam Elliott." He extended his hand.

"Nice to meet you, Mr. Elliott."

"Likewise," Sam said. "Have a blessed day." And with that, he turned and abruptly walked off, leaving Emma frowning.

"Now that was strange," she mumbled to herself.

Strange, but deliberate.

Sam knew he couldn't come at Emma full-on. He had to plant a seed and wait for it to sprout.

The following Sunday, when service was over, Sam joined the line of congregants. When he reached Emma, he barely glanced at her as he took her hand into his, wished her a blessed day, and then fled. Sam did this for three consecutive weeks. The fourth week, he didn't attend church service at all.

By Tuesday, word reached him that the reverend's daughter was asking around town about him.

"Yeah, what she asking?"

"Who your people. Where you live. What you do."

"Is that right?"

On the fifth Sunday, Sam arrived at the church early enough to snag a seat in the front pew. When Emma looked up from the organ keys and spotted his smiling face, she became all thumbs. Flustered, she stumbled clumsily through the last scale of "All God's Chillun Got Wings," garnering annoyed glances from Lucille and other members of the choir.

After service, Emma took her place in the receiving line alongside her mother, distractedly greeting parishioners as she searched for Sam's brown face.

But that Sunday, Sam wasn't in the line. He was across the street, secretly watching her.

Afterward, he trailed Emma and Lucille to Schlesinger's Confectionary, a place popular with the young after-church crowd. When Emma and Lucille exited the store, each holding a waffle cone piled high with vanilla ice cream, Sam finally made himself known by sidling up alongside the pair and offering a sunny, "Good day, ladies."

Emma's face brightened. "Good day to you too," she called back to him as he passed.

"He the one?" Lucille asked.

Emma's face warmed. "Yes!"

Chapter 5

Emma couldn't be seen keeping time with a man who wasn't her father or one of her three brothers. It wasn't proper behavior for a Christian girl, especially the daughter of a minister.

Since Lucille's character had already been sullied—what with the low-down music she sang and the paint she wore on her face—she had nothing to lose and so volunteered to play decoy for Sam and Emma.

Lucille was with them on Saturday mornings at the open-air farmers market, as they grinned at each other over woven baskets filled with yams, string beans, and beets. She accompanied them to the picture shows, sat one row ahead of them, which was never far enough, because Lucille could still hear Sam's whispered sweet nothings.

Months collapsed and advanced. Soon it was Christmas and then the champagne-popping welcoming of 1917.

On Friday, April 6, 1917, President Woodrow Wilson declared war on Germany, officially entering America into World War I.

In response, Reverend Tenant Robinson opened his church and announced that the next seventy-two hours would be dedicated to prayer for those soldiers called to defend life, liberty, and the pursuit of happiness. Faith-filled Maconites answered, arriving by the carriage load, on foot and bicycle. To shelter the overflow of people, tents were erected on the church lawn.

From Friday midday straight until Sunday-morning service, the Cotton Way Baptist Church rang with prayer and song.

Emma, Sam, and Lucille went to the confectionary shop following the Sunday service. Ice cream in hand, they sat outside on the benches, shading their eyes from the sun.

Around them, worried faces hovered over the afternoon edition of the *Macon Telegraph*. And it was quiet, as if the thirty-seven million dead and wounded had already been prophesied, leaving Macon hush with anticipatory bereavement.

"I'm moving," Lucille uttered beneath the lull.

Emma dragged her napkin over her lips. "What you say?"

Lucille's voice climbed an octave: "I said I'm moving to Chicago."

Emma's mouth fell open.

"What's in Chicago?" Sam asked casually.

Lucille blushed. "Bill."

"What?" Emma chirped, wide-eyed.

"Oh, that your beau?" said Sam with a wink.

Lucille nodded and turned to Emma's blank face. "He done asked me to marry him and I said yes."

"What?" Emma echoed again as if she'd gone deaf.

"She said she's getting married," Sam laughed, nudging Emma in her waist. "Congratulations, Lucille."

"Thanks." Lucille dropped her eyes from Emma's shattered gaze.

"Well, ain't you gonna say something, Em?"

Emma's eyes closed and opened in a slow and deliberate blink.

"What's there to say?"

"Oh, Em, don't be like that!"

"Like what?"

"Like *that*. Can't you just be happy for me?"

A wide, leering smile rose on Emma's lips. "See, Lucille," she pressed the tip of her index finger to the corner of her mouth, "look how happy I am for you."

Lucille stood. "Lord, Emma, can't you think about someone other than yourself for once in your life? You've got every damn thing, can't I have this?"

The patronizing grin vanished from Emma's face. "What are trying to say, Lucille?"

"I think you know."

Emma rose, propped her hand on her hip, and narrowed her eyes. "I think I don't," she stated pointedly. "Maybe you should tell me."

"Now ladies..." Sam started, stepping between the friends.

"The only reason you're even a tiny bit upset that I'm leaving is because of Sam. Without me, there's no him."

Not only had Lucille hit the nail on the head, but she had driven it deep into Emma's core, and she erupted. "Well, I thank you very kindly for your assistance. I wouldn't have asked if I knew you'd be throwing it back in my face like a filthy rag. A real friend wouldn't stoop so low. Thank you for showing me your true colors!" And with that, Emma marched off, leaving Sam and Lucille blinking.

Lucille shook her head. "You sure she's what you want, Sam?"

Not peeling his eyes from Emma's retreating back, he replied, "I've never been more sure about anything in my entire life."

Chapter 6

Sam convinced Lucille to make peace with Emma, and eventually she did.

The night before her best friend left Macon forever, Emma asked her parents if she could spend the night with Lucille. It was a risky request because, best friend or not, sleepovers were not allowed on weeknights.

If Louisa knew that the pleading in her daughter's eyes had less to do with the heartbreak of losing her longtime friend to Chicago and everything to do with the ache and throb of blossoming love—Louisa would have turned Emma down flat. But Louisa didn't know and so she agreed.

After dinner, the two friends closed themselves away in Lucille's room, climbed into bed, folded their arms around each other, reminisced about what was, and swooned over what could be. Before long, it was midnight, time for Emma to leave.

"I'm gonna miss you so much," Emma moaned, rubbing her wet eyes.

"Me too," Lucille concurred.

"You'll write, won't you?"

"Of course I will, Emma."

Emma climbed out of the bed, smoothed her dress, and finger-combed her hair back into place.

"How do I look?"

"Beautiful as always, Em." Lucille raised herself up onto her elbow.

"I'll stay here tonight if you want me to."

"And hate me forever?" Lucille laughed. "No thank you." Emma rolled her eyes. "You promise to write?"

"As soon as I get there."

Emma quietly opened the window and climbed out. She blew a kiss at Lucille and disappeared into the night.

Beneath a black sky strewn with stars, Emma hurried toward her destiny. When she reached the rooming house, Sam was on the porch waiting, just as he had promised.

In his bedroom, the flame of the kerosene lamp cast their shadows long and dark against the walls and lace curtains covering the window.

Sam thought sitting on the bed would seem suggestive or presumptuous so he offered Emma the only chair in the room, while he remained standing.

"I-I got us some Coca-Cola," he said, pointing at the two bottles perspiring on the dresser.

"Oh, that's nice," Emma said, nervously wringing her hands.

Her eyes darted between Sam and the door, certain that at any moment her father would come bursting in, swinging his belt like a lasso.

Sensing her uneasiness, Sam said, "If you wanna go, I'll understand."

Emma shook her head and exhaled. "No, I want to stay."

He handed Emma a bottle of Coke.

"So," Sam started, shifting his weight from his right leg to his left, "is Lucille all packed?"

"Pretty much."

"I guess you're really going to miss her, huh?"

"Yeah," Emma sighed.

Silence pulsed between them.

Sam finished his soda and set the empty bottle on the dresser. "Emma?"

She looked at him expectantly. "Yes, Sam?"

"I, um, I just want to say that I really, really like you."

Emma's face flushed. "I like you too, Sam."

He took a measured step toward her. "I know you probably don't think I'm good enough for you—"

"I think you're a fine man, Sam. As good as any out there."

It was Sam's turn to blush. "Well, thank you, Emma."

Feeling warm, Emma leaned toward the window, hoping to catch a breeze.

"I want you to know that I ain't never felt about no woman the way I feel about you."

Emma shot him a bashful look.

"Emma Robinson, I'd—"

"Yes, Sam?"

"I don't want you to think me too forward, okay?"

"Okay, Sam."

"Emma, may I kiss you?"

All she knew of kissing were the brush of lips against cheeks and the modest pecks newlyweds bestowed one another after her father pronounced them man and wife. Although there was that one time when she was walking with her mother and, out of the corner of her eye, she spied a couple in the alleyway that separated the feed store from the barbershop. The woman's back was against the wall, the man pressed against her, their lips tightly locked; Emma wondered how in the world they were able to breathe. The scene never left her and every time she thought of it, her intestines wiggled in her gut.

"I would very much like you to kiss me, Sam Elliott," she uttered breathlessly.

The kissing quickly escalated and before Emma knew it, she was on the bed, skirt rolled up to her brassiere, bloomers dangling from her ankles, Sam on top of her panting like a racehorse.

It was over as quickly as it had begun.

Afterward, they lay very still, listening to each other breathe. Sam touched her waist. "Emma?"

"Yes?"

"You okay?"

"Yes."

He pulled her to his chest, brushed the hair from her face, and kissed her wet cheeks.

"Why are you crying?"

"I can't say. It's so stupid."

"Are you sorry we did this?"

"N-no."

"Then what?"

"I'm just worried that people will know."

"How would they?"

"I heard that people can tell by looking at the back of your knees."

Sam chuckled. "I think that's an old wives' tale, Emma."

"Maybe."

"The only way people will know is if you tell them."

"Well, I'm not gonna tell a soul—are you?"

"Of course not."

"Good, then we don't have anything at all to worry about." Sam kissed her again. "Not one thing."

Chapter 7

"You're what?" Tenant boomed, carefully setting his Bible onto the sofa table.

"Pregnant," Emma repeated timidly, gripping Sam's hand.

"*Pregnant?*" Tenant uttered stupidly as if he'd never heard the word before. He turned confused eyes to Louisa. "Pregnant?"

"Yes, dear," Louisa said sadly. "Three months."

Dumbfounded, Tenant dropped down heavily beside his wife. He winced at Sam. "I know you, don't I?"

"Yes sir, I'm—"

Tenant wagged his finger at the young man. "Aren't you Lucille Nelson's beau?"

"No sir, I'm not, I—"

"What in the world are you doing in my living room..." Tenant trailed off, his eyes bouncing from Emma's face down to their tightly linked hands. "Oh, no. No, no, no," he lamented, shaking his head.

"Daddy, we—"

Tenant raised his hand and turned to his wife. "Well, we'll just have to send her away."

"Away?" Louisa said.

"We'll send her up to Atlanta or maybe down to Jacksonville!" The words tumbled from his mouth. "She'll have the baby and put it up for adoption—"

"Adoption?" Louisa reeled back in horror.

"Yes. And then she'll go off to Howard University and complete her education."

"I'm not putting my baby up for adoption!" Emma screeched.

Louisa shot her a hard look. "Now Tenant, there's no need for all of that. Sam is willing to marry Emma."

"Marry?" Tenant barked, jerking his thumb violently in Sam's direction. "Him? Who is he? He's nobody. Just a carpenter. Certainly not good enough for our Emma!"

Emma started to protest, but Sam quieted her with a gentle squeeze of her hand.

Stepping toward Tenant, he said, "Sir, I believe Jesus was a carpenter too, was he not?"

Chapter 8

Three weeks later, Sam and Emma exchanged vows. Tenant officiated the ceremony.

The day of the nuptials, thunder rang through the heavens and lightning knifed the sky, dumping buckets of water. Emma was near tears.

Louisa said, "Don't worry, it's good luck."

The reception was held at the Robinsons' home. People had never seen so much food and flowers in one place.

Emma wore a girdle beneath her simple white dress. It did wonders concealing her bulging stomach, but nothing at all to dissipate her glow. Louisa dusted Emma's face with so much powder that for a few moments, the girl looked like a ghost. In the end, all of Louisa's efforts were for naught, because minutes later, Emma's radiance burned right through that mask of powder, bathing her face luminous once again.

It made Tenant nervous whenever he saw a guest looking too hard at Emma. During these moments he would bellow boisterously, "Look at my beautiful daughter, she's just glowing with happiness!" And any mother in earshot would roll her eyes and spit, "Who he think he fooling? I been pregnant before, I know what it looks like!"

Sam, who was not a drinking man, had two glasses of fine champagne at the reception—the bubbles were still floating in his head as he and Emma entered her bedroom.

Everything was pink: the canopy bed, walls, and window treatments. Everything.

Sam looked around the room and fell apart with laughter. "Shhhh," Emma warned, reaching for his zipper.

"What you doing, girl?"

"What you think? It's our wedding night, you know."

Sam backed away from her. "You jumped the gun on that. I gave you your wedding gift a few months back, remember?" he slurred drunkenly, aiming his chin at Emma's midsection.

"No, I don't quite remember, so I guess you gonna have to remind me now, won't you?" Emma giggled seductively.

Before God blessed them with abundance, Tenant and Louisa had been sharecroppers, living in a one-room chattel house with two other couples and their three children. That life wasn't so distant a memory that they couldn't recall having to offer privacy in a home where there was no privacy to be had. They'd turn their backs on the grappling lovers, push their fingers into their ears, and pray for a hasty conclusion so they could snatch some shut-eye before it was time to head back to the fields.

But in 1917 there were no fields for Tenant and Louisa to fret over, just the squealing bedsprings and love talk slipping through the thin wall that separated their bedroom from Emma's.

That first night and the nights that followed, Tenant and Louisa lay in bed, spines touching, palms pressed over their ears, minds ringing loudly with the familiar appeal: *Hurry up and be done now. Hurry up!*

Chapter 9

As promised, Lucille did write. She and Bill Hegamin were planning to leave the bone-chilling cold of Chicago for the endless sunshine of California. There was talk of her making a record.

Can you imagine, Emma? Me on somebody's record?

But for now it was still just talk. If it did happen, Lucille would be the first black female vocalist in history to do so.

Emma wrote back that Sam was a good and kind husband. He had built a beautiful crib for the baby. Emma said that if she gave birth to a girl, she would name it Lucille and perhaps, when the baby was old enough, they would all come out to California for a visit. In the meantime, she and Sam were making plans to start their new life somewhere north of Georgia.

One night, she announced casually over dinner that she and Sam were planning to leave Macon after the baby was born.

Louisa lowered her fork. "And go where?"

"The capital," Emma spouted excitedly.

"Atlanta?" Tenant said, his voice bright with hope.

"DC," Sam corrected.

"Why DC?"

"Got an uncle there, seems as good a place as any to start a new life."

"Why can't you start here?"

"Oh, Mama, we can't start a new life in an old place," Emma snorted.

"Washington, DC is an old place," Tenant countered. "Older than Macon. DC was established in 1790, Macon in 1823—"

"Daddy, you know what we mean!"

Tenant shoveled a mound of mashed potatoes into his mouth.

Louisa folded her hands onto the edge of the table. "What are you going to do in Washington, DC?"

Emma shifted her eyes away from Louisa's excavating gaze. "Sam's going to find work and I'm going to give piano lessons."

"Piano lessons? Really?"

"Yes, ma'am."

Part II

He is born

Chapter 10

The baby arrived on Christmas Eve, right there on the parlor floor between the piano and the Christmas tree.

Emma was hanging an ornament when she was struck with the first knee-shaking pain. Setting the ornament on the arm of the sofa, she cautiously spun around, intent on moving into the kitchen where her mother was kneading dough for bread. The second pain sliced across her lower back, and her head went light. She opened her mouth to scream, but found she couldn't raise her voice above a whisper.

Her water broke, gushing fluid everywhere. Surprised, Emma careened backward into the mantle and crumpled to the ground, taking the Christmas stockings down with her. By the time Louisa heard the commotion, Harlan's head was crowning.

"Easy now, easy, Emma," Louisa cautioned, squeezing her daughter's trembling hand.

Emma pushed twice and the baby boy slid out as easily as jam from a jar. Louisa had to pop his buttocks three times before he made a sound. And when he finally did open his mouth, he yawned.

Louisa reeled back with astonishment. "Well, ain't he a grand piece of work!" she cried. "Been here a hot minute and already bored!"

They named him Harlan, after Sam's deceased father.

Copper-colored with a mane of slick black hair, Harlan kept

his eyes closed for two whole months—as if he couldn't care less about what the world had to offer. Considering how his life would turn out, perhaps Harlan knew, even in infancy, just what the universe had in store for him.

"Is there something wrong with my baby?" Emma asked the doctor.

"No, he's perfectly healthy, just lazy."

Chapter 11

Spring swept into Georgia, gartered in green, yellow, and blush. In honor of her arrival, Maconites began sprucing up their homes: replacing roof shingles, stripping away dreary weather-beaten paint from shutters and porches, recoating them with light, bright colors.

New bonnets filled the display window of the millinery shop, colorful spring frocks crammed boutique racks. Flowers sprang from garden beds, lush leaves exploded from the tiny brown nubs of tree limbs. The days stretched and warmed and the cobalt winter sky paled to a powder blue.

"Mama, we gonna leave next week!"

Louisa had suspected as much and invited the bright-eyed couple into the drawing room to voice her concern. "I think it would be best to leave the baby here with us," she said. "Just until you all get settled."

Emma went rigid. "You don't think I... we... can take care of Harlan on our own?"

Louisa shook her head. "That's not at all what I'm saying, Emma. You and Sam are wonderful parents. I just think it would be easier on everyone if Harlan remained in a stable environment."

Emma chewed on her bottom lip as she contemplated this.

Louisa presented cream-colored palms. "Just until you're settled," she repeated.

43

Upstairs, Harlan started to wail in that languid way of his. With Louisa's words twirling in her mind, Emma rose from the sofa and started toward the staircase.

As it stood, they would be staying with Sam's uncle, Daniel; sleeping on a Murphy bed in a room that was as tiny as an outhouse, or so Sam had told her. Where would she put a crib? And Daniel was an old bachelor, no doubt firmly set in his ways. How would he adjust to having a crying baby in his space? Maybe Louisa was right.

Halfway up the stairs, Emma paused, glanced at the polished wooden banister, and dropped the decision into her husband's lap. *Whatever Sam decides is okay with me*, she thought to herself.

They left Macon on a bright May morning.

The entire family went to the train station to see them off. Emma and Sam clung to Harlan like a drowning couple to a life raft.

Harlan, belly full of milk and the tiniest bit of farina, slept straight through the shower of tears.

The next day, Louisa had Emma's bedroom painted blue. She swapped out the pink and cream bedding for mint green and white. The dolls and dollhouse were replaced with a wooden rocking horse, softball, bat, and catcher's mitt, and Harlan and his grandparents settled into life as if it had always been just them three.

Chapter 12

They promised to come back for Harlan as soon as they were settled. But they never quite settled.

In DC, clothed in a smart dress and dainty hat, Emma marched into a cabaret that was advertising for a new pianist. She introduced herself to the manager, a big, black, thick-lipped man, heartily shook his meaty hand, and advised him, quite confidentially, that she was exactly who he was looking for.

Amused, he rolled his long cigar from one corner of his mouth to the other. "Are you now?"

"Yes."

The man pointed at the piano. "Show me."

Back straight, head high, Emma marched to the piano, situated herself on the bench, floated her hands above the keys, and froze. Every note of every song she had ever played flew right out of her head.

"I'm waiting."

Emma shot him a weak smile, cleared her throat, and cracked her knuckles. Still, her mind remained blank.

She left in tears.

"Maybe you coming down with something?" Sam said.

"Maybe."

Sam made her a cup of hot tea. "They'll be other auditions," he assured her.

"Yes, I suppose so."

45

There were indeed other auditions and Emma froze each and every time.

"DC ain't worth squat," she declared after the seventh disappointment. "I think I'd do better someplace else. What you think, Sam?"

Sam thought what Emma thought.

When they moved to Baltimore, Emma experienced the same paralysis. Philadelphia was no different.

"Baby, I think you got the stage fright."

"That don't make no sense!" Emma snapped. "I been playing the organ in church ever since I was four years old and this ain't never happen!"

"Perhaps," Sam offered cautiously, "that was because you were doing the Lord's work. These clubs is the devil's playground."

Emma glared at him. "Now you sounding like my daddy."

Sam shrugged his shoulders. "Make sense to me."

"God is everywhere!" Emma screamed.

"Except where He ain't."

"I ain't hearing this from a man whose sole purpose for attending church was to find a woman."

"Not just *any* woman." Sam slipped his fingers between hers. "You."

Emma melted. "You a stone-cold fool, Sam Elliott."

"But I'm *your* fool, Emma Elliott."

The couple returned to Macon to celebrate the holidays as well as Harlan's first birthday.

They arrived empty-handed, sans luggage. All the moving around had depleted their meager savings. They didn't even have enough money to buy Christmas and birthday gifts for Harlan.

Tenant paid for their train tickets.

When Emma walked into the house and removed her coat, Louisa almost cried. Emma was thin, her once-full hips now sheared down to the bone; dark half-moons hung beneath her eyes.

Sam didn't look much better.

Furtively avoiding the shock shining in Louisa's eyes, Emma forced a smile. "Where's Harlan?"

"Upstairs napping," Louisa squeaked.

In the bedroom, Emma and Sam stood over the crib, marveling at the little life they'd created.

"He's getting so big," Emma whispered in wonderment.

Sam grinned, reached down, and touched Harlan's hand. "He's amazing, Emma, thank you."

A lump rose in her throat. "He is, he is," she managed.

"Maybe it's time we take him with us."

"Maybe," Emma said.

Days later, as the family prepared to head out to Christmas Eve service, Tenant turned to Emma and asked if she wouldn't mind accompanying the choir on the organ. "Like old times."

The words barely left his tongue before Emma barked, "No!"

Tenant flinched at the severity of her response, but said nothing. He had no idea that Emma was damn mad at the Lord for taking away her ability to play in front of an audience of strangers, and so she had ousted God and His religion from her life.

"S-sorry, Daddy," Emma mumbled as Tenant shuffled sadly away.

Chapter 13

They'd decided that the next best place to start again would be Louisville, Kentucky, home of the Kentucky Derby, the Hot Brown, bourbon, and Sam Elliott.

"Kentucky?" Tenant scratched his head. "I don't understand why y'all keep jumping from state to state like a pair of jackrabbits."

"I guess we haven't found the right fit is all," Emma retorted.

"Fit?"

"Yes, Daddy. We trying to find a place that feels like home."

"Well, if that's what you're looking for, you should just stay right here in Macon. Don't Macon feel like home?"

"We've already been through this, Daddy."

Tenant folded his lips.

During the visit, Emma didn't spend much time with Harlan. Not the amount of time you'd think a mother would spend with a child she hadn't seen for seven months. She barely even held him, though that part wasn't all her fault—whenever she reached for him, Harlan would scream bloody murder.

And really, what did Emma expect? Louisa was the only mother Harlan knew. She was the one who bathed him, fed him, read him bedtime stories, comforted him when he was scared, spanked him when he was ornery, and kissed him no matter what.

Who was Emma? Mostly a gray face in a grainy photograph, a name scrawled at the end of a letter or on the inside of a sentimental greeting card. Those things didn't mean anything to Harlan. As far as he was concerned, Louisa was his world.

Louisa tried her best to comfort Emma. "He's got to get to know you; that's all."

"But Mama, he don't behave that way with Sam."

It was true; Harlan was always quiet and content in Sam's arms.

"Some babies just take to men easier than they do to womens," Louisa said, even though she didn't actually know that to be true. But what else was she to tell her wounded daughter?

The morning of the day Sam and Emma were scheduled to leave, Louisa crept into Emma's room with Harlan balanced on her hip. Emma was standing over her suitcase, staring solemnly down at the neatly folded clothing.

"I got his bag all packed," Louisa announced brightly, even though her heart was breaking.

"About that," Emma began without looking up, "where we'll be staying, there's barely enough room for Sam and me, I don't know where we'd put Harlan. So I think it's best if he stayed here."

Emma had gone round and round with Sam about leaving Harlan behind until she'd finally convinced him that it was the best thing for them and their son. Even so, having seen how Emma was (or wasn't) with Harlan, Sam couldn't help but ask the dreaded question that had been tormenting him since they'd returned to Macon: "Don't you love him, Emma?"

"Sam! Of course I do. How could you ask such a thing?"

"Because I love him and I want him to be with us. That's how I can ask."

"Well, I love him too, love him so much I'd rather leave him here safe and sound with my parents. Suppose I get a job playing in a club or with an orchestra, huh? With you working days and me working nights, who's going to look after the baby?"

Sam knew that was never going to happen, but he loved Emma too much to say so.

When Emma told her mother she was leaving Harlan behind, Louisa nearly fainted with happiness, but was careful to keep the joy out of her voice. "That's no problem. We're happy to have him."

50

Chapter 14

They hadn't been in Louisville six weeks before Emma's hurt feelings riled her roaming spirit, and they were off again. This time, however, Sam chose Grand Rapids, Michigan—there was steady work to be had up there in the furniture factories.

They hitched a ride in a truck owned by a family who were moving to Detroit. The husband and wife had both secured jobs at the Ford Motor Plant.

They arrived in the middle of winter and rented a cold-water at on the top floor of a four-story clapboard house that was bullied day and night by bone-chilling winds blowing off Lake Michigan and the Grand River.

The streets were covered in snow and ice until April. When spring arrived, Emma's spirit soared along with the temperature. June, July, and August were more glorious than she could have even hoped for. But after Labor Day, her happiness dulled with the waning light of autumn—a season she'd come to believe was little more than a pretty word yoking September and October.

For a while, Emma made money teaching piano to colored children, but after two or three lessons, the money that was usually wrapped in a handkerchief and pinned to the inside of their jackets or stuffed into their socks was replaced with slips of paper, lettered: IOU.

Before long, the children stopped coming altogether.

Emma became friendly with a young woman named Maxine Black, who lived in the first-floor apartment with her husband and six children. Maxine took in laundry to supplement her husband's salary. As a result, her hands were as wrinkled and spotted as a woman three times her age.

Sometimes the two women would visit in Emma's apartment. Over tea and saltines slathered in jam, they'd gossip and listen to the radio.

Once, after weeks of casting furtive glances at the piano, Maxine finally ambled over and touched the keys.

"You interested?" Emma asked. "If you like, I'll teach you. No charge."

The light that flashed in Maxine's eyes came and went as quickly as a shooting star. She withdrew her hand and swiped it across the skirt of her dress as if she'd touched something dirty. "And when I learn to play, then what?" she scoffed. "Carnegie Hall?" She tossed her head back with laughter. "Like white folks gonna let a nigger on that stage!"

"Well," Emma responded slowly, "Sissieretta Jones is black, and she sang at Carnegie Hall."

"Sissy who?"

When the weather broke, Emma began prowling Main Street, waylaying white women window-shopping with their children.

"That your little girl?"

A nod, a smile.

"She's stunning." Emma always started with a compliment. "She's got lovely long fingers. Great piano-playing fingers."

The mother beamed.

"Oh, I see where she gets them. You have beautiful hands

too."

More smiles.

"I teach piano," Emma would say, presenting a business card.

"Oh?"

"Yes, ma'am, I do. And I must say that I'm better than most. And I don't charge much. Just a dollar and a quarter per hour."

"Is that so?"

"Yes, ma'am."

Some mothers took the cards and dropped them in their purses only to toss them into the first garbage can they came upon. Others laughed openly and mockingly as they walked off.

One woman sneered, "What can you teach my child? Dixie? What in the world is she supposed to do with that?"

Emma's face warmed. "Ma'am, I assure you I am proficient in the classics—Beethoven, Bach, Mozart, and Chopin."

"How nice for you."

***

So while they weren't living like royalty, Sam was making enough money to keep the rent paid, food on the table, and Emma in new dresses and sheet music.

One evening in 1920 Sam came home from work, gray. The whites of his eyes had turned yellow and his knuckles were swollen and painful.

The doctor didn't know what to make of it. Emma followed him out of the apartment and into the drafty hallway.

"I ain't never seen nothing like it," he said. And then as an afterthought: "You got a burial policy on him?"

Emma broke down in tears.

By the end of the month the pantry was empty, the rent was coming due, and Emma needed to refill the prescription medicine that didn't seem to be helping Sam. She found a dollar in his wallet, sixty cents in the mason jar beneath their bed, and a dime stuck to a forgotten piece of hard candy at the bottom of her purse. Not enough.

Too prideful to ask her father for help, Emma finally decided to look for work. She bought the newspaper and circled jobs seeking women for hire in dress shops and diners. She didn't know how to type, but couldn't see it being any more difficult than playing the piano, so she circled those jobs too.

She'd arrive at interviews promptly, wearing a proper dress, hair pulled back into a conservative bun, and only the slightest trace of color on her lips. She was turned away at the dress shops and the fine-dining restaurants; the greasy spoons seemed to have all of the help they needed. If she made it past an office secretary or receptionist, the interviewer wouldn't even look at her application.

"We don't hire Negroes. Well, at least not for this position."

With a notice of eviction burning a hole in her purse, Emma gritted her teeth and succumbed to the very thing she was trying to avoid. "I'll take whatever job you've got for Negroes, then."

"We don't have anything here, but I do know a few people who are looking for good help."

That first day, Emma wept with shame all over those rich white people's floors, silverware, and bed linen. And if you had seen what the washboard and Borax did to her lovely hands, you would have cried too.

Emma returned home that evening, dead on her feet and filled with lament. She stripped out of her uniform, climbed into bed, and sobbed into her husband's chest.

"Look at me, Sam," she sniffed, "raised in silk and now living in burlap."

"I'm sorry," Sam muttered tearfully.

"Aww, it ain't your fault. I'm the one who dragged us all over creation chasing a stupid dream. You just went along for the ride."

"So you ready to go back to Macon now?"

"No."

Meanwhile, Emma's eldest brother Seth was a well-respected teacher. The middle boys, John Edward and James Henry, had followed in Tenant's footsteps and were successful ministers in their own right. And Lucille had made a record called *Crazy Blues* that sold a million copies in under a year. She wouldn't go down in history as the first blues singer to record, but she would hold second place.

At this point in 1920, Emma wasn't second place in anything, and she refused to return to Macon until she had accomplished something more spectacular than basic survival.

As it turned out, her return to Macon, two years later, would be spawned from tragedy, not triumph.

Chapter 15

1922

Wednesday, the day Tenant had put aside to visit the sick and shut-ins, he arrived home in a jovial mood. He removed his favorite pair of brown shoes, put on his slippers, washed his hands, and sat down to a supper of roasted lamb, new potatoes, sweet corn, and blueberry pie for dessert. Afterward, he and Harlan went into the study and shut the door.

It had become a custom of theirs, not unlike Saturday-morning pancakes.

"What y'all in there talking about?" Louisa would tease.

"Man stuff," Tenant always replied.

After the dishes were washed and put away, the family gathered in the sitting room to listen to the *Amos'n' Andy* radio show and laughed themselves to tears.

Later, Harlan kissed his grandparents goodnight, and headed up to bed—leaving Louisa darning socks and Tenant reading his Bible.

At eight o'clock Tenant's eyelids drooped. When Louisa heard him snoring, she patted his knee. "Reverend, you sawing wood."

"Am I?"

"Yes."

He set his Bible and reading glasses on the nesting table beside his chair and clapped his hands against his legs to get the blood flowing. When he was able to stand, he walked over to Louisa and touched her shoulder. "Will you be much longer?"

"No, I'll be up soon."

He kissed her and headed up to bed.

When Louisa finally entered the bedroom, Tenant was snoring like a freight train. Smiling to herself, she changed into her nightgown and slipped in beside him. Soon, she was fast asleep as well.

***

You don't spend decades of your life with a man and not become so familiar with his behaviors and sounds that when something changes, you fail to notice.

It was closing in on three in the morning when Tenant's body went silent. The silence was as loud as a church bell, as earsplitting as a siren; it tore Louisa from her sleep. She turned onto her side, floated her palm over Tenant's open mouth, and felt the worst thing of all.

Nothing.

Chapter 16

It had been a couple of years since Harlan last saw his parents, so when they showed up at the front door, he treated them as he had the last forty strangers who had come to give their condolences to the widow Robinson.

"Hello, I'm Harlan. Please come in."

Truth was, Emma didn't know he was her child until he said his name. After all, the last time she'd seen him, he was still small enough to fit on her hip. The boy standing before her was all limbs—clad in gray knickers, a white dress shirt, and a navy-blue bow tie.

Emma gasped in surprise. "Harlan?"

"Yes, ma'am. My grandmother is receiving guests in the parlor," he said, sweeping his hand through the air.

Emma and Sam exchanged looks. Even though it was one of the saddest days of her life, Emma couldn't help but giggle at Harlan's gallantry. "Well, aren't you the little man!" Stooping down before him, she added, "I know it's been awhile, but you really don't know who we are?"

Harlan glanced at Sam's smiling face and then back to Emma. "No ma'am."

Her heart cracked. "I'm your mother, and this is your father." Sam extended his hand. "Hello, son."

"Oh," Harlan muttered skeptically, "nice to meet you."

They followed Harlan into the parlor where Louisa was

seated on the sofa, surrounded by her sons.

Louisa smiled out through a fog of grief. "Oh, babies," she whispered, wringing her hands, "he's gone... he's gone."

The *Atlanta Constitution* published an editorial dubbing Reverend T.M. Robinson's funeral the largest and most imposing colored funeral ever held in Macon.

After Louisa had read the words a dozen times, she climbed back into bed and remained there for five days.

Emma's brothers Seth, James Henry, John Edward, and their wives, along with Emma and Sam, did all they could to comfort the grieving Louisa, but she waved them away, keeping her gaze fixed on the sky outside her bedroom window.

Grappling with his own grief and despair over the loss of his grandfather, and terrified that God was coming to take Louisa from him too, Harlan made a pallet on the floor beside Louisa's bed, refusing to leave her side.

Since Emma and Sam returned, Harlan had paid them little mind—treating them like the strangers they were.

"He hates us," Emma fretted to Sam.

"No, he doesn't."

"Well, he may not hate you, but he certainly hates me."

"That's not true."

"Do you see how he looks at me? Like he wishes I was dead."

"It's all in your mind, Emma."

"He thinks we don't want him, that we abandoned him!"

"You're just emotional because of your father, and Harlan is overwhelmed too. Tenant's death took a lot out of both of you."

"You think so?"

"I know so. Give him time, he'll come around."

One afternoon, Harlan wandered into the kitchen to find Emma standing at the window. He tried to back away, but it was too late, she'd already sensed his presence.

"Harlan?"

"Yes, ma'am?"

Emma spun around to face him. Her eyes were bloated and red from crying. She didn't expect sympathetic words, though she did hope to see a glint of pity in his dark eyes. But there was nothing there.

"Yes ma'am," he repeated flatly.

Incensed, Emma shook her fists, barking, "I lost someone too, you know! He was her husband, but he was my father. I hurt too!" A fresh torrent of tears spilled from her eyes.

Harlan stared passively at her, unsure of what was expected of him; he droned once again, "Yes, ma'am."

"I am not your *ma'am*. I'm your mother!"

Harlan fled from the kitchen, up the stairs, and back into the safety of Louisa's bedroom.

Chapter 17

Finally, the day came when Louisa, dressed in mourning black, joined the family in the dining room for breakfast.

Setting a plate of sausage and eggs down before her, Emma asked, "How you feeling, Mama?"

"How you 'spect I feel? I ain't never gonna feel right, ever again. Pass me them stewed apples, I need something sweet in my mouth."

Emma handed her mother the bowl.

"I see you all packed up and ready to go," Louisa said, scooping the apples onto her plate.

"Well, yes. Sam has to get back to work and I—" Emma stopped. There was really no reason for her to leave. She could stay a few more weeks; Sam could make do without her. But since Harlan hadn't made her feel especially needed or wanted in the house, she didn't see the sense in staying on. "Sam has to return to work or he won't have no job to go back to."

"I see. When y'all planning on leaving?"

"Tomorrow. First train."

Harlan's face broke into a smile so wide, it showcased every tooth in his head. It was all Emma could do to keep from slapping that grin clear off his face.

"You gotta stay till Friday, Emma," Louisa said. "That's when the lawyer will be 'round."

"Lawyer? For what?"

"To read the will."

Turned out, Tenant owned not just the family house in Macon but acres of land in Warner Robins and a warehouse in Milledgeville. He held savings accounts in two different banks, war bonds, and a life insurance policy worth five thousand dollars.

While the lawyer rattled off Tenant's assets, Emma and her brothers were slack-mouthed with astonishment.

The lawyer went on to say that it was Tenant's wish that all of the property (except for the family home) be sold off, and the proceeds split between Louisa and their children.

Emma was aghast. "Mama, did you know Daddy had all this?"

"That we had all this? Yes, of course I knew."

"But how... how did he... you all acquire so much?"

Louisa sighed wearily.

"Mama?"

Louisa reached for Emma's hand. "Let's just say that God has been very, very good to us."

Sam and Emma didn't return to Grand Rapids, not even to collect the clothes they'd left behind. Emma said it wasn't worth the train fare.

"Well, what about your piano?"

"That old thing?" She waved her hand. "Why would I go back for that when soon I'll have enough money to buy a brand-new one?"

It took five months to settle Tenant's estate. In May of 1923,

Emma and Sam took her inheritance and set off for New York to visit Lucille.

Chapter 18

The Greyhound bus arrived in the bowels of the Manhattan night. Country mice that they were, Emma and Sam couldn't help but gawk at the throngs of people swarming along the city streets, lit bright by marquees burning hundred-watt lightbulbs.

They were met by Lucille and her husband Bill—a tall, nut-brown man with a smile almost as stunning as Sam's.

Almost.

After hugs and handshakes, the couples climbed into Bill's late-model car and set off for Harlem.

When they stepped into Lucille and Bill's large home, Emma's mouth dropped wide open. "This all yours?"

"Well, me and the bank!" Lucille cackled as she toured them through rooms replete with chandeliers and miles of shining hardwood floors. "These rugs come straight from Turkey."

"Turkey?"

They wandered beneath the fourteen-foot ceilings, past built-in bookshelves, into one of five bathrooms where Sam pointed at the sink and jokingly commented, "That faucet look like real gold."

"That's because it is," Lucille said with a smirk.

Lucille's parents and siblings were now living with her. "You got a house full," Emma commented. "Me and Sam could get a room somewhere."

"Chile, please," Lucille replied. "Even with all these folks up in here, I still got one empty bedroom."

A mixture of pride and awe for Lucille swelled in Emma's chest, but then, rather suddenly, it was drowned in a sea of unworthiness. Her mood darkened; embarrassed, she feigned a headache and retired to a bedroom so lavish that she lay awake fighting back tears until dawn.

***

At breakfast the next morning, Lucille glanced up from her plate of pancakes and bacon to find herself in the crosshairs of Emma's starry-eyed gaze. She calmly rested her fork on her plate, folded her hands beneath her chin, and said, "Emma Elliott, will you please, please stop looking at me like that!"

Startled, Emma blurted, "Like what?"

"Like you just now making my acquaintance. Like you only know me from my records. Like we ain't come up together making mud pies."

A hush settled around the table.

"Huh?" Emma offered quietly.

"I'm just Lucille from down home, okay?"

Emma's cheeks burned. "Okay," she murmured.

Envy soon replaced that pride and awe, and in order to keep her feelings at bay, Emma had to drink three tall glasses of water swimming with bitters.

Sam cocked his eyebrows. "Your stomach upset?"

"A little."

"Maybe you pregnant!"

"No, I don't think that's what it is."

A week later, Lucille threw Emma and Sam a "Welcome to Harlem" party, attended by the black glitterati.

Emma was too busy swooning to fully enjoy herself.

No one would believe that she—little Emma Robinson from Macon, Georgia—was at a party, given in her honor no less, talking bread pudding recipes with blues singer Alberta Hunter. She'd be branded a liar if she told the folks back home that pianist Jelly Roll Morton had slipped her his number and pinched her bottom. And those same folks would just cut their eyes at her claims that country-blues guitarist Sylvester Weaver was as snazzy a dancer as he was a musician.

"Sylvester, thank you so much, but I'm going to have to sit this song out, my dogs are barking!"

"Okay, da-hling," Sylvester said, dancing away.

Emma spotted space on one of the four cushioned sofas, hobbled over, and sat down between two white women wearing brightly colored flapper dresses. The women were pointing and howling with laughter at Lucille's father, who was toting an open bottle of gin, snake-hipping his way from one guest to the next, offering to top off their drinks.

Emma slipped her feet from her shoes and pressed her burning soles against the cool wood floor. When she finally looked into the women's laughing faces, she was stunned to find that she had sandwiched herself between blues songstress Marion Harris and actress-turned-singer Esther Walker.

She was still reeling when Bessie Smith walked in, trailed by an entourage of the most beautiful men and women Emma had ever seen at one time.

Lucille dragged the famous singer over to Emma, who didn't know if she should bow or curtsy and so awkwardly combined the two, which raised more guffaws from Marion and Esther. Finally, grinning like a clown, Emma presented Bessie her trembling hand. "Very nice to meet you, Ms. Smith."

After an exaggerated eye roll, Bessie threw her fat arms around Emma's neck and squeezed the breath out of her. "We hug here in Harlem!" she bellowed.

The party didn't end until every drop of liquor was gone and the sky was soupy with misty morning light.

As Sam and Emma climbed the stairs toward their bedroom, Emma laid her head on Sam's shoulder and announced dreamily, "Harlem is definitely where I want to restart our lives."

Chapter 19

Nine months later they were back in Macon.

Louisa opened the front door to find Emma and Sam standing on the porch, glistening like movie stars in their expensive leather shoes, fine hats, and his-and-hers raccoon coats.

Seeing all of that new finery, Louisa feared that they'd run through every blessed cent of Emma's inheritance. "Well, don't y'all look like new money," she gulped. "Come on inside."

Harlan came bounding down the stairs. When he saw his parents standing in the foyer, he paused and stared, but said nothing.

Louisa shot him a stern look. "What do you say, Harlan?"

"Hello," he whispered.

"*Hello*? Get your butt down here and greet your parents properly." Harlan drifted over slowly and gave them each a weak hug, then planted himself at his grandmother's hip.

The family moved into the parlor. Sam and Emma sat in the wing chairs, Harlan on the sofa alongside Louisa.

"How's Lucille doing?"

Emma shrugged. "You know Lucille, she's just fine. Sends her love to you. Says she's sorry she couldn't make the funeral, but she was on the road. She did send flowers, though. Do you remember getting them?"

Louisa nodded. "And the husband?"

"She got a good man," Sam responded.

"Aww, Sam just likes him 'cause he let him drive his fancy car!" Emma laughed. "But he seems nice enough, I guess."

Louisa reached over the sofa table, plucked a white-and-red-striped peppermint ball from the glass jar, and handed it to Harlan. "And her parents? How they like living in New York City?"

"They seem to like it just fine."

Steadily eyeing Emma, Harlan rolled the mint ball across his tongue.

Emma smirked at him. "So how's school, Harlan?"

"Fine," he gurgled.

Louisa rubbed his head affectionately.

"Me and Emma got news," Sam croaked suddenly.

"Oh?"

"Go on, tell her, Emma."

Emma straightened her back, planted smiling eyes on Louisa's anxious face, and squealed, "We bought a house!"

"A house?" Louisa sputtered. "Where?"

"In Harlem. Well, not a house like this one, a row house. Brick. Three floors."

"Three floors? My goodness, it sounds like one of those mansions in Vineville."

"No, Mama, this house ain't quite as big as those—"

"Got a tenant on the top floor," Sam interjected.

"To help pay the mortgage," Emma added quickly. "A mother and her two children—a boy and girl." She looked at Harlan. "I believe the boy is just about your age."

Harlan peered down at the floor.

"Sounds very nice," Louisa said, casually crossing her ankles. "And what about work? Any one of you got a job?"

"Yes, ma'am," Sam replied proudly. "I snagged me a job with Applebaum and Sons Construction Company."

"Yep, he starts in two weeks," said Emma, reaching down to squeeze Sam's knee.

"Ain't that nice," Louisa sighed with relief.

"Anyway," Emma waved her hand, "our place is not as grand as Lucille's, but it's perfect for us. It's got a backyard and a bedroom for Harlan."

"A backyard? Ain't that something," Louisa offered.

"And a room for Harlan," Emma repeated, before prattling on. Harlan looked at his grandmother, anticipating the moment Louisa would raise her hand and bring Emma's foolish talk to an end. He waited and waited, but Louisa just sat there nodding and smiling as if she didn't have a brain in her head.

Finally, Louisa uncrossed her ankles and spoke: "Sounds to me like Harlan will be very happy there."

Harlan's jaw dropped—the peppermint candy rolled off his tongue and onto the floor. "What?" he blurted.

Harlan was not a child prone to fits of outrage, but on that day, he stood, screeched his disapproval and contempt, and then dropped to his knees and locked his arms around Louisa's legs.

"I hate you and I ain't going nowhere with you!" he wailed at his parents.

The adults looked on, stunned.

Her feelings decimated, Emma fled from the room in tears. For a moment, Sam forgot Harlan was his seed and glared at the boy like a bully sizing up his victim. Mouth twisted in anger, he rose, walked over to Harlan, and caught him roughly by the collar.

"Get your black ass up off that floor right this minute," he sneered.

Louisa's eyebrows furrowed. Speaking softly and gently patting Sam's clenched jaw, she said, "No need for all of that, Sam. Just leave him be."

After Sam had gone upstairs to check on Emma, Louisa uncoiled Harlan from her legs, pulled him onto her lap, and rocked him against her bosom the way she used to when he was a chubby baby. "You carrying on as if New York is as far away as the moon!" She laughed and tweaked his nose. "Us will visit all the time. You'll come here and I'll go there. And in between, we'll write letters."

Harlan remained defiant.

"Look here, Harlan," Louisa continued, "this is just the way things are. You have to stop all this crying and showing off and behave like the big boy your grandpappy and I raised you to be."

Water sprung from Harlan's eyes.

"You remember what the Good Book says about your parents, don't you?"

Harlan nodded his head.

"Lemme hear it."

"*Honor thy father and thy mother: that thy days may be long upon the land which the Lord thy God giveth thee*."

"That's right. Now, you dry those tears and go upstairs and apologize to your mama and daddy."

"But Grannie, ain't you gonna miss me when I'm gone?"

"Sure 'nuff. I'll miss you like a hooked fish miss water."

Part III

Harlem

Chapter 20

To Harlan, New York City was as chaotic and thrilling as the three-ringed circus that came through Macon each spring.

No matter which direction his head spun, there was something new and exciting to behold: white men with long beards and black hats as tall as chimney stacks; poor people begging for money; rich people walking white poodles tethered to long leather leads; blind people tapping walking sticks; fat people munching soft, salted pretzels; and middle-of-the-road people like themselves.

Harlan had never seen an Oriental, so he gawked openly as six Chinese men—mandarin-collared and skullcapped—bore down on him. Sam jerked Harlan out of the way, rescuing him from being trampled beneath their slippered feet. The group hurried along, leaving Harlan gazing at their long, inky-colored braids, swaying like tails against their backs.

In the checkered cab Harlan sat with his forehead pressed to the window, silently ogling the tall buildings, trollies, and fancy automobiles.

His new home was a three-story brick row house on East 133rd Street, between Fifth and Madison avenues, right near the Harlem River. The house was resplendent with wood moldings, parquet floors, and replaces. Harlan's bedroom was on the second floor, in the rear of the house, just down the hallway from his parents' bedroom. It was small and made smaller by the mountain of toys and games heaped in the center of the floor.

The backyard was a disappointment—just a rectangle of dirt enclosed by a short wooden fence. No matter, all playing—stickball, catch, hide-and-seek, hot peas and butter, tag—happened out front on the sidewalk or in the middle of the street.

When Harlan first arrived, the tenants—the mother and her two children—came down to make his acquaintance. The family paraded into the parlor, brother and sister flanking their mother like bookends.

"Harlan, this is Miss Mayemma Smith," Emma said, stringing the woman's two first names together like harlot beads. "And her children, John and Darlene."

All three had identical beak-shaped noses, slanted eyes, and full lips. Mother and son were the color of coconut husks. The girl was much darker, as if she had been slathered in crude oil. John was clutching a book to his chest; Darlene's hands were locked tight behind her back.

"So nice to finally meet you," Mayemma beamed.

"Hey," said John.

Darlene mumbled a greeting.

"Hi," Harlan piped.

"John is one of my students," Emma said. "He plays very, very well."

Chapter 21

It didn't take long for Harlan to settle into his new life.

His easy disposition and Southern civility made him popular with the neighborhood children and parents alike. Despite being far from an astute student, those same attributes endeared him to his teachers, and they happily promoted him from one grade to the next.

Needless to say, Emma felt guilty for having missed out on Harlan's formative years and so indulged him to the point of ruin. When Harlan misbehaved, she refused to take a switch to his behind and threatened Sam with divorce if he did.

"The Bible is specific," Sam reminded her. "*Spare the rod and spoil the child.*"

Emma just sucked her teeth.

This is not to say that Emma never hit Harlan. She did. Just once—in 1928 when he was eleven years old. They were at Lucille and Bill's on a hot, muggy Saturday evening. The air inside the house was as still as a painting. Harlan, bored with watching the adults play spades, wandered outside.

The streets were alive with playing children, the stoops crammed with adults fanning themselves with newspapers, rolling cold bottles of beer over their foreheads before emptying them in one long swallow.

Harlan walked a few houses away, stopped to watch a pair of old men hunched over a chessboard before continuing on to

77

the corner. He dawdled there for a while—counting passing cars and debating whether he should defy his parents and cross the street to discover what mysteries might be lurking on the next block. Deciding against that, Harlan turned around and started back to the house.

Parked in front of the Hegamin home was Bill's 1926 black and cream Ford coupe. Harlan peered through the driver's-side window. There were some playbills on the front seat and a few candy wrappers on the floor. His eyes popped with surprise when he saw the key dangling from the ignition. He glanced nervously over his shoulder, jiggled the handle, and found that the door was unlocked. Another quick look to make sure he wasn't being watched and then, as swift as a cat, he creaked the door open and slipped inside.

Harlan sat in the driver's seat, hands tightly gripping the wheel, imitating the roar of an engine. "*Brrrrrrr... b-b-b-b-b... Brrrrrrrr!*"

He reached for the key. His intention was to bring the car to life, quickly turn it back off, slip out, and leave it unmoved. But Harlan hadn't even completed that thought before he found himself slamming two feet down on the brake to keep from hitting a kid who had dashed out into the street to retrieve his ball.

Having no idea how to put the vehicle in reverse, with three cars now behind him honking their horns, the panicked Harlan pressed hard on the accelerator, sending the car down the street, through the intersection, and directly into a police car.

The cops hauled him to the local precinct. Harlan had never been so frightened in his life. When the officer asked his name, he said: "Jack Black." When they asked for his parents' names,

Harlan said he didn't have any.

Three hours passed before the adults realized Harlan was missing. Sam's eyes swept the street. "Where in the world is that boy?" Bill took a swig of Scotch from the glass he held, blinked, and roared, "Where's my goddamn car!"

All eyes fell on the empty parking space.

Emma ran down the steps screeching Harlan's name. Sam followed. "Where the fuck is my goddamn car?" Bill said again, glaring at Lucille as if she had something to do with its disappearance.

"How am I supposed to know, Bill?"

Emma and Sam scoured Lucille and Bill's neighborhood and then their own. They looked into the faces of every black boy they encountered. They checked with friends and acquaintances.

Harlan here?

You seen my boy?

They ended up at Harlem Hospital. Sam asked the admitting nurse if any eleven-year-old black boys had been brought into the emergency unit in the past four hours or so. The woman let out a tired sigh, as if it was the hundredth time that night she'd been asked that particular question. After lazily flipping through a binder filled with pages, she looked up and spoke without a hint of compassion: "I think you might need to check the morgue."

Emma, who was standing beside Sam, nervously chewing on her bottom lip, stumbled back into the wall, whimpering. After she had taken a few sips from the water fountain and three deep breaths, she and Sam followed a lanky male attendant down a wide corridor to a bank of elevators.

The morgue was located in the basement of the hospital, where the air was sharp with the scent of formaldehyde and bleach, aggravating Emma's already churning stomach. She closed her hand over her nose and mouth to keep from throwing up.

The morgue was a large, square room filled with a desk and dozens of metal gurneys, bearing corpses veiled in white sheets. The walls were lined with doors that looked very much like the door of any kitchen icebox. And it was cold in that room. Cold enough to turn breath into clouds.

When they walked in, a doctor was shining a penlight down a dead woman's throat. Emma's eyes jumped frantically from the woman's massive, flaccid breasts to the doctor's blood-splattered scrubs before she was finally able to look away.

The doctor looked up from the corpse and frowned.

"They're looking for their son," the attendant announced casually, as if Emma and Sam were searching for something as insignificant as a scarf or glove.

Whistling to himself, the attendant walked over to the desk and retrieved a green sheet of paper. He studied the page, every now and again glancing at the drawers.

Emma was shivering so hard, Sam thought she was going to shake right out of her skin. He wrapped his arm around her shoulder, pulling her into him.

"Okay," the attendant said, walking across the room, "this is the first one."

When he reached for the door handle, Emma's eyelids instinctively snapped shut. She heard the click of the lock, the squeal of the slab wheels, and Sam's deep inhale. It was just a few seconds, but it felt like hours before she heard Sam's grateful voice exclaim, "No, that's not Harlan! That's not our son."

The second and third dead boys also proved not to be Harlan.

When the attendant's hand fell on the silver handle of the fourth and final door, Emma pushed her open palms at him. "Wait, wait a minute, please."

Each and every time she'd heard Sam utter those magical words—"That's not our son"—Emma felt like she'd hit a jackpot. She wasn't a gambling woman, but she figured the odds were in favor of Harlan being in that fourth drawer because they'd rolled the dice three times, and each time—lucky seven. Four in a row? No way that was going to happen. God wasn't so kind to colored folks; snake eyes had to be on the horizon, because winning streaks always came to an end.

"Go ahead," she whispered.

When the attendant slid the body into view, Sam broke into sobs. Emma peered down into the dark, still face and promptly fainted.

Chapter 22

While Sam was gently shaking Emma back to consciousness, Bill and Lucille were at the police station filing a report for their stolen vehicle. After handing the two-page statement to the police officer, Bill bid him goodnight, and he and Lucille started toward the exit. But the officer quickly called them back.

"Says here the vehicle is a 1926 black and cream Ford Model T. Is that right?"

"Yeah," Bill said.

"License plate 15 32 44?"

"Yeah."

The officer chuckled. "Well, we towed that car from the scene."

Bill narrowed his eyes. "Towed?"

"The scene? The scene of what?" Lucille asked.

"Well," the officer started, folding has arms across his chest and leaning way back in his chair, "the driver rammed it right into a police cruiser."

"What?" Bill blurted, wide-eyed.

"Yep, we got 'im locked up in the back."

"Well, I wanna see the thieving son of a bitch," Bill bellowed. The officer rose from his chair, hitched his pants beneath the swell of his belly, and said, "Sure, follow me."

Harlan was sitting on the floor with his back against the

brick wall of the tiny holding cell. From his tearstained cheeks, it appeared as though he'd cried himself to sleep.

"Aw, shit," Bill sighed.

Lucky for Harlan, Bill and Lucille weren't your regular Negroes, but well-known celebrities—well, at least Lucille was. The police chief himself held a standing invitation to their weekly Sunday dinners, of which he took full advantage.

Needless to say, the officer waived Harlan's bail, the incident report was destroyed, and Harlan was released into Bill and Lucille's custody.

Lucille thanked the officer, caught Harlan by the ear, and tugged him screaming toward the exit. Bill followed, biting his lip, pulling his belt free from his trousers. They damn near ran right into Sam and Emma who had just dashed into the station.

"Harlan!" Emma cried, rushing to her son and crushing him to her chest.

Relieved to see his son, Sam dragged his hands over his wet face and shook the perspiration to the floor. The episode had left his eyes red and face etched with deep worry lines.

Bill snaked the belt back through the loops of his trousers and stepped hastily to Sam. "Look here, can I have a word?"

Sam looked at Bill's pinched face. "Yeah, yeah."

Lucille watched the men walk off to a quiet corner before turning her attention back to Emma, who was blubbering and fussing over Harlan.

"You know he tore up the car?" Lucille said, tapping Emma on her shoulder.

Emma's head snapped up. "What you say?"

"I said he tore up the car. He stole it and crashed into a police car." Emma's eyes fluttered and she folded her lips into her mouth. For a moment, she thought she was going to pass out again.

Off to the left, Sam's angry voice bounced off the police station walls: "He did *what*?"

Chapter 23

They walked all the way home. Sam's anger reached a state he hadn't even known existed. Walking helped relieve some of that rage. Had it not, Harlan would still have stood a chance out in the open, where witnesses were plentiful and he had space to run.

They trudged home in tense silence. When they reached the house, Sam sat down on the stoop and dropped his head into his hands. "I'll just stay here for a while," he mumbled through splayed fingers.

Emma nodded understandingly, unlocked the door, and followed Harlan into the house.

Once inside, the boy scurried up to his bedroom without a word. Emma closed the parlor drapes, switched on a lamp, and slowly climbed the stairs. In her room, she opened the closet door, rested her chin on the back of her hand, and stood pondering Sam's belts.

Harlan figured his parents' smoldering, disapproving silence was the worst it was going to get. So it took him by surprise when a wild-eyed Emma burst into his room whipping a belt through the air.

Thwack!

The stinging lash sent him running for his life.

Emma beat Harlan around the room, up and down the hallways, into the parlor, and around the piano.

Thwack! Thwack! Thwack!

Outside, the crack of the belt and Harlan's terrified squeals raised a satisfied smile to Sam's lips. Later on, he'd feel sorry for his son, but for now, it was all he could do to keep from cheering.

Harlan managed to keep a length ahead of Emma, but he couldn't escape the reach of the belt. Like a sprinter hurtling toward the finish line, Harlan summoned all of his speed and exploded down the hallway into the bathroom, where he shut and locked the door.

Emma pummeled the door with her fists and feet. She threatened and cussed and demanded, but Harlan refused to let her in.

And then, just as suddenly as the madness had seized her, it slipped away. Out of breath and drenched in sweat, Emma flung the belt down to the floor and collapsed backward into the wall.

Harlan's wounded howls pierced her heart, nearly splitting it in half. Soon, she was bawling too.

That was the first and last time she ever beat that boy.

Chapter 24

"The problem is," Lucille complained to her husband, "they treat Harlan like a man, not a boy."

"A friend, not a son," Bill grunted in agreement.

"They let him listen to all that grown-ass music. Mine included. He knows all the words. You hear him, don't you? Singing 'bout moochers, rolling lemons, and warming wieners!"

"Yep."

"That boy needs some religion in his life, 'cause the devil's watching and waiting."

Church had not been a staple in Sam and Emma's lives since they'd left Macon. Once they'd settled in Harlem, their religion became swing, jazz, and bebop, ministered by Satchmo, Calloway, and Gillespie.

"What that boy needs is more Our Father who art in Heaven and a little less *Hi-dee-hi-dee-ho!* and *Hep! Hep! Hep!*"

"A-yuh."

"Of course he's going to do and say as he pleases. There ain't no consequences to his behavior."

"Uh-huh."

"What parents you know don't beat their kids? Even white folks beat their damn kids!"

"Uh-huh."

"If they don't make that boy mind his manners, you know who will, right?"

"The po-lice."

"Say it again.

"The PO-LICE."

"You got that shit right."

"Uh-huh."

"And you can't tell him nothing. You notice that? Any good advice you try to sling his way, before you can get it out your mouth, he hollering, *I know, I know!*"

"I got a nephew just like him," Bill huffed, "know everything and don't know shit."

Well, that wasn't an entirely true statement. Harlan did know how to con his mama out of money—it only took a smile and a, *Aww, Mama, please!* As he grew older, he would use the same formula to coax women out of their drawers: *Aww, baby, please!*

The other thing that he would become proficient in was playing the guitar.

Chapter 25

You can't expect a child not to become a product of his environment. If you're a drinker, you'll raise a drunk. If you're a single mother, traipsing men in and out of your bedroom in front of your girl child—mark my words, in time she'll claim a corner and charge money for what you gave away for free. Kings and queens raise princes and princesses. That's just the way it is.

So who knows why Sam was floored when Harlan—barely fifteen—walked into the house, dropped his school books on the floor, and declared, "I'm done with school, gonna pursue guitar-picking full time!"

"Say what now?"

While Emma had finished high school, Sam had only made it through the fifth grade. Being one of ten children, he'd had a responsibility to his younger siblings, or so his father had reminded him every morning as Sam headed off to work, leaving the senior Elliott splayed on the couch balancing a jar of corn liquor on his chest.

Harlan would have been the first in a long line of Elliotts to attend and graduate high school. Now, his decision to drop out all but dashed Sam's dreams to silt.

"Well, let's see what your mother has to say about all of this," Sam said.

When Emma came home, Harlan repeated his plans.

Sam braced himself for the fury. Instead, he was treated to

a delighted response from Emma worthy of a million-dollar windfall.

"He don't have to drop out of school to play guitar. He could do that after he graduates," Sam stated meekly.

Emma waved her hand at him. "Oh please, Sam! You know the boy ain't good with books and numbers. What he's good at is playing the guitar. So let him do that."

It was ironic, to say the least—Harlan abandoning the very institution that had introduced him to his calling.

Harlan had studied piano in Macon. In New York, he continued to practice under his mother's tutelage, but it was soon clear to Emma that he didn't possess the same passion and talent she had. On top of that, he didn't really like it.

Frustrated and disappointed after one of their lessons, Emma caught Harlan by the chin. "Well, if not the piano, then what?"

Mayemma's son John had taken up the trumpet—this after witnessing Louis Armstrong's magic at one of Bill and Lucille's Friday-night parties. Harlan figured if John could blow, so could he. "The trumpet, I guess," he replied with a shrug of his shoulders.

The experiment had been a failure: Harlan clearly didn't have the lungs for the instrument.

It was in his high school music class that he first became acquainted with a battered caramel-colored Stella Parlor. When Harlan raked his fingers over the six strings, his entire body vibrated. He'd never thought of himself as incomplete—one half of something he could not name—but there it was, the very thing that had been missing from his young life.

Emma ran right out and bought Harlan his very own Stella Parlor and promptly signed him up to study with Vernon Craig, who at that time was considered a master of the guitar.

It cost a small fortune for Harlan to train with Vernon, but Emma didn't see the dollars and cents of it, just the glow of happiness on her boy's face.

Chapter 26

Before long, Harlan and John carried their combined talents to the streets, performing on corners in and around Harlem. The boys couldn't decide which was more thrilling—the money tossed into the cigar box resting at their feet, or the hip-bumping, finger-popping joy their music inspired in the people watching them.

When the two friends weren't practicing or performing, they were doing boy things: reading comics, play fighting, or, locked away in John's bedroom, pulling on their dicks until they were as rigid as metal rods. Which is what they were doing on that rainy Saturday afternoon when John's sister Darlene completely unraveled.

John aligned the wooden ruler alongside his penis and squinted at the black numbers. "I still got you by a half-inch," he laughed.

"What? Lemme see." Harlan stooped over to scrutinize the fading black number on the ruler just above the dome of John's penis. It wasn't quite a half-inch, but it was close. "Whatever," Harlan offered dismissively as he tugged the waist of his trousers over his hips.

John shoved his member back into his pants, dropped onto the bed, raised his foot, and joggled it near Harlan's face. "Big feet, big dick," he goaded, laughing. "It's the law of nature." John's feet weren't just big, they were boats. His mother complained that she needed a third job just to keep him in shoes.

"I'm going back downstairs," Harlan grumbled miserably.

John sat up and the grin on his face widened. "You sore at me because I got a bigger dick?"

"Nope," Harlan snapped.

"I think you are."

"Think what you want."

Harlan opened the bedroom door to find Darlene standing in the hallway, head cocked to one side, hands on her hips like she was grown—like she was someone's mama—gazing in that creepy way that raised the hairs on your neck.

Emma, not one to bite her tongue, had come right out and called Darlene bewitched.

"She'll grow out of it," Mayemma assured her.

And it wasn't just the creepy way she looked at people. There was that other thing about her, the dangerous thing. She had a fascination with matches. Lit ones. In fact, it was Emma who had discovered Darlene's compulsion.

When other kids were spending their coins on soda and candy, Darlene was saving her pennies to buy Ohio Blue Tip Kitchen Matches. Up until she was caught, Darlene had been content sitting by her bedroom window, striking matches, and watching the blue flame burn to smoke. But on the day that Emma discovered this, the pigeons were especially distracting, and Darlene had got it in her head to make the matches fly.

Emma was downstairs, standing at the kitchen window, pondering the tomatoes she'd planted in the backyard. When the first match came careening into view, she didn't know exactly what to make of it. "What in the world," she murmured, slamming through the back door just in time to see Darlene's black hand drop another match.

Back in the house and up the stairs, Emma shot into Mayemma's unlocked apartment like a rocket.

Darlene's head spun around—eyes wide with surprise.

"You black roach! Are you crazy!" Emma bellowed, spraying Darlene's face with spittle.

"I—"

Emma caught Darlene by the arm and slung her brutally onto the bed.

"I-I'm sorry, I was just playing," Darlene sobbed.

"Matches ain't toys; they're not to be played with. I know you're simple, but you ain't so simple that you don't know that!" Trembling with anger, Emma spun widely around the room. "Where is it?!"

Before Darlene could respond, Emma spotted the box of matches on the floor, snatched it up, and shook the box angrily in Darlene's face. "Is this it? You got any more?"

Darlene shook her head.

"Don't lie to me, girl!"

"That's the only box I have, I swear," Darlene sobbed.

"Wait till your mama gets home! I hope she beats the black off you!"

Days later, her behind still sore from the whipping Mayemma had dealt her, Darlene procured another box of matches and moved her hobby into the bathroom. No windows there, just a skylight.

She seemed helpless to stop. No amount of cuss words, threats, or lashes from a belt could force her to end that thing that Mayemma's former boyfriend, Will, had started.

He'd been gone from her life for years. Mayemma had moved on, but Darlene was still pining, longing for those times when Will pulled her into his lap and slipped his hand between her legs. As he fondled her, he blew breath as hot as steam onto her neck, murmuring: "D, you the best thing this side of the moon."

Afterward, he'd lean back in the chair, satisfied, slip a cigarette between his lips, strike a match, and dance the flame close to Darlene's face. "Ain't it beautiful?"

"Uh-huh."

"But you prettier."

No one had ever called her pretty, not even her mother.

She took the compliment to school and tossed it at the feet of those girls who told her she would never have a boyfriend because she was spook black, ink black, turn-off-the-lights-and-she-would-vanish black.

Their denigration outweighed Will's adulation, and Darlene began to experience sudden bursts of anger and uncontrollable sobbing. The peculiar look came and stayed, and soon, peering into Darlene's eyes was like watching the sun set from behind a filthy window.

Mayemma dismissed Darlene's behavior as adolescent growing pains, a prelude to the arrival of her monthly friend. But if Mayemma had taken the time to really look at her child, she would have realized that Darlene was unspooling, and Will was the one pulling the string.

Before she could put two and two together, Will up and quit Mayemma like a bad habit. He packed up his few rags and left without even a goodbye. The only thing that suggested he'd ever been in their lives was the box of Blue Tip Matches he'd left behind.

That day, when Harlan opened the bedroom door to find Darlene standing in the hallway, the evidence of what she had been doing was hanging thick in the air.

"Pee-u!" Harlan sounded, fanning his hands. "You sure are hardheaded. You must enjoy getting whooped."

John leaped from the bed. "Goddamn, Darlene, why can't you mind?"

Darlene ran into the parlor and planted herself firmly between Harlan and the door leading out of the apartment.

"Save me!" she squealed girlishly.

"C'mon now, I don't feel like playing."

Darlene pushed her lips out in an exaggerated pout.

"Get out of his way, Darlene!" John shouted as he pounded toward them.

Darlene raised her hands. "But I got something I wanna show y'all."

Harlan rolled his eyes. "What is it?"

"Man, don't pay her no mind," John said. "Darlene, get outta his way before I get the belt and whoop you myself!"

"Just two minutes," Darlene whined. "Pleeeeasaase!"

"You ain't gotta—"

"It's okay, let's just see what it is," Harlan interrupted.

Darlene grinned. "Okay, sit down, I'll be back," she said, before moving to the phonograph.

The boys flopped down onto the couch, clasped their hands behind their heads, and stared at the ceiling.

Soon, "Flamin' Mamie" by the Six Black Diamonds filled the room.

John and Harlan tapped their feet; they liked that song.

Darlene cupped her hands around her mouth. "I won't be

back!" she yelled, and skipped out of the room.

"What she say?" Harlan asked.

John shrugged. "I dunno."

She's Flamin' Mamie, the surefire vamp / The hottest baby in town...

The music was so loud, Harlan was sure he'd soon hear Emma shouting from the bottom of the staircase for them to turn it off. With that thought, he rose from the couch, went to the phonograph, and lowered the volume.

When it comes to loving / She's a human oven...

A bloodcurdling yowl echoed through the apartment. Startled, both boys looked at the phonograph. A second ear-piercing scream followed, this time accompanied by violent, erratic thumping that rattled the walls.

"What the—" John started, but Harlan was already running through the apartment calling Darlene's name.

Smoke foamed from beneath the bathroom door.

Inside, Darlene shrieked in terror and pain as the ravenous flames consumed her body.

Harlan jiggled the hot knob and John threw his weight against the door. While they were fanning smoke, shouting, and pleading for Darlene to open the door, Sam appeared at their backs and shoved them roughly aside. He hit the door, felling it with one blow.

They found Darlene smoldering in the tub, her body lurching and shuddering with shock. Sam removed his shirt and smothered the dying orange flames flickering on her scalp.

Emma had followed Sam up the stairs and into the apartment, but Darlene's screams stopped her like a wall, leaving Emma cemented to the parlor floor, hugging her shoulders and trembling, as the phonograph needle skipped repeatedly over one phrase: *She's a heart scorcher/Loves torture...*

Darlene languished in Harlem Hospital for weeks before transitioning. A steady stream of visitors came through daily, bringing with them flowers, prayers, and words of encouragement.

Even the cruel girls from school came to see. They gathered at Darlene's bedside, secretly wondering if beneath all those layers of gauze, Darlene was finally free of that awful dark skin—now a pinkish-white, the same color the tops of their ears turned when the hot comb slipped and seared them.

Chapter 27

"The service was lovely. Closed casket, of course."

"Of course. I wouldn't have wanted to see that child all burned up."

"You ain't never seen a burned body?"

"No, ma'am. Have you?"

"Girl, I'm from Mississippi, stringing niggers up and setting them afire is the official state pastime."

"Well, I'm glad I'm from Chicago. Anyway, I wish I could have made the funeral, but you know I had to work."

"But you made the wake, right?"

"No, Mrs. Trellis had a dinner party that day. She asked me to work it, even though it was my day off. What was I supposed to say? *No, Mrs. Trellis, I gots a wake to attend?*"

"Who you think you fooling, girl? Just say you did it for the extra money."

"Well, I ain't never said no to a dollar!"

"You say no, and somebody right there next to you saying yes." "You got that right, Lenora!"

"Lemme ask you something, Josephine: can you imagine setting yourself on fire?"

"'Course not! And I don't want to believe such a thing!"

"What a horrible way to die."

"Terrible."

"Why you think she did it?"

99

"Girl, that is the question for the ages. But you know she never did seem right to me. A little off in the head, if you know what I mean."

"You're kind. Bless your heart. Tell the truth now, the girl was strange. The way she just stared... Honestly, I didn't like being 'round her."

"I felt the same."

"So what else?"

"Well, the repast was at the Elliotts'."

"Was it now?"

"I tell you one thing, that Emma Elliott knows how to lay a table!" "Hmmm, well, you know, she always down for a party. You ever pass her house on Saturday night? Music blaring and folks jumping 'round like frogs."

"Well, Lenora, I would not consider a repast a party."

"Okay, okay. How's the mother holding up?"

"Mayemma? She a mess, of course. Any mother would be."

"Yes."

"And the boy, her son... What's his name again?"

"John."

"John? Such a simple name, I don't know why I can't ever remember it. How is he doing?"

"He sad. Blew his horn in his sister's honor."

"At the church?"

"Nah, outside on the sidewalk. Stood straight as a soldier, aimed his horn to the heavens, and blew like an angel."

"Aww, that's nice. What he play?"

"Don't know, but the tune sho' was sad. Mayemma had to be carried away."

"You go upstairs?"

"Don't think terrible of me now, but I was just dying to see!"

"So you did go upstairs?"

"I did."

"Is it like they say? She did it in the kitchen?"

"Whoever they is, they got their information wrong. She did it in the bathroom."

"In the bathroom? Why they say she did it in the kitchen?"

"'Cause that's where she got the can of grease."

"Grease?"

"Uh-huh. I hear she poured grease over herself before she... well, you know."

"Lawd Jesus, fix it."

"Too late for that. Lucky she did it in the bathroom. If not, the whole house would have gone up in flames."

"Why the bathroom so special?"

"'Cause she lit herself up in the tub. Cast iron, don't you know."

"Oh yeah. So you saw it. The bathroom?"

"You know I've always been light on my feet."

"Like a dancer, you are!"

"Uh-huh. I tipped right up them stairs and was back down before anyone missed me."

"What'd you see?"

"First, it stinks to high heaven up there. You can still smell the smoke, and her..."

"What?"

"Skin. Flesh. Whatever you wanna call it."

"Oh."

"And the bathroom tile is as black as I don't know what."

"Like she was?"

"It ain't right to talk ill of the dead."

"Just trying to lighten the mood. Go 'head on."

"Well, Emma is just torn to bits. You'd think she lost her own child. And Harlan, well, he ain't handling it any better. Emma say every other night he wakes up screaming Darlene's name."

"He dreaming 'bout her? Make sense. How Sam holding up?"

"You can never tell with him. But I suspect he hurting too."

"So sad."

"Ain't it though? Anyway, Mayemma and that boy of hers moving out to New Jersey."

"New Jersey!"

"Mayemma say she done with Harlem."

"My goodness, there are other places in New York she can move to. Brooklyn, for example."

"Brooklyn? Who in their right mind wanna live in that ass-backward place? Nothing but bumpkins live in Brooklyn."

"True."

"When she leaving?"

"She's already gone. Left two days after the funeral."

"Aww, that's a shame. I sho' would have liked to have said goodbye."

After the tragedy, Emma placed their Saturday-night house parties on hiatus, but word of mouth was slow to spread. The following weekend some folks showed up as usual, bottles in hand, ready to party. Even though the house was dark and as quiet as a tomb, they still rang the bell.

When Emma opened the door, her solemn face said it all.

But some people just aren't very perceptive.

"Girl, you look like someone died!" a woman cackled. Emma didn't crack a smile.

"Wait, someone died for real?"

Emma closed the door without a word.

Chapter 28

"I'm thinking about enrolling in nursing school," Lucille announced suddenly while she and Emma sat in her kitchen sipping sweet tea and chomping on fried bologna sandwiches.

Emma's mouth dropped open. "Nursing school?"

The good times, Lucille explained, were rolling to an end. "With the Depression and things being the way they are, we ain't selling records like we used to." She shrugged her shoulders. "My manager says my style of music is going the way of the dodo bird." A wounded chuckle escaped her.

"Nursing school?" Emma echoed.

"Um-hum, what else am I gonna do? Day work?"

Emma slowly shook her head. She'd traveled that road, and it had been bumpy and unforgiving.

"I can see it now," Lucille spoke dreamily, "me walking into some white lady's house in my starched maid's uniform, all ready to attack the baseboards and her husband's dirty drawers, and then..." She paused dramatically; her eyes stretched saucer-wide and when she spoke again her voice was shrill and animated: *"Oh my! Is that Lucille Hegamin? The Lucille Hegamin? Why, I saw you perform at the Panther Club, and I have all of your records!"*

The women howled with laughter.

Lucille wiped tears from her eyes. "I won't put myself through that type of embarrassment."

"And the house?"

Lucille's face clouded. "Gonna have to let it go."

Emma reached across the table and closed her hand over Lucille's.

"I'm sorry."

"Don't be. I... we all had some good times here. It served its purpose and served it well. My season is over. Seasons come to an end. Don't the Good Book say as much?"

Emma nodded.

"Besides, it wasn't always easy being Lucille Hegamin—"

"The *great* Lucille Hegamin," Emma corrected with a smile.

"So they say," Lucille sighed. "People don't know how hard I had to work. How much I had to give up."

"I know," Emma said.

Lucille turned toward the window—sunlight lit the tears swimming in her eyes. "You know, it wasn't easy being in Mamie Smith's shadow."

Emma squeezed her hand.

"You don't get no parade for being second," Lucille huffed. Emma, eager to brighten the grim mood that had befallen the kitchen, hurriedly changed the subject. "So, when you gonna start nursing school?"

"Hmmm, I don't know yet. Right now, it's just a thought. Until I make up my mind, I'm going to ride this train until it runs out of steam."

"Oh?"

"Umh-hm. I'm booked solid for the next six months."

"That's good."

"God is good." Lucille winked and raised her glass of sweet tea in salute. "I've got some dates booked down south, and I was wondering if you think Harlan might wanna come along."

Emma was struck. "Really?"

"After all he's been through, seeing that child doing what she did..." Lucille trailed off, shaking her head. "I just think it would be good for him to get away."

Emma grinned.

"Best he see for himself that this life ain't as easy or as glamorous as folks think. Best he see the for-real-deal before he jump in with two feet." Lucille drained her glass, slapped her chest, and belched. "What you think, Emma? You think he ready for the road?"

Emma beamed, "Yeah, I think he is."

Chapter 29

Harlan, all of sixteen, having only really been in Macon and Harlem, hit the road green, brimming with delight.

In a rickety bus that had seen better days, the veteran musicians and their entourage rolled out of New York on a spring morning thick with the scent of flowering things.

They traveled for days, covering mile upon mile of open road and ever-changing countryside. Harlan watched with amazement as emerald pastures gave way to fields choked with cotton stalks, plantation estates, and ramshackle shotguns.

Their first stop was Wilson, North Carolina, and even though the country was crawling through the muck and grime of financial ruin and despair, you wouldn't have known it by the number of people who came out to see them.

"Man, you look as green as a frog!" the squat, flat-faced drummer named Cecil laughed. "You scared?"

They were about to perform on a makeshift stage in a dilapidated barn that reeked of livestock. Lucille was on the bus, donning her dress for the evening.

Harlan looked down at his sweaty, trembling hands. "No," he gulped nervously.

The drummer shoved a half-empty jar of corn liquor at him. "Drink this, it'll calm you down."

The swig Harlan took would have been too much for a drinking man, much less a young boy who'd only stolen sips of beer. He gagged. The drummer laughed again, slapped Harlan hard on the back, and told him to take another. "You'll get used to it," he said.

Harlan's hands stopped shaking, but now his head was spinning.

"Come on." Cecil grabbed him by the elbow.

On the stage, the guitar strings felt like spaghetti against his fingers. Sweat as biting as lime juice streamed into his eyes as he clumsily strummed chords that might have belonged to some other singer's song, but not Lucille's.

After the show, an angry Lucille pressed her lips together and stomped past Harlan without a word.

Bill was the one who took him aside. "If you can't handle your liquor, you shouldn't drink," he warned angrily.

Shamed, Harlan dropped his head and stammered an inaudible apology.

By the time they reached South Carolina, Harlan hadn't had a swig of anything harder than Coca-Cola and he was beginning to perform like a pro.

After a show in Charleston, Cecil loudly proclaimed, "You did great out there!"

"Thanks."

He pulled a cigarette from behind his ear and held it out to Harlan. "For you."

Harlan scrutinized it for a second. "Naw, I don't smoke."

Cecil's eyes narrowed. "Aw, you think this is the tobacco type of cigarette?"

Harlan shrugged his shoulders.

"This here," Cecil announced grandly, "is a reefer cigarette.

One puff of this and you'll know Jesus." He slipped the cigarette between his lips, pulled a silver lighter from his suit jacket, and fired the tip.

Harlan watched the flame swell and collapse as the drummer puffed.

"You gotta hold it in," Cecil instructed in a strangled voice. After a few seconds, he blew a stream of smoke into Harlan's face. "Just try it. One toke, that's all. That's all you'll need."

Harlan smirked. "Naw, that's okay."

"Don't you wanna know Jesus, boy?"

Craig, the piano player, swaggered by, nodding in their direction. When his nose caught the pungent scent, he turned back. "May I?" he asked, grinning.

Cecil passed him the joint.

Craig inhaled deeply and then exhaled. "Damn, that's some good shit," he coughed.

"The best," Cecil said, thrusting the joint at Harlan for the second time. "You'll play better than you ever thought you could."

"Sure 'nuff," Craig agreed.

Three tokes later, Harlan couldn't stop laughing at his shoe-laces. An hour after that, he was stumbling up and down the dark aisle of the bus, begging for food to quell his ravenous appetite.

Their arrival in Augusta, Georgia coincided with the National Baptist Convention, so all of the colored guesthouses were full. Bill informed them that they would have to spend the night on the bus.

Harlan watched the musicians remove their shoes and fold their jackets into makeshift pillows. "But we passed a hotel not a mile down the road that had a vacancy sign in the front yard," he said sleepily.

"You talking 'bout the Partridge Inn?" Bill questioned.

"Yeah, I think so."

Bill laughed.

Lucille pulled a purple scarf over her curls and knotted it behind her neck. "Boy, this ain't Harlem," she said. "Down south, you can't walk through the front door of any establishment you please, sit down, eat and drink your gut full. Down here, if your bladder begs, you got to search high and low for a bathroom marked *Colored*. This here is Jim Crow territory—the rules down here are different. That vacancy sign you saw was for white folks, not us."

Chapter 30

The following night, they performed under a massive tent raised in the middle of a cow pasture. Before taking the stage, Harlan sought out Cecil and his magic cigarettes.

"Um, you got some more of that weed?"

Cecil eyed him amusingly, crowing, "You done had all the freebies you gonna get from me. You want some more, it's gonna cost you."

"How much?"

"Fifty cents."

The band opened with "Chattanooga Man" and moved into "Down Hearted Blues," "Always Be Careful Mama," and "Dinah." After two hours, they closed the show with "Reckless Daddy."

It was Harlan's best set to date. He knew it before Bill and Lucille even told him. He had felt like a king on that stage—unstoppable and all-powerful.

And best of all, that night when Harlan bedded down on the cramped bus seat, Darlene was nowhere to be found and he slept soundly.

In Mobile, Alabama, the entire band stayed at the home of Clarence and Joy Temple, a wealthy white couple who had befriended Lucille early in her career.

"They ain't your run-of-the-mill white folks," Lucille called out over the laboring engine as the bus chugged its way up the halfmile-long driveway. "These people are free thinkers. *Liberals* is what they call themselves."

The home came into view. Stacked porches, Greek columns, and a sweeping verandah. Harlan had never seen anything like it.

"How many people live there?" he whispered in awe.

"Just them two," Lucille said. "Not counting the help."

Clarence and Joy were well into their seventies, silver-haired and wrinkled. Their matching green eyes made them look more like siblings than husband and wife. They seemed hungry for the company. Unwilling to let their guests retire. After the sumptuous meal, the Temples coaxed everyone out onto the rear porch to sip cognac and deliberate on all things musical.

It was near midnight when Harlan, yawning, excused himself and headed up to the room he was sharing with Craig. Before retiring, he slipped into their private bathroom and red up one of the three joints he'd purchased from Cecil.

Head spinning, floating more than walking, he crossed the room and dove onto the goose-feathered mattress, slipping into blissful slumber.

Just at the tip of three, Cecil stumbled noisily into the bedroom, hissing, "Pssst!"

The room flooded with yellow light.

"Pssssssst! Harlan!"

"Shit," Craig mumbled angrily.

Harlan sat up, shielding his eyes.

"Turn that light off!" Craig growled. "Ain't you got your own room to go to?"

Alongside Cecil was a curvaceous raisin-colored woman.

Cecil dragged her toward Harlan. "You gotta see her eyes." He was giddy. "I ain't never seen no shit like this in my life!"

The two reeked of whiskey, reefer, and something else Harlan couldn't put his finger on.

Craig sat up. "Man, you crazy or what? Here these nice white folks welcome us into their home, and you bring a whore up in here?"

"Aw, man, shut the fuck up and mind your business," Cecil snapped.

"It's 'cause a niggers like you that good, decent black folk get a bad rap!" With that, Craig punched his pillow, lay back down, and turned his back on the sordid affair.

"Go show him," Cecil urged. "Wait till you see this, Harlan."

The woman wobbled forward. The hem of the tight black and red dress she wore inched up her thigh with each step. When she reached Harlan's bedside, she uttered a breathless, "Hi," before flopping down on his thighs.

"Show him," Cecil urged again.

"Okay, okay, damn," the girl giggled. "See," she sang, pushing her face into his and stretching her already large eyes wider.

Swimming in the dark pond of her face were two watery blue orbs, ringed in gold.

"You ever seen anything like that in your life? A nigger with blue eyes?" Cecil slapped his thighs, chortling. "That's some wild shit right there!"

Harlan's lips flapped. The woman raked her fingers across his bare chest. "You a scrawny something, huh?" she purred. "How old you is?"

Harlan looked stupidly at Cecil, who was still bent over

laughing.

"Eighteen," Harlan coughed.

"Sixteen!" Craig yelled from his bed. "Too young for your old ass."

"I ain't gonna tell you again, Craig," Cecil warned. He looked back at Harlan and licked his lips. "Hey, she a pretty thing, don't you think?" Harlan nodded.

"I thought you'd feel that way. That's why I brung her up here for you to have."

Harlan blinked. "*Have*?"

"Yeah!" Cecil laughed.

Harlan's eyes bulged.

"Nigger, this is where you say thank you," Cecil admonished.

"Say thank you, nigger, so I can get some goddamn sleep!" Craig cried.

The girl took Harlan's face into her hands. "Tell me something, boy. You still a virgin?"

Harlan swallowed hard. "Yes, ma'am."

The woman giggled, rolled back the quilt, and pressed her hand against his groin. "Oh my," she crooned seductively. "Well, that there ain't scrawny at all, is it?"

Cecil turned off the light and backed out of the room, whispering, "And to all a good night."

Harlan woke to the scent of flapjacks and bacon. Upon opening his eyes, his stomach growled. He lay there for a moment, trying to figure out if the woman had been a dream spurred on by the reefer. But that notion was quickly put to rest when out of the corner of his eye, he spotted a pair of blue panties crumpled on the pillow beside his head.

Chapter 31

Sam and Emma waited all day for the bus—taking turns leaning out the window, standing on the stoop, walking from one corner of the block to the next, and pacing the parlor floor like parents awaiting the birth of their first child.

"You see anything?"

"Nope, not yet."

It was nearly eight o'clock when the bus finally arrived. They nearly tripped over one another getting through the door and down the steps to greet their son.

When Harlan stepped off the bus, Emma stalled. Even in the fading summer light, she saw in Harlan what she had seen in Lucille the first time she'd gone away and come back. "Oh," she mumbled miserably, "he's pissing straight now."

Not only that—Harlan was taller and heavier, and there was a shadow of dark hair above his upper lip. Gone was the carefree, arm-swinging gait, replaced now by a confident swagger historically hitched to men who frequented pool halls and whorehouses, drank whiskey before noon, and kept a lit cigarette dangling from the knotted corners of their mouths. Those men carried switchblades in their coat pockets, pistols stuffed behind the waistbands of their trousers. They smoked dope, had women in every city and children they would never claim. Those men worshipped jewelry, money, and pussy. They lived fast and died young.

Harlan opened his arms. "Hey, Mama, Daddy," he called sluggishly.

Sam took his hand and pumped it exuberantly. "Welcome home, son. Welcome home."

Emma folded her arms across her chest. "Hello, Harlan," she offered coolly.

Oblivious to the chill, Harlan leaned in and planted a wet kiss on her cheek. "Did you miss me?"

Emma turned her face away from his alcohol-soaked breath. "Um-hum."

Harlan chuckled, kissed her again, and started up the steps. Sam followed close behind, happily lugging his son's suitcase.

Later, over a hefty plate of boiled potatoes, pig tails, and black-eyed peas, Harlan regaled them with stories from the road. He went on and on about the venues, the audiences, sleeping on the bus, pissing and shitting in the woods, and that time the bus broke down beneath a big sky. Lucille had spat on the ground and called that place the "middle of nowhere," but it was beautiful and green and quiet in a way Harlan didn't know the world could be. He left out the blue-eyed black woman and all the other ladies who followed, and the reefer.

Emma listened quietly, suspiciously. Sam, however, was so enthralled that he forgot about his food, leaning over his plate, lapping up every word that tumbled out of Harlan's mouth. When Sam finally scooped a potato into his mouth, it was cold.

Harlan dropped his fork into the center of the plate, fell back into the chair, and slapped his gut like an old, sated man. "That was good, Mama, thanks," he yawned.

"Yeah, baby, that was good," Sam chimed, smacking his lips. Emma nodded, rose from her chair, and silently cleared the table.

Harlan cocked his eyebrow. "You okay, Mama?"

"Yeah, you okay?" Sam echoed.

"I'm just fine," Emma responded tersely, evidence that she was not fine, not fine at all.

Father and son exchanged a cautious glance. When Emma was out of earshot, Sam scooted his chair closer to Harlan. "So, tell me 'bout the gals."

That night, Emma's nose caught the scent of something foul. She sat up, sniffing the air and rubbing sleep from her eyes. The scent was unmistakable: reefer.

"Not in my goddamn house," she grumbled angrily, slapping Sam on the shoulder. "Get up!"

They found Harlan in bed, his back propped against two pillows, one hand behind his head, the other holding a joint.

"What's wrong?" he sputtered when they rushed into the room.

Emma's eyes narrowed; she aimed a stiff index finger at the joint. "Is that what I think it is?"

A wisp of a grin surfaced on Harlan's lips. "That depends. What do you think it is?"

"Now look here—" Sam started just as Emma exploded.

"Don't you sass me, Harlan Elliott! You're not too old for the switch, you know!" She turned wild eyes on Sam. "Tell him!"

Sam's lips flapped, but before a word could cross his tongue, Emma was shrieking again.

"Dope? Dope! In my house? You think 'cause you got your dick wet, you grown? Well let me tell you something, Negro, you must have left your whole mind down south somewhere, if you think you gonna sit up in my house smoking dope!"

Harlan's face warmed with amusement. "Aww, Mama, this ain't dope. I seen dope, and this ain't it." He turned to his father. "Pop, will you please tell her that it's no big deal?"

"I think—"

"You know like I know," Emma interrupted. "You better not ever smoke that shit in my house again."

And with that, she stormed from the room, leaving Sam standing there looking at the tops of his feet. Finally, when he was sure there was no threat of Emma interrupting him again, he mumbled, "Listen to your mother, boy," and walked out of the bedroom.

Emma lay in bed seething until the sky paled and the streets came alive with the chattering of domestics hurrying to catch the downtown bus. After Sam headed off to work in Greenwich, Connecticut—a town he claimed to be so wealthy that the butchers wrapped meat in hundred-dollar bills—Emma washed and put away the breakfast dishes, wrote a letter home to her mother, put a roast in the oven, swept and mopped the floors, and played Chopin's "Marche Funèbre"—three times.

When she looked at the clock and saw that it was half past one and Harlan still hadn't made an appearance, she went up to his bedroom, shook him awake, and picked up where they had left off.

"Aww, Mama," Harlan whined, "why you making such a big deal about this? All the musicians smoke it."

"I don't do it," Emma snapped.

"Of course you don't," Harlan remarked smugly. "That's because you ain't no real musician, you just a piano teacher."

If Harlan had spat in her face or called her a dog, it still wouldn't have been as cutting.

"What did you say?"

Harlan saw too late the hurt crouching in her eyes. "Mama, I didn't mean—"

Emma raised her hand. "Don't say another word." She walked stiffly from the room.

That night, Sam came home to a dark and quiet house. Harlan was out; Emma was in bed, under the covers, sobbing.

Sam tried and failed to pry from her the name of the person who had hurt her so badly, but Emma refused to say; she just clung to him and wept.

Chapter 32

Pussy: hypnotic and narcotic. It had toppled dynasties, initiated wars, transformed boys into men, men into idiots, led husbands away from their good wives, turned sons against their dedicated mothers—had Harlan believing he was kin to Christopher Columbus, as if he'd discovered sex, as if it hadn't existed before he was born.

Fool.

Four years of steady fucking, combined with a daily, healthy dosage of reefer and Scotch, had raised in Harlan a level of conceit that people (mostly grown folk) found difficult to endure.

Him, coming to rehearsal late, stinking of weed, liquor, and self-regard, boldly directing the great Lucille Hegamin on just how she should sing her own damn songs.

Scandalous.

Lucille had kept Harlan on after the tour, not because he was such a great guitarist—he was adequate at best—but because she loved his mother like a sister. But even love has limits, and Harlan had managed to breach every one.

In September of '37, four years after Lucille first took Harlan out on the road and returned him to Harlem with his nose wide open and narrow ass propped high on his shoulders, Lucille decided that enough was enough.

Harlan stumbled into rehearsal, high and late, and Lucille wagged an angry finger at him, yelling, "Just turn your black ass around and go on back where you came from."

A lopsided grin rippled across his face as he continued to move unsteadily toward her, bouncing his hands in the air. "I... know, I know I'm late, but lemme tell you what happened—"

"Nah, ain't interested. You're done," she spat.

"Is it about the fine? I got the money," he slurred, slapping the pockets of his pants. "Oh yeah, I moved it." He chuckled, lifting the black Stetson from his head and removing a few dollars from the interior band. "Here you go." Harlan flung the bills at her.

Lucille watched in open-mouthed astonishment as the money fluttered down to the scuffed wooden floor.

The musicians shifted uncomfortably, their eyes skating between Harlan, Lucille, and the wilted dollar bills lying at her feet.

"Out. Get out and don't come back," Lucille ordered in a trembling voice.

"Psshhh," Harlan sounded, dismissing her with a wave of his hand.

She flew at him, rushed him like a linebacker, howling, "I said get the hell out!"

Les Parker, the clarinet player, caught her by the arm and swung her out of striking distance. "Calm down, Ms. Lucille."

Harlan reared back. "You serious?" He was genuinely miffed. "I gave you the money, didn't I?"

Les said, "Just go man, okay?"

"But I gave her the money."

"You're fired," Lucille rasped, trying to wiggle free of Les's grip. "Get the hell out!"

Harlan looked around the room, helplessly searching for

support, but none of the men would meet his pleading gaze. "So that's the way it is, huh?"

"Yeah, that's the way it is," Lucille shot back.

They stood glaring at one another until Harlan arrogantly cocked his Stetson to the side of his head. "Forget you then. Forget all of you."

Harlan spent the remainder of the day roaming through Harlem, dragging Lucille's name through the streets like a mangy dog.

Somewhere between the Midnight Bar and the pool hall, his guitar went missing. Lost, stolen, or gambled away in some backroom game of craps—he couldn't recall.

By the time he got home, he was so intoxicated he could barely manage the steps. After several attempts, he finally reached the front door, but was unable to fit his key into the lock and so gave up, slumped down onto the stoop, and promptly fell asleep. His Stetson toppled off his head and careened down onto the sidewalk. Without missing a beat, a passing pedestrian scooped up the hat, placed it in the crook of his arm, and hurried away.

An hour later, Sam arrived home from work to find Harlan slouched over and snoring. He had a mind to leave him right where he slept, but he knew Emma would never forgive him. He hooked his hands under Harlan's armpits, dragged him into the house, and dropped him in the hall. The commotion startled Emma, who was in her bedroom changing the linen. She appeared on the top landing—head crowded with pink, foam rollers—brandishing a hammer.

"Oh my goodness, what happened to him?" she exclaimed.

"He's fine, just drunk."

"Are you sure?" Emma checked Harlan's face and neck for

bruises.

Finding none, she sighed with relief.

"Hey, you been crying?" Sam asked.

Yes, Emma had. The tip of her nose was as bright as maraschino cherry and her eyes were puffy. Her lips quivered. "Oh Sam, it's awful," she sniffed. "Bessie Smith is dead."

Part IV

Coming to America

Chapter 33

SEPTEMBER 26, 1937
BESSIE SMITH, QUEEN OF THE BLUES, HAS CHANTED
HER LAST INDIGO LAMENT...

Beneath the headline of the week-old newspaper was Bessie Smith's smiling black face. Ethel studied the photo and with a shrug of her shoulders muttered, "So what," and then folded it in half and laid it across a white dinner plate. "Gwen! Gwen! Your tea is getting cold, gal!" Ethel's shrill voice echoed through the apartment like an alarm bell.

"I'm coming!" the girl called back. From her bedroom, she soft-shoed her way through the living room and into the kitchen. Just about five feet four inches in height, thick-legged, the color of warm honey, Gwen was an exact replica of her mother at that age: fourteen.

When Gwen made her raucous entrance into the kitchen, Ethel turned on her, wagging the spatula. "Stop all that noise, girl!" she scolded. "Have some respect for the people downstairs."

"Sorry," Gwen mumbled.

Ethel smiled in spite of herself. "What me going do with you, heh?" She slipped the spatula into the frying pan and carefully flipped the half dollar–sized Barbadian staple made out of water, flour, sugar, nutmeg, and baking powder. Bakes were usually served with fried fish, but there was no fish that morning, so Gwen would have to make do with bacon.

Ethel lifted the bakes from the pan and placed them on the newspaper to drain. She watched, unbothered, as the oil seeped across Bessie's face, then set the plate on the table before Gwen.

"Where's your food, Mum?"

"I already ate. Hurry up or you'll be late." Ethel retrieved her teacup from the table and went to stand in the spray of sunlight coming through the window. Even after a decade, she was still amazed at how the air could be cold even when the sky was clear and the sun dazzlingly bright. In Barbados, clear or cloudy, rain or shine—it was always hot. Shuddering, she pulled the panels of her robe closed over her chest.

Ten years?

Ethel shook her head in wonder. The decade had run off like sand through a sieve. Quick. When she'd left Barbados she hadn't one gray hair—now she had a headful. "I picked up half of them on the trip over," Ethel chuckled to herself.

Gwen stopped chewing. "Mum?"

"I'm just talking to myself." The memories of the crossing, those first hard years, were still fresh in Ethel's mind; she could recall them with ease, as if she'd just stepped off the ship last week.

It was December. It was a Tuesday. The wharf was packed with weeping and cheering people waving handkerchiefs and miniature Barbadian flags. Ethel's young daughters, Irene and Gwendolyn, hadn't known that they were supposed to feel sad about leaving Barbados, and so smiled and waved back at the crowd. Ethel thought that was okay because she had enough tears for all three of them.

When the SS *Munargo* was so far out to sea that Barbados was little more than a shadow on the water, the passengers turned their attention to the setting sun. When the fiery ball disappeared, they focused their sights on the ever-darkening sky, the tremendous ocean rolling beneath it, and forced themselves to imagine how life would be in America.

Two weeks later, the ship floated into New York on a frigid, cloudy morning. The Hudson River was swimming with ice and tugboats. Overhead, seagulls squawked and swooped frantically across the slate sky.

Layered in the scratchy wool blankets provided by the shipping company and every stitch of clothing they owned, the passengers rushed on deck. They gasped at the cold, and the sound floated out of their mouths in frosty white clouds.

When the Statue of Liberty came into view, some passengers broke out into song: "*Oh beautiful for spacious skies...*" Others dropped to their knees in gratitude, threw their hands up in celebration, grabbed hold of their loved ones and squeezed.

Little Gwen, just four years old at the time, glanced shyly at Lady Liberty, pressed her cheek against Ethel's thigh, and softly chanted, "America, America, America..."

Chapter 34

Aubrey Gill had only one suit. It was navy blue. He only wore this suit on special occasions—night-watch service and Easter Sunday. The day he went to collect his family from Ellis Island was as special as any of those days, so Aubrey donned that blue suit, sprinkled a few drops of Old Spice cologne on the lapels, and headed off to Manhattan.

In the receiving area, upon seeing their family members, people whooped with joy and broke into dead runs, flinging themselves into the arms of their beloveds.

Ethel watched in wonder.

Extravagant expressions of affection were not her way. Not the way of any Barbadian she knew. Barbadians prided themselves on their reserve, just like that of the island's ruling royal English family.

When Ethel spotted Aubrey's six-foot-six frame floating above the throng of people, she gently squeezed her daughters' hands. "There's your daddy."

"Daddy!" Irene yelped with excitement.

"Daddy!" Gwen echoed, even though she had no memory of Aubrey, who had left Barbados when she was just three months old.

Aubrey and four other fathers in earshot turned around, faces plastered with wide smiles.

Both hands waving, Aubrey hurried toward his family.

Husband and wife beamed at each other. "I glad to see yuh," he said.

Ethel curled her fingers around his forearm. "I glad to see you too."

Aubrey rested his hand on top of hers and grinned down at his daughters. "Who deez pretty ladies, Ethel?"

Irene blushed. "It's me, Daddy!"

"Me? Me who?" Aubrey laughed.

"Irene!" Irene cried.

Aubrey pressed his palms against his cheeks and rocked on his heels in mock amazement. "My little Irene? Can't be!"

Irene nodded vigorously.

"And this little one. What is her name?"

Irene's face went slack, her tone turned serious. "Daddy, don't you remember Gwendolyn?"

Aubrey winked at Ethel, who pressed a calloused palm over her smile.

"Are you telling me that this is Gwenie?"

"Yes, it is," Irene responded earnestly.

Aubrey bellowed with laughter and scooped both girls up into his arms. "You think I could forget you all?" He planted kisses on their foreheads, then looked at Ethel. "They're sweet enough, heh?"

Their new home was located in Brooklyn, on a long east-west street called Fulton that was lined with dreary gray and redbrick mixed-use buildings. Monday through Saturday the sidewalks teemed with peddlers, hawking all manner of pickled things, jams, vegetables, freshly baked bread, and hard and soft cheeses.

The street itself was a hazard. Daily, some unwitting

pedestrian was mowed down by a horse and buggy, bicyclist, kid on a pogo stick, or trolley snaking its way along the latticework of silver tracks. At night when all other Brooklyn streets had been put to sleep, Fulton still sparked and sizzled with life: marauding stray dogs, ravenous rats, and drunkards loudly serenading the streetlamps.

Located above a butcher shop, the apartment originally intended for one family was now rented out as rooms, accommodating three families.

Their room was average size, consisting of a pair of double beds, one chest of drawers, one closet, and a pale blue wooden rocking chair. The dull oak floors were pocked and dimpled with wear, and the once-white walls were yellow with age and veined with cracks. At the center of the distended ceiling hung a single sputtering lightbulb.

Certainly not the home Ethel had hoped for.

Aubrey saw disappointment sweep across his wife's face. He dropped his head, shoved his hands deep into the wells of his trouser pockets, and mumbled ashamedly, "It's just until we can do better."

Ethel nodded, forced a smile, and heeded her mother's warning:

When you get there, I don't care if he living in a box, you hold your tongue. No quarreling, hear? Yuh lucky he sending for you and the chirren. You see how many wives here without husbands? How many women here without men?

The lure of the American dollar had slowly emptied Barbados and her sister islands of most of their able-bodied men. Soon enough, the women left behind looked up from their bubbling pots of rice, from hands plunged deep into galvanized tubs of soapy water, up from the scaling of fish and plaiting of hair, and were astonished to find that their men were all gone.

On Thursday evenings and Sunday mornings, fingers banded in rings of Guyanese gold, the women filled church pews, babies propped on their laps, older children sitting at their hips silently watching their mothers flip frantically through battered Bibles in search of a psalm that could provide comfort for a lonely soul awaiting the return of her man.

At the end of the American harvesting and planting seasons, some Caribbean men did return, and those women who could steal away from work to meet the ships did. Clothed in vibrantly colored dresses and skirts, they swarmed the wharf like hungry rodents, congesting the air with their spirited chatter, perfume, and scented hair grease.

For some, however, the joy was fleeting. Not all of the men came home. Within weeks, the sad truth arrived by post, telegram, or the worst delivery of all—gossip—advising the waiting woman that she should pawn her wedding ring and get on with her life, because he had gotten on with his in the land of the free and home of the brave.

But not Ethel's husband. Not Aubrey Gill. When his letter arrived, it contained American greenbacks and said: *Buy passage for you and the girls and come.*

So Ethel did as her mother told her—held her tongue as best she could—and set both feet in the well of gratitude.

She looked at the four blank walls. "No window?"

"It's just for a little while, Ethel," Aubrey repeated.

Ethel bobbed her head thoughtfully. "Who in the other rooms?" Aubrey pointed at the wall to his left. "A family from Trinidad.

Husband, wife, daughter, and son." He aimed his chin at the wall to the right. "A couple from Haiti."

Ethel frowned. A fine way to start a new life, she thought, pulling back the dull brown bedspread to examine the cleanliness of the sheets. She did not like Trinidadians. Her baby sister had married one. Three years and two children later, she was running for her life, the husband hot on her heels, swinging a cutlass. *Trickster-dadians*, Ethel called those people.

She reached for the pillow, raised it to her nose, and sniffed. The Haitians would be another problem altogether. Black-magic dabblers, voodoo practitioners fond of raising the dead, like Jesus Christ himself. *Cross a Haitian on Tuesday, wake up blind Wednesday morning*, Ethel always said.

She grunted and dropped the pillow onto the bed. She would be polite, but she would never call them friends. She and those women would never, ever be souly-gals. If they happened in while she was preparing a meal, Ethel would offer them food— but she would never accept a grain of rice from any of them.

"Where's the toilet?"

"Down the hall," Aubrey announced excitedly.

The bathroom was nearly as large as their bedroom. Bright white ceramic tiles covered the floor and walls.

The girls oohed.

"Watch this," Aubrey said. And with the dramatic flair of a magician pulling a rabbit from a hat, he tore back the blue and white cloth curtain to reveal a claw-foot bathtub.

Ethel grinned, the girls squealed with delight.

Aubrey whirled the faucet handles until crystal-clear water rushed from the silver spout. "We don't go to the water, the water come to we!"

The girls clapped their hands with joy.

"See there?" Aubrey pointed at the toilet. "That is where you do your business and then flush it clean away." And with that, he pressed the lever and they all watched the water swirl round and round in the bowl before draining down its porcelain throat.

Running water and a flushing toilet were luxuries for Ethel and her children. Back in Barbados, they used an outhouse and fetched water for cooking, washing, and bathing from the community standpipe.

"G'dear," Ethel moaned, genuinely pleased.

Beyond the bathroom was a small, sunny kitchen, outfitted with one table, four chairs, a stove, a double sink, and an icebox.

Outside the window, the wind howled and the bare tree limbs shivered. Ethel shivered too. Taking Gwen's hand, she started back toward their room. "Let's get unpacked," she said.

They'd moved twice since that first place. With each move the living situation improved, and now they were living in a spacious apartment in a prewar building with plenty of windows.

The previous apartments, the crossing of the Atlantic, and Barbados were often topics of dinner conversation—conversation Gwen could not participate in. She had not forcibly shaken from her memory the sound the rain made against the rusted roof of their tiny brown and beige chattel house, the fragrant, colorful bougainvillea that grew wild along the winding roads, the musty smell of the ship, the pitch of it atop the rolling Atlantic, or the sound of her father's snoring, booming like thunder in that first small bedroom they shared.

"You really don't remember?" her sister would whine.

No, she did not.

Gwen hadn't intentionally rid her mind of those memories, but they were gone just the same and she had to endure the pitiful looks from her sister and parents whenever they talked about "back home," "the crossing," and "that first place," while she sat there with nothing at all to offer.

The lack of recall didn't much bother Gwen. Even though West Indian blood pulsed in her veins, her heart strummed "The Star-Spangled Banner"—she was an all-American type of girl who preferred apple pie to West Indian black cake, franks and beans over rice and peas, mashed potatoes to the Barbadian mixture of cornmeal and okra known as coo-coo.

With her family, Gwen spoke in the rapid-fire melodious way of her motherland, but when she was with her peers, the notes in her voice disappeared, and she dropped her Rs—*what-ev-a, wa-ta*—just like any other self-respecting New Yorker.

Chapter 35

On that morning, a week after the world of blues began mourning the death of their queen, Ethel crumpled up the oily newspaper carrying the headline and tossed it into the trash. She scrubbed clean the frying pan, dried it, and set it onto the stove for the next meal.

Noon arrived and the day warmed enough for Ethel to raise the window a bit, allowing fresh autumn air to blow in. Still, she reached for the yellow sweater draped on the back of the kitchen chair and pulled it on.

In the front hall, the jangle of keys announced that Aubrey had returned home for lunch. "Afternoon," he offered lightly. "Mail come early today." He tossed the stack of letters onto the kitchen table. "Going to wash up for lunch."

Ethel reached for the mail as she heard the gurgle of water emanating from the bathroom. A letter from home, light bill, the credit account she had at Martin's department store, and... what was this? She took a moment to admire the pretty pink envelope and the exquisite cursive. It was from the Mary Bruce School of Dance where Gwen took classes.

Saturday mornings, Gwen and a half-dozen other Brooklyn girls, all skirts, bobby socks, and Vaseline-polished knees—a giggling mess of femininity—boarded the uptown train to Harlem. Drunk with freedom, they fell into each other, stumbling through the moving cars in search of a section large enough to accommodate the lot of them. During those trips there was not much talk of school, but plenty boy talk—who liked who, who was going with who, who kissed who, who allowed whose hand beneath her blouse.

The men on the train snatched glances at the girls, at their pretty knees, and smiled to themselves, while the women who had daughters of their own aimed sharp-as-knives eyes at them, glaring until the girls were shamed silent.

The Mary Bruce School of Dance was founded by its namesake, a petite brown-skinned woman who hailed from the Windy City. Mary Bruce addressed the art of dance with all of the gravity of a mathematician tackling calculus. "My time is not playtime," she reminded the girls each week. "Dancing is serious business, not to be taken lightly, and if you feel different, then you're in the wrong place."

Not long after Gwen started attending the school, Mary Bruce advised Ethel that her daughter was not suited for the graceful elegance of ballet (Gwen was big-boned with large feet) and should take tap instead.

"No skin off my nose," Gwen had spouted at the news. "I prefer hoofing anyhow." Bill "Bojangles" Robinson was her hero.

Gwen had gone to see the movie *The Little Colonel* four times, committing to memory Robinson's famous step dance, which she then reenacted for her parents, Mary Bruce, and anyone else willing to sit and watch.

Ethel tore open the flap and removed the announcement card:

> *I am pleased to inform you that Gwendolyn Dorothy*
> *Gill has been chosen to participate in the Star Bud*

Recital, which will be held at Carnegie Hall on Monday, April 25, 1938, at 7p.m.

Ethel swelled with pride. Gwenie would be so happy, she mused, turning the card over and over in her hand.

Chapter 36

They usually practiced with records, but Mary Bruce said she'd be bringing in live musicians. "You won't be dancing to records at Carnegie Hall!"

In addition to their regular Saturday class, those chosen to participate in the recital were now required to attend rehearsals on Wednesday and Thursday evenings. And when they weren't rehearsing at the dance school, Mary Bruce encouraged them to practice every free moment they had.

Well, Ethel couldn't have Gwen tap dancing up and down the halls and marble steps of the Eastern Parkway apartment building they lived in. Those white folks wouldn't tolerate that noise, no matter how pleased they were with Aubrey's work or how many compliments they dropped in Ethel's ear about her polite and clean daughters.

Ethel knew that all of the praise would disintegrate, right along with their radiant smiles, and those tenants would march their disapproval, their downright infuriation, straight to the landlord, Mr. Leo Rubenstein, who lived a few blocks away in a mansion on New York Avenue. And, before any one of them could blink, Aubrey would be out of a good job and he and his family turned out into the streets.

So no, Gwen couldn't practice in the apartment or anywhere in the building. "Take that outside," Ethel said.

"But I need steps."

"Cheese on bread, child, then go to the library, it got plenty of steps!"

"The library? But Mum, you're supposed to be quiet in the library."

"I'm talking 'bout the steps outside the library."

Gwen went, but halfway through her routine, a librarian rushed out and shooed her away.

There was a playground on Sullivan Place, just a fifteen-minute walk from her apartment building. The playground sat high off the sidewalk; one had to climb seventeen sprawling stone steps to reach the grounds.

It was perfect.

All of that dancing muscled Gwen's already thick thighs and raised her behind high onto her back.

"My goodness," Ethel cried, swatting Gwen's bottom, "your boxy is getting big enough!" As if it wasn't a family trait. As if big legs and broad backsides didn't run as thick as molasses through the family line.

Unfortunately, though, the trait had skipped Irene, who was tall and lanky like her father—all limbs, no ass, and barely any breasts to speak of. She had tried and failed to put on weight, evidence of which cluttered an entire shelf in Ethel's kitchen cabinet. Pills and potions, powders and capsules—all promised results that always failed Irene. She couldn't even eat herself fat. Blame her overly sensitive stomach that rejected spice, salt, and portions larger than the palm of her hand.

So now, as Gwen bloomed and curved, Irene found herself swallowing her envy when she and her sister were out together. Gwen drew all the attention, all the favorable glances and cheeky comments from men who beckoned her as if she wasn't a girl at all, but a cat.

Pssssst.

Gwen may have had the body of a woman, but a man didn't have to kiss her to taste the film of mother's milk on her tongue—he could look her in the face and see she was still just a child.

Not that this mattered to Harlan and the other musicians who were tuning their instruments when Gwen and her friends came rushing through the door of the Mary Bruce School of Dance.

Chapter 37

Shy girls don't look at men the way the bold ones do. Shy girls steal camera-shutter-quick glances—time enough to capture the fan of eyelashes, the jut of a chin, lips.

Gwen didn't have a shy bone in her body. She didn't giggle behind her hand or blush like the other girls when the musicians' admiring looks turned hard and probing.

Gwen enjoyed being leered at. Welcomed it. Provoked it.

During the warm-up exercises, all for the entertainment of the handsome guitar player, Gwen floated her arms extra-wide like a swan vying for a mate. She rested the heel of her foot atop the wooden rail, arched her back, presenting Harlan with the most exquisite view of her beseeching ass.

When Mary Bruce called for a five-minute break, Gwen joined the other girls around the water cooler. Amidst sips of water from paper cups, giggling, and gossiping, Harlan caught the music riding her tongue.

"Shit, she's a West Indian," he groaned.

The West Indians thought quite highly of themselves; those dark people from those hot islands viewed black Americans as vultures, hawks, dung beetles, and blowflies—*Eh, you come along and fill your guts after someone else has done all the hard work—scavengers, born of slave stock. Lazy and worthless, just like the white man claimed.*

But whether it took a day, a month, or a year, they soon

learned that their pretty talk, high regard for themselves, claims of being children of Mother England, children of God, or both—here in the land of amber waves of grain, none of it mattered. If you were black-skinned, you were a nigger no matter where you hailed from.

All of that aside, Harlan still thought Gwen was very cute. So by the third rehearsal he was dropping praise at her feet like confetti.

"You look nice today."

"What's that scent? It sure smells good on you."

"New hairdo? It really fits your face."

Gwen looked through him.

The other musicians shook their heads in pity.

"Give it up, man, can't you see she ain't studying you?"

"Anyway, why you running behind a coconut when you got down-home ass right here under your nose?"

"And she ain't even that good-looking!"

The other guys thought Gwen was easy on the eyes, but not drop-dead.

"Man, you'll break your mama's heart if'n you come home with a monkey on your arm."

Monkey or not, coconut or peach, Harlan wanted her.

Chapter 38

In 1938, just in time for Gwen's dance recital, spring arrived and sprawled her loveliness all of over New York. Crocuses, marsh marigolds, tulips—all rose to greet the steadily warming sun.

Gwen and her family exited the subway station and joined the caravan of smartly dressed black folk, all making their way toward Carnegie Hall.

In Weill Recital Hall, the smallest theater in the Carnegie complex, Ethel took a seat beside her husband and immediately began to fret about the massive chandelier dangling high above her head. "Waa-lah," she exclaimed, "I sure hope that ting don't fall and kill me."

The houselights dimmed. A spotlight flooded the stage and Mary Bruce appeared in a shimmering purple sheath. "Friends and family, welcome to the Mary Bruce School of Dance's sixth annual spring recital. The dancers you'll see today were chosen exclusively by me, and you all know how I am..." She let her words trail off with a sly smile.

A titter rippled through the audience.

"But seriously, these dancers are the best and brightest in my school. You all are in for a real treat."

With that, the stage went dark. The audience took a collective breath, drowning out the click of Mary Bruce's heels as she headed into the wings. The orchestra struck up, the footlights glowed, and the curtains parted, revealing a magical woodland scene.

Forty minutes into the performance, Ethel reached over Aubrey and tapped Irene on the knee. "When is Gwen coming on?"

Without taking her eyes off the stage, Irene shoved the program at her mother.

Ethel slapped the program. "Me ask you something 'bout a program?" she spat. "Me ask you when she coming on!"

A couple in the row of seats ahead of them turned and shot Ethel a menacing look. To that, she sucked her teeth and glared until they looked away.

Onstage, the dancers brought their routine to an end, bowed, and walked off to applause. The curtains slowly closed and the houselights came up.

"Is this the end of the show? But Gwenie didn't perform yet. What's happening?" Ethel raged.

"Mother," Irene calmly replied, "it's not the end of the show, it's intermission."

"Intermission?"

"A break in the show."

"A break?"

"To use the toilet or get a glass of wine—"

"You know I don't drink," Ethel snapped.

Exasperated, Irene collapsed into her chair.

Ethel watched her for a while before turning her attention to Aubrey. "Who dey make these chairs for? Not me, not you." She slapped at her knees and fixed her gaze once again onto Irene, who was trying to disappear into the bloodred upholstery of her seat. "Look at your father. His knees are in his throat!" Ethel shrieked.

"Lower your voice, Mother, please," Irene implored, glancing around to see if anyone was watching.

"I'm fine, I'm fine," Aubrey coughed.

Ethel caught him by the wrist and tugged. "You are so lie-ard. Get up. Get up and stretch your legs before you get a blood clot and die!"

Irene closed her eyes in shame.

Aubrey pulled himself to his feet, offering apologetic smiles to those who openly stared.

Using the program to fan her neck, Ethel called out to Irene.

"Yes, Mother?"

"Look at your program and tell me when your sister going to perform."

On the stage, the lights were brighter than Gwen expected, and hot. Racing heart, shaky hands, her feet felt like blocks of cement cast in lead. Worse still, the big toe on her right foot was throbbing.

This left shoe is fine, she thought as she walked to the mark on the stage, *but the right one is too tight. This right shoe can't be mine. How am I going to dance? I won't be able to dance. I won't be able to dance...*

The audience applauded, the music swelled, and to her amazement, Gwen's feet began to move.

Did I put on deodorant?

What is that pain in my side?

Why won't my hands stop shaking?

Smile, Gwenie, smile.

I'm going to be sick.

Remember to smile, keep your head up, smile!

Is this the right music?

Don't forget to smile.

This doesn't sound like the right music.

Oh my god, Ms. Bruce gave them the wrong music!

Head up. Smile, smile.

I'm going to puke all over this nice stage.

Why won't my hands stop shaking?

I think my toe will have to be amputated. Whoever switched my shoe is dead!

Smile. Smile. Smile...

Chapter 39

The warm spring faded into a humid summer.

Newly graduated from high school, but with no jobs available to them, Gwen and her friends whiled away the steamy summer on Coney Island's hot beach, splashing about in the salty blue Atlantic Ocean, gorging themselves on Coca-Cola, Nathan's Famous hot dogs, and fried shrimp on a stick.

At Steeplechase Park, they rode the Lindy Loop and Roll-O-Plane with their hands stretched high above their heads, screaming themselves hoarse.

On the Coney Island Cyclone, they favored the first or last car of the coaster because that's where they felt, most intensely, the blossoming sensation in the pit of their stomachs when the coaster dove over the camel humps in the tracks. The girls didn't know what to call it, how to label that thing that felt so good, they just knew that they longed for it, and worked to recreate that unnameable thing in the dead of night while hidden beneath bedsheets, fingers between their legs, prodding and stroking.

The effort left them damp; the reward, however, was so much more than the amusement park ride could ever bring.

When there was no more money for hot dogs, pretzels, and ice cream, they trolled the boardwalk in search of lost coins.

Gwen's friends wouldn't touch the pennies they found tails up. "It's bad luck," they warned her.

"That's silly," she said, plucking up the pennies and dropping them into her pocket.

"You'll see," her friends hummed.

And yes, Gwen would.

By the end of the summer, Harlan was little more than a cobweb in Gwen's memory. The last time she had seen him was at the final rehearsal before the recital.

He'd followed her to the subway station as usual, asked for her telephone number for the hundredth time, and Gwen had replied, just as she had so many times before, "I told you, we don't have a telephone, and even if we did, the answer would still be no."

"Well, good luck this weekend," he said as Gwen started down the steps of the station.

Gwen had looked over her shoulder. "Won't you be there?" she heard herself ask before she was even aware the question had formed in her mind.

"Nah," Harlan replied, "the house band will be playing for you."

Gwen had tried to cloak her disappointment with a smile, but Harlan seemed to see through the screen. Grinning, he tipped an invisible hat and wished her well.

"Break a leg."

Chapter 40

Other than job hunting and church, Gwen's life moved along quietly and uneventfully, until Halloween Eve cast its eerie eye over the land, raising goose bumps on America's flesh.

On October 30, 1938, Ethel walked to the far corner of the living room and switched on the Zenith console radio. It was the proud centerpiece of their home.

Ramón Raquello and his orchestra were performing "La Cumparsita" from the Meridian Room of the Park Plaza Hotel in Manhattan.

"Tango!" Gwen squealed. She grabbed Irene, and the two tangoed from one end of the living room to the other.

Aubrey applauded. Irene and Gwen bowed and curtsied.

"You two are so foolish," Ethel laughed. "Now come. Sit and eat." When a special broadcast interrupted the soothing music, the family fell quiet as they listened to the newscaster's description of fluorescent gas explosions on the planet Mars.

"Mars?" Ethel clucked.

The music resumed, and so did their dinner conversation. Ramón Raquello's orchestra segued into the romantic "Star Dust." Aubrey winked at Ethel, who side-eyed him bashfully.

"You want another piece?" she asked, pointing to the platter of chicken.

"A piece?" Aubrey smiled furtively. "Maybe later."

Ethel flashed him a coy look before lowering her eyes.

Irene didn't miss her father's insinuation. Her eyes darted to Gwen. Had she caught it too? The expression resting on Gwen's face suggested otherwise. Irene sighed with relief.

Once again, the music was interrupted. The newscaster's voice took on a level of anxiety: *"We have arranged an interview with noted astronomer Professor Pierson, who will give us his views on the event."*

Aubrey set his fork down; his face darkened with concern.

"How do you account for those gas eruptions occurring on the surface of Mars at regular intervals?"

"Mr. Phillips, I cannot account for it."

"By the way, professor, for the benefit of our listeners, how far is Mars from earth?"

"Approximately forty million miles."

"Forty million miles," Irene gasped. "That's a long way."

The music resumed.

After dinner, Ethel and her daughters carried the platters and plates into the kitchen. Aubrey slid back from the table, crossed his legs, and stared at the radio, his head slightly lolling to the music.

Above the rush of water and the clatter of silverware came the newscaster's panicked voice: *"A special announcement... a huge, aming object, believed to be a meteorite, fell on a farm in the neighborhood of Grover's Mill, New Jersey, twenty-two miles from Trenton."*

"What he say?" Irene asked, looking fearfully at her mother.

"We take you now to Grover's Mill, New Jersey."

Ethel turned off the water and followed Irene and Gwen back into the living room.

"*The ground is covered with splinters of a tree it must have struck on its way down.*"

Ethel wrapped her hands around her neck, Irene clenched her teeth, Gwen moved to her father's side.

The newscaster declared that something large, gray, and snakelike was wriggling out of the shadows.

"Oh Lawd!" Ethel cried out, dancing back from the radio.

An unearthly screech hurtled from the radio speaker. An explosion followed, and Aubrey's heart skipped three full beats.

The radio air went dead.

Seconds turned into minutes, and then, suddenly, soft piano music.

It went on like that—minutes of comforting music, interrupted by horrific reports of destruction and mayhem.

The listening audience was informed that aliens from Mars had journeyed forty million miles, through a multitude of galaxies, landed in New Jersey, and were steadily moving toward New York City.

Seven thousand troops had been deployed, but only 129 had escaped slaughter. The other 6,871 soldiers had been burned to death by the aliens.

Irene emerged from the bathroom in time to see her family drawing curtains and stacking the dining room chairs in front of the apartment door.

Afterward, they huddled on the couch, joined hands, and recited the Lord's Prayer.

Uptown, Sam retrieved his loaded gun from the shoe box beneath the bed, released the safety, and joined Emma on the settee in the dark parlor, leaving Harlan locked away in his bedroom, drinking himself numb.

All across America, people took shelter in closets, in sheds, and dank, dark basements.

Other people—the believers, the stupid, the curious—took to the streets with binoculars, offerings of fruit, buttered toast, waving signs that read: *WELCOME TO EARTH. WE ARE YOUR FRIENDS!*

The next day, they'd all feel foolish when they learned that the broadcast was a hoax, nothing more than a dramatization of the novel *The War of the Worlds* by H.G. Wells.

Many of those foolish-feeling people, including the ones who'd been so terrified they'd soiled themselves or piled into their cars in an effort to escape the inescapable—many of them would call for the head of the person who perpetrated the fraud.

In the end, Orson Welles would not give them his head, just an apology for the prank that catapulted him to fame.

The real monsters were much closer than Mars. The real monsters were right across the Atlantic. They did not have black serpent eyes or tentacles; they were two-legged, two-armed, beating-heart beasts who were methodically scaring all of Europe to her knees.

The terrified people of Europe didn't have to watch the skies for monsters or flaming objects because the monsters were their neighbors, and synagogues were burning right there on the ground.

Part V

The World's Fair

Chapter 41

In July of '39, on the day commencing the onset of Negro Week at the World's Fair, a short white man dressed in a gray suit jacket, black shirt, and white slacks walked into Mary Bruce's dance school.

Mary was in her office going over invoices and new applications. The smell of cigar smoke alerted her to the fact that she was not alone. She stepped silently into the studio, her right hand shoved deep into the square pocket of her navy-blue smock, fingers tightly gripping the wooden handle of her small pistol.

From her vantage, Mary could see the ceiling light's reflection twinkling on his highly polished black shoes and dark, oily hair. He was admiring himself in the wall of mirrors when Mary made herself known.

"May I help you?"

"You Mary?" he said to her reflection.

"May I help you?" she asked again.

He turned to face her. "Are you Mary Bruce?"

"Yes, I'm Ms. Bruce. And you are?"

He thumped his cigar. "Mike Todd," he announced smugly. Mary watched the ashes scatter across the floor.

When she didn't respond, he repeated himself: "Mike Todd. You know: Mike. Todd."

Mary's index finger stroked the smooth metal of the gun

trigger. "I heard you the first time, Mr. Todd. How can I help you?"

He made a sound in his throat. "Mike Todd. *Hot Mikado*?"

Mary frowned. "Hot who?"

"*Hot Mikado*, on Broadway? That's the musical I produced. Surely you've seen it." He pulled a business card from the inside pocket of his jacket and held it up for Mary to see.

Her eyes quickly scanned the gold-embossed letters. "Oh, oh yes," she announced gaily, loosening her grip on the gun. "I have seen the show. Twice. What a lovely production." Mary took the card and slipped it into the pocket alongside the gun.

Hot Mikado was the Negro spin on Gilbert and Sullivan's comic opera The Mikado. Bill Bojangles was the star of the production; his showstopping performances had garnered rave reviews from audiences and critics alike.

Mike Todd offered a smile wide enough to swallow his face, then thumped another pile of ash onto the floor.

"Excuse me a moment," Mary said, turning and walking back into her office. She returned holding a heavy crystal ashtray which she set atop the piano.

"Thank you," Todd muttered.

"You're welcome."

"You got a nice place here." His eyes roamed around the studio. "Real nice."

Mary knew his type. Short in stature, sky-high ego. Worse yet, a Chicago man. Mary had detected the accent as soon as he opened his mouth—Chicago was her hometown too. "Thank you," she said.

Todd set the cigar in the ashtray, folded his arms over his chest, and rocked back on his shoe heels. "I've heard good things about this place. And you. You know?"

"Oh?"

"Yeah. An associate of mine was at the recital at Carnegie Hall a few months ago."

"Last spring," Mary corrected.

"Yeah, whenever it was. Anyway, he said you got some real talented dancers."

Mary nodded gracefully.

"I trust this person. We're like family, you know? So when he say's you've got talent, I believe him."

Again, Mary nodded.

Todd unfolded his arms, made a reach for the cigar, decided against it, and instead thrust his hands into the pockets of his slacks. He looked down at his shoes, staring at them for so long that he seemed to have forgotten that Mary was even in the room.

The seconds ticked off; the silence was suffocating. Mary cleared her throat and the man snapped back to life. "Mr. Todd, I'm sure you didn't come all the way up to Harlem to commend me on my dancers."

He scratched the back of his head, glanced at the cigar. "Nah, I wouldn't come all the way up here just for that," he chuckled. "I did want to tell you that I'm bringing *Hot Mikado* to the World's Fair."

And what does that have to do with me? Mary resisted shrugging her shoulders. "Well," she breathed, "that's exciting news."

"Okay," Todd spouted, "so you're on board then?"

Her eyes widened. "On board for what? I don't even know what it is you're talking about."

He winked at her. "Ha! I just wanted to make sure you were

listening!"

Mary smirked.

"I want the best dancers in the city to perform in the show, and since you have the best dancers in the city, I want *your* dancers to be a part of my World's Fair production."

The light in Mary's eyes set off an explosion in Todd, and he was off, pacing the floor, hands flailing, breathlessly sharing his vision.

"In addition to *Hot Mikado*, I'm going to have three cabarets and a dancing campus—"

"Dancing campus?"

"Yes, a big stage with nothing but dancing, all sorts of dancing. A communal-type thing, professional dancers and amateurs all on one stage..." He rambled on excitedly, pausing only to puff on his cigar. At the end of his soliloquy, he tilted his head back and blew four smoke rings into the air. "So what do you think about that?"

There were countless thoughts spinning through Mary's mind, but only one toppled from her mouth: "It sounds expensive."

Todd nodded. "Oh, it will be very, very expensive—and worth every cent." He looked at his wristwatch. "Well, Mary, it seems I am late for my next appointment. I hope I didn't take up too much of your time, I get real excited about things and then..." He trailed off for a moment. "Sometimes I don't know when to reel myself in, you know?" He offered his hand. "It was a real pleasure meeting you, Ms. Mary Bruce."

"And you, Mr. Todd."

"I'll be in touch," he said, hurrying toward the exit. "I'll look forward to hearing from you."

The door closed noisily behind him.

Mary brought her hand to her forehead. She felt weak; Todd had sucked all the air out of the room.

Suddenly, the front door swung open again. Todd stepped in and pointed his cigar in her direction. "Oh!" he exclaimed. "I forgot to tell you that I'd like you to choreograph one of the shows." He shoved the cigar back into his mouth and walked out.

Mary watched the door warily. When it remained closed, she twirled across the floor, squealing.

Chapter 42

Not the same type of weariness her father felt when he was a younger man, picking beans and fruit beneath a merciless Southern sun. Not even the fatigue he experienced now, after a day of pushing a mop as tall as an average-sized man across the lobby's marble floor, washing windows, polishing brass banisters, fixing leaky pipes, painting, and any other number of things the landlord wanted him to do, and any other number of things the tenants asked of him, including running errands to the corner store. Some days, Aubrey was so tired he had barely enough energy to smile at his wife and daughters.

So not that kind of exhaustion, but certainly close to it, Gwen claimed.

After Mike Todd's visit, Gwen was one of the first dancers Mary reached out to. By September, Gwen was a key figure in Mike Todd's Dancing Campus. In thirty-two shows a week, Gwen alternated between high-octane solo tap performances and dancing with a chorus of men and women who were required to coax the audience onto the stage to join them in the jitterbug, fox-trot, and Big Apple routines.

During her breaks, Gwen visited the other Todd Production venues. The Streets of Paris and Gay New Orleans cabarets were amongst her favorites. The women who performed in those shows wore barely anything at all, save for towering plumed headdresses, sparkly thongs, and tassels that dangled from nipple-concealing pasties. One woman danced with a boa constrictor curled around her neck and torso; another skillfully manipulated two enormous fans constructed of ostrich feathers.

Gwen longed to perform those erotic dance routines; in fact, she had spent hours in front of her bedroom mirror, dressed in nothing but underwear, perfecting every sensual move. But she knew that her performance, as good as it was, would never be seen outside her bedroom because her mother would never allow it. According to Ethel, women who flaunted their bodies in that way—onstage or elsewhere—were just one short step from becoming prostitutes.

It wasn't in Gwen to tell lies.

Ethel said, "If you lie, you'll thief. If you thief, you'll kill!"

Those words rang in Gwen's head whenever she set her mouth to tell an untruth. But she was eighteen years old now, done with school, holding down a job, and still her mother continued to treat her like a child.

Boyfriend? What was that? The word better not even come up in conversation or Gwen risked being whacked across the mouth.

Some of Gwen's school friends were planning spring weddings. At least two were pregnant—Gwen was sure of it. They'd disappeared at the end of June and no one, not even their parents, would say where they'd gone off to. Other girls her age were going to dances and house parties. The only parties Gwen was ever allowed to attend were those held in the basement of the church she attended with her parents and ones hosted by trusted family friends who also attended their church.

"So what, you're eighteen," Irene scolded Gwen whenever

she heard her grumbling. "I'm twenty-four, living under the same roof, following the same rules, and you don't hear *me* complaining."

Irene didn't go anywhere but work and church, more than happy to stay home, puttering around the house behind Ethel. She didn't have many friends to speak of, and those she did have were much like herself, content with Jesus being the only man central in their lives.

Gwen was different; she yearned for something more, although she wasn't completely clear on what that something was. What she was certain about, however, was that the longing was growing with every blessed day; and she was sure the growth would eventually split her in two.

Perhaps it was this impending rupture that drove Gwen to say yes when the slender, cat-eyed dancer named Patsy invited her to a party in Harlem.

They heard the music before they saw the house—a tired-looking limestone structure with filthy windows and crumbling steps.

Gwen hesitated at the door. "Who lives here?"

Patsy rolled her eyes, caught Gwen by the arm, and yanked her over the threshold. "Does it matter?"

Stationed inside the dark foyer was a young man with conked red hair and a face splattered with freckles. When Patsy and Gwen stepped inside, he pushed an open palm beneath Gwen's nose. "One dollar."

Gwen looked at Patsy. "We gotta pay?"

Patsy's nodded and presented a five-dollar bill. "You got change?" she asked the man.

Freckleface smiled, revealing a sparkling gold incisor. "Yeah, honey. I got change and anything else you want." His eyes floated to Gwen. "She got you too?"

"Excuse me?"

"No, she has her own money. Don't you, Gwenie?"

In the hot, shadowy house, Gwen stood squinting into the parlor trying her best to make out the faces of the couples grinding their way through a woeful ballad. Hands riding high on rib cages or low on hips, the twosomes hitched themselves to the melody and slow-dragged their way through it. The boys groaned hungrily, tiny gasps rose from the girls like bubbles. Both male and female prayed that the song would go on forever; the virgins among them hoped to God that the real thing would be somewhere close to that dry-humping high.

When the song came to an end, Gwen glanced over to find that Patsy was no longer at her side, replaced now with a pair of hand-holding strangers. Her eyes frantically scanned the shadows, roaming from one unfamiliar face to another.

No Patsy.

Uneasy, but trying her best to feign otherwise, Gwen cradled her elbows in her hands, swayed unsteadily to the music, waiting in quiet anticipation for some young man to ask her to dance.

The front door swung open and closed. As the house swelled with people, it seemed to shrink in size. One record replaced another, shrinking violets of all hues and sizes were pulled from the wall onto the dance floor, yet still no one asked the dancer to dance.

Rivulets of sweat trickled down the center of Gwen's back; she tugged uncomfortably at the dainty collar of her white blouse, smoothed her palms over the sharp pleats of her plaid skirt, cast an embarrassed eye down at her size-nine Oxford shoes, and realized with stark embarrassment that she looked either like an overgrown child—or someone's grandmother.

No wonder she was ignored. Gwen looked so bland, she was invisible. Teetering on the verge of tears, she spotted a lit room at the end of the hallway and moved toward it like a moth.

The bright kitchen was jam-packed with people; cigarette smoke hovered above their heads like rain clouds, conversation buzzed at a deafening pitch. Liquor bottles were everywhere— on the table, the windowsills, on top of the stove.

When Gwen walked in, heads turned and eyes combed over her, but no one said hello. Patsy was standing near the back door, some man pressed into her with his face buried in her neck.

Gwen moved toward her. "I think I'm going to leave."

Patsy shrugged her shoulders. "See you tomorrow, then."

"You're not coming with me?"

"Na-ah."

Feelings mangled, Gwen spun around and walked right into Harlan. "Hey!"

A familiar face.

Gwen's levies broke, spilling tears down her cheeks.

Harlan immediately took her hand and guided her outside.

"Sit down," he ordered tenderly, passing her his handkerchief.

Harlan didn't know what else to do, so he sat down beside her and waited for her to stop sobbing.

Behind them, the door opened; foot-stomping music burst from the house like a colorful bird, its wildly flapping wings catching the attention of pedestrians who slowed their gait to look at the house and the young people milling about on the steps.

Harlan turned around to find the woman he had come there

to meet standing in the doorway, arms crossed over her bountiful bosom, eyebrows arched, lips pulled grotesquely to one side of her face. She didn't utter a word, didn't have to, her entire being bellowed: *Nigger, who is she?*

Harlan raised his index finger. "Gimme a minute."

The woman rolled her eyes, yanked the door open, and disappeared inside.

Gwen dragged the handkerchief over her face. "I-I'm sorry," she mumbled into the cloth, too embarrassed to look at Harlan.

"You feel better?"

Gwen nodded.

"You wanna tell me about it?"

She shook her head.

"Do you want to go back inside?"

Another shake of her head, then she stood. "Thanks," she muttered, folding the handkerchief into a square. "I'll take this home, wash it, and give it back the next time I see you."

"So there'll be a next time, huh?"

Even though her eyes still glistened with tears, she managed a warm smile. Harlan grinned back at her.

"You sure you don't want to go back inside? We could show them how to really get down." Harlan pursed his lips and rolled his shoulders in a clownish fashion. Gwen couldn't help but laugh.

"No, I better get home."

"Brooklyn, right?"

"Yeah."

Harlan looked at the door. "I can ride with you if you like."

Gwen's eyes widened. "All the way to Brooklyn?"

"Yeah, why not?"

Chapter 43

In the Gill household, fixed on the wall above the refrigerator was a clock with a white face and green arms in the shape of palm fronds. At six o'clock, Ethel glanced at the clock and then at the door of the apartment, expecting Gwen to come bursting in, babbling about her day.

At six-fifteen, Ethel went to the door, opened it, and poked her head into the hallway. By six thirty, she was nervously pacing the floor. Irene arrived home from work at seven o'clock; Aubrey followed not too long after.

"She probably had trouble with the trains," Irene commented nonchalantly. Aubrey nodded his head in agreement.

When nine o'clock arrived and Gwen still hadn't come home, Ethel pulled her winter coat over her nightgown and took her worried pacing out onto the sidewalk.

It was mid-October, Indian summer had its torrid grip on the city, and within minutes, Ethel was soaked in perspiration. Her concern slowly melted into anger, and even at a distance, Gwen could spot the scowl on her mother's face as soon as she and Harlan rounded the corner.

She rushed ahead of him. "I have to go."

"Call me!" Harlan hollered after her.

Gwen's feet may have been walking, but she was sailing on air. Ethel, drenched from two hours of stalking the neighborhood, looked up and saw Gwen racing toward her—grinning no less—and instantly her already foul mood turned rank.

When Gwen reached striking distance, Ethel's arm catapulted into the air, her closed fist punched the left side of her daughter's face and then the right, sending Gwen scrambling into the building.

Ethel trailed Gwen up the stairs, her coat billowing out behind her like a cape. She raised her fist again, catching Gwen on the crown of her head, the second blow hitting the center of her back.

They exploded into the apartment and Aubrey, who had been sitting reading the paper, jumped straight out of his chair. A slicing look from his wife warned him that he'd better mind his business—this was mother-daughter stuff, no men allowed or needed. So Aubrey just stood there, quiet.

Ethel chased Gwen into the bedroom, where she unleashed a barrage of bad words before striking her again, this time across the mouth.

After Ethel charged from the room, Irene, who had been watching silently from her bed, sucked her teeth and spat, "Chuh, you feel you is a big woman now? Running the streets like some wildcat? You deserve them licks!"

Gwen said nothing. She stripped out of her clothes, climbed into bed, and gave Irene her back.

Yes, Gwen's feelings were bruised, and her lip was split, but none of that could take away from the hour or so she had spent on the train with Harlan. Even as she lay with her face buried in her pillow, still sniffing from her mother's blows and insults, Gwen was able to smile through her tears. The memory and feel of Harlan's thigh knocking against her own when the train sped around a bend in the tracks or came to a stuttering stop in the station helped to ease the pain.

And oh, how they had talked! They had talked about near everything: her parents, his parents, music, his grandmother who had recently passed away.

"In her sleep," he had said. "Just like my grandfather."

A sadness gripped his face and Gwen wouldn't swear on it, but she thought she saw water in his eyes.

"We just got back from the funeral a few days ago."

"Where did she live?" Gwen asked.

"Macon, Georgia. You ever been to Georgia?"

"No."

"It's nice," he said, bobbing his head.

How dainty her hand had looked cradled in Harlan's big one when he scrawled his number in blue ink on her palm.

She played and replayed the feel of his arm around her waist as they ascended the subway steps and his plea as she hurried toward home: "Call me!"

Chapter 44

If Ethel thought she'd knocked some sense into her daughter, she was wrong. All of those angry cuffs to Gwen's head and face had done little else but empty her of all the good sense she might have once had.

The next day, lips still pulsing in pain, Gwen dropped a nickel in one of the pay phones scattered around the campus of the World's Fair and dialed Harlan's number. When he answered, she asked if he wouldn't mind meeting her after work, and he agreed.

And so it began.

Gwen, telling lies, sneaking off to be with that mess of a man-child who favored dark liquor, who smoked reefer and Viceroy cigarettes. Who frequented illegal card and dice games in rooms hidden behind false walls and had so many women, he couldn't bother to remember their names so just called them all baby.

Three weeks into their courtship, Harlan convinced Gwen to give up that part of herself that Ethel warned she'd better save till marriage or be fated to spend eternity in the underside of heaven.

Ethel's threats fell on deaf ears and on a Thursday evening, Gwen found herself in Harlan's bedroom, sitting on his bed.

"C'mon," he coaxed, floating the lit joint near her mouth. "Just take one pull."

"I better not."

Eyeing her seductively, Harlan slipped the joint between his lips and pulled. After a few seconds, he blew a stream of smoke into her face. Gwen fanned it quickly away.

"Stop," she whined girlishly.

"Just one," he urged. "You'll like it, I promise."

Gwen's eyelids fluttered. "Okay."

Harlan guided her through it. One puff, two. "Hold it, hold it," he cautioned, laughing.

The smoke bit her throat, her eyes watered, and she gagged. Harlan rubbed her back, smiling. "How do you feel?"

At first Gwen felt as if her chest was on fire. When the flames subsided, she became supremely aware of her heart's steady drumming. At first the sound only filled her head, then it filled the room. Covering her chest with her hands, she turned wonder-filled eyes on Harlan.

"Do you hear that?"

"What?"

She fell back onto the mattress and closed her eyes. "It's so loud."

"Is it?" Harlan leaned over and pressed his mouth against hers, using his tongue to pry her lips apart. Somewhere beneath the thump of her heart, Gwen realized she was experiencing her first kiss.

His fingers slowly, expertly undid the buttons of her blouse. Gwen was barely aware of her undressing, focused as she was on her heartbeat. When his fingers grasped hold of the button closest to her navel, Gwen's eyes flew open, she caught his hand and sat up. Her eyes swept over the chaos of the room. Molehills of dirty laundry, shoes thrown here and there, an open suitcase spewing clothes.

"Are you going somewhere?" she asked.

Harlan's mouth fell into his lap. "W-what?"

Gwen nodded at the suitcase.

Harlan barely glanced at it. "Nah, I haven't unpacked from Georgia."

"Oh," Gwen moaned, falling back on the bed again. Her blouse spread out around her, providing Harlan with a full view of the white cotton brassiere she wore.

"You're so beautiful," he announced thickly.

Gwen covered her face in giddy shame.

Harlan rose from the bed and hurriedly shrugged off his trousers and T-shirt.

Outside, the evening sun faded from the sky. Inside, on top of freshly washed sheets—that Emma herself had pressed and placed on his bed—Harlan suckled Gwen's breasts and drowned his fingers in the river of warmth between her legs.

When she started mewing, he climbed atop her and the sound of his panting drowned out the knocking of her terrified heart. If Gwen had been a seam, she would have burst.

A few penetrating strokes later, and sweet mercy—that roller-coaster feeling swept through Gwen like a rogue wave. Every cell in her body erupted, setting her limbs to rattling.

Afterward, when they saw the blood shimmering on Harlan's penis, Gwen flew into a panic because he seemed as shook by the sight of it as she was.

Harlan gasped. "You're a virgin?"

To which Gwen responded, "Do I need to go to the hospital?"

An hour-long explanation and nearly a pack of cigarettes

later, Harlan was finally able to convince Gwen that no, she didn't need to go to the hospital, and no, he hadn't done anything wrong.

"It's normal to bleed the first time," he kept assuring her.

Emma and Sam came through the door, laughing and teasing each other in that way that long-married couples do. Gwen had never met them and wouldn't meet them that night because Harlan hustled her down the stairs and out the door like an embarrassment. At the subway station, he hesitated at the top of the stairs.

"You gonna ride to Brooklyn with me, right?"

"Not tonight, I'm tired." His lips barely brushed hers. "All right, baby, get home safe."

Part VI

The Future Has a Past

Chapter 45

Well before Harlan had ever laid eyes on Gwendolyn Dorothy Gill, he'd walked into the Powder Room on 138th and Madison Avenue determined to drink himself blind.

Tuesday evening, only a few people were seated in the brown leather-clad booths. At the bar, three men balanced on low stools, staring silently into their drinks. Cigarette smoke drifted eerily along the embossed copper ceiling, found refuge beneath the metal skirts of the pendant lights, and faded slowly away. A torch song spilled from the radio behind the bar; Oscar Meade, the fat, balding proprietor, polished water glasses and sang along.

When Harlan walked in, the murmur of conversation collapsed. He raised a hand in greeting and slid onto the stool closest to the door.

Oscar lumbered over. "Whaddya have?"

"Whiskey, straight."

Oscar set a short glass before Harlan and filled it, then proceeded to make small talk, but his mouth clamped closed when he saw the festering gaze in Harlan's eyes. He turned to leave, but Harlan wrapped his knuckles noisily against the wooden bar, demanding another.

After Oscar refilled the glass, he lingered in anticipation, but it seemed Harlan was taking his time with the second drink. He'd started away again when Harlan grumbled incoherently. Oscar cocked his ear. "Say what now?"

"I said, you think people got your back, but they don't."

Although weeks had come and gone, Harlan was still bitter about being fired from Lucille's band.

Oscar shrugged. "It bees like that sometimes," he chuckled.

Harlan bobbed his head and raised his glass and bitterly mimicked Oscar's declaration: "It bees like that sometimes." He threw a crumpled ten-dollar bill on the bar. "Keep pouring until it's all used up."

Seated two stools left of Harlan was a slim, smartly dressed light-skinned fellow who had been nursing his drink for some time.

Oscar ambled over to him. "Another?" he asked, even though the man's glass was still full.

"Ah, yeah," the guy said, lifting the glass and draining the contents. The man seated between Harlan and the mulatto slipped off his stool. He thumped the bar and said, "See you tomorrow, Oscar."

"Sure thing, Joe."

Oscar removed the empty glass and dropped it in the sink. Harlan glanced over at the light-skinned man. His profile looked familiar, but Harlan couldn't conjure a name to go along with the soft jawline. He took a sip of his drink and pondered. Within seconds, a name popped into his head. "Percy Lester?" he called out.

The man turned to face him. "Who?"

Harlan carefully studied the stranger's face. His eyes lingered on the prominent callus on his top lip. "Sorry, man. From the side, you looked like someone else."

"No problem."

Harlan emptied his glass; Oscar quickly refilled it.

A callus on the top lip usually meant one thing: trumpeter. Harlan leaned back in his chair and spotted the battered burgundy trumpet case resting on the stool next to the man. "That yours?" he asked, pointing.

The man glanced at the case. "Yep."

Harlan grinned. "Music man, huh?"

The man nodded.

"Me too." Harlan picked up his drink and moved to the empty stool between them. "Harlan," he said, offering his hand.

"Lizard."

Harlan rocked with laughter. "Your mama named you Lizard?"

"Nah, it's a nickname. My mama named me Leo, but I prefer Lizard."

"Well then, Lizard it is."

Bolstered by the whiskey and their shared love of music, the men slipped into easy conversation.

"Who you like?"

Lizard offered a sheepish grin. "The king, of course."

"Satchmo?"

"Yeah," Lizard said. "Yeah, he's the man for sure."

The two clinked glasses.

"I know him," Harlan boasted.

Lizard's eye twinkled with suspicion.

"For real, I do," Harlan said, raising his hand. "May God strike me dead if I'm lying."

"He's telling the truth," Oscar interjected from the corner of the bar. Lizard didn't look convinced.

"He been to my house and everything. Known him for years. Know him so well, I call him Uncle Satchmo!"

Lizard didn't even try to dim the astonishment glowing on his face.

"Aww, man, he comes by the house sometimes just for my mama's red beans and rice," Harlan chuckled.

Lizard was speechless.

"Another for me and the Lizard," Harlan called out jovially.

Oscar waddled over. "You got any more money? 'Cause you done run through that ten spot."

Harlan burped. "Already?"

"Don't worry, I got it," Lizard said, wrenching a wad of bills from his pocket.

Harlan's eyes stretched. "Hey, man," he whispered, "you betta stop flashing that cash 'fore someone relieves you of it."

Lizard looked thoughtfully at the money and then at Harlan's soupy eyes. "You think so?" he said with all of the naïveté of a country boy.

"Yes, I do. Where you say you from again?"

Lizard set two dollars on the bar. "St. Louis."

"St. Louis? I ain't never been, but I heard it ain't sweet. You should know better."

Lizard nodded. "I guess you're right." He stuffed the money back into his pocket. "And you're right about another thing too: St. Louis ain't sweet—that's why I've got this." He stretched out his right leg and tugged up the pant leg. Strapped to his ankle was a .22 snub-nosed revolver.

"Nice," Harlan said admiringly. "Good to know you're not a punk." He patted his stomach. "You hungry? I'm hungry."

Lizard said, "I could eat."

***

They ended up at Jimmy's Chicken Shack, a Harlem eatery known for its food, but celebrated for its late-night jam sessions.

"Who's your friend?" the curvy, brown-skinned waitress asked Harlan as her eyes crawled all over Lizard.

"Lizard, Davette. Davette, Lizard," Harlan stated distractedly. Davette batted her false eyelashes. "Lizard, huh?"

"Uh-huh."

Her eyes dropped casually to his crotch. "Why they call you that?" she purred.

Lizard didn't miss a beat: "If we get to know one another, I might show you."

A sultry smile curled Davette's lips.

"Over there." Harlan pointed anxiously to an empty table near the band. "We want to sit there."

They spent the latter part of that Tuesday night reveling in the music, munching on whiting sandwiches, and slurping down Schlitz beer.

One musician after the next was invited to the stage to jam with the band. Some were good, most were mediocre, two were booed off. Near one a.m., Lizard licked grease from his fingers, opened the red case, and retrieved his instrument.

Harlan eyed him. "You gonna try?"

"Sure. I came to Harlem to play with the best."

He mounted the small stage and told the musicians what he was going to play; his selection provoked dubious glances.

Lizard pulled a white handkerchief from his jacket pocket and clutched it firmly in his hand. The white handkerchief was Louis Armstrong's signature. The audience shook their heads in sad amusement.

"Aww, man, please!" someone yelled.

"Don't tell me this white-as-rice-looking Negro think he's as good as Satchmo."

Harlan dropped his head into his hands.

Lizard raised the horn to his mouth and pressed a smoldering kiss onto its brass lip. The move raised a squall of laughter from the band. Lizard blew a few magical notes, dropped the horn to his hip, and began to sing. "*Got no shoes on my feet, ain't got nothing to eat, but I've got a heart full of rhythm...*"

He didn't completely possess Armstrong's gravelly timbre, but his imitation was strong enough to bring the audience to their feet, clapping, hooting, and fanning the air with napkins.

Harlan lifted his face from his hands, bona fide surprise radiating on his face.

When Lizard stepped off the stage, Harlan scrambled to him, slapped him heartily on the back, proclaiming, "Lizard, you a baaaad man!"

Hours and many beers later, the new friends stepped from the eatery onto the sidewalk and headed down the street toward the sunrise.

"That was some kind of night," Lizard beamed.

Turning up the collar of his shirt, Harlan yawned his response: "Every night in Harlem is some kind of night."

To say they became fast friends would be an understatement— *attached at the hip* paints a better picture. Within a short span of time, they became as close as brothers, and that's how Harlan introduced him around Harlem. "This is my brother from another mother."

Emma took a liking to Lizard immediately. "My goodness," she gasped the first time Harlan brought him home, "if you don't look like my brother Seth!"

The only similarities Lizard shared with Seth were their complexions, silky-to-the-touch hair, and the labels used to describe black people shod in white skin: *half-caste, mulatto, light-bright*.

Lizard soon became a fixture in the Elliott household.

During the week, he joined them for dinner. On Saturday nights, white hankie in hand, Lizard showcased his gift— blowing high notes that scraped the ceiling, notes so low people half-expected to see clefts and trebles scuttling across the floor. Happy notes, sad notes, sexy notes, deep-in-the-bone-weary notes. Notes that recounted stories so primal, Lizard couldn't have had any earthly acquaintance with them—but there they were, streaming from his trumpet like ribbons.

Chapter 46

It made all the sense in the world to marry their magic, bottle it, and put it out for profit. All they needed was a piano player, a drummer, and a nice-looking girl with a decent voice, pretty legs, and straight teeth. None would be difficult to find in Harlem. One could throw a penny out a window and it would ricochet off one and hit another.

"A band?" Lizard said and burped. "You and me?"

They were in the parlor, sprawled on the sofa, nursing their bloated Sunday-dinner bellies.

"Yeah, man. We out here playing with all of these other cats, making them look good. We should have our own group."

Lizard scratched the bridge of his nose. "You think?"

"You goddamn right I do. You and me would blow the lid off this town!" Harlan slapped his chest.

Lizard silently pondered his friend's words.

"So you wanna do this thing or what?"

"I dunno." Lizard looked down at his hands.

Harlan waited for more, but Lizard offered nothing.

Taking his friend's silence as rejection, Harlan huffed cavalierly, "Whatever, man, I ain't gonna beg you. I don't even beg for pussy." Dejected, he rose from the couch and went to sulk at the window.

Lizard laughed. "You're such a baby. Waaaa-waaaa!" he teased, rubbing his eyes. "Yeah, man," he announced after a pause with a clap of his hands, "of course we should start our own band."

"You serious, man? For real?"

"Yeah, I'm serious. Let's blow the lid off Harlem!"

Harlan went on to recruit Lincoln Watson, who had been making a name for himself playing piano in musical battles known as Cutting Contests, held at rent parties and boutique nightclubs. The color of strong coffee and round, Lincoln wore black thick-framed bifocal glasses which painted him with a comical facade that often excluded him from romantic considerations. That was until he opened his mouth and slayed them with his silky baritone, reducing women to crimson cheeks and giggles.

Harlan enlisted Bruno Franklin on drums. Bruno was a towering, serious-looking, chain-smoking fellow who was not only a skilled barber but claimed to have also mastered six instruments, including the mbira.

"What the hell is a mbira?" Lizard asked.

"Hell if I know," Harlan shrugged. "I'm just selling it the way I bought it."

When Ivy Reid strolled into Harlan's favorite watering hole, he hadn't seen her in years. Ivy had been Harlan's eighth-grade crush. His heart had been broken when she went to live with an aunt in the Bronx.

Harlan had heard that she'd married at eighteen. By then, of course, whatever it was about the thirteen-year-old Ivy that had stolen his heart was now buried beneath layers of time and the dozens of women who'd cycled in and out of his life. He hadn't thought of Ivy Reid in years, so it had to be kismet that steered her into the Powder Room and to the stool next to Harlan.

Completely engrossed in his conversation with Lizard, Harlan didn't notice her, although he was vaguely aware of the sweet perfume clouding the air. Lizard, however, couldn't keep his eyes off the woman.

Harlan smirked. "You listening to me?"

"Uh-huh," Lizard said pensively.

Harlan snatched a glance. He thought she was cute, but not to the point of distraction. Turning back to Lizard, he picked up where he'd left off: "So, like I was saying, if we—" He was interrupted by a tap on his shoulder. Harlan twisted around to face the woman. "Yeah?"

"Harlan Elliott?"

"Yeah?"

The woman offered a wide, sparkling smile. "C'mon now, Harlan, you don't remember me?"

He stared at her. Suddenly, his face brightened. "I-Ivy?"

"Yep!"

It hit him then why it was he'd been so taken with her. It was a school performance, he couldn't remember exactly what, but Ivy had sung the lead and her voice had caused his heartstrings to quiver.

"Ivy Reid," Harlan breathed, "you still married?"

She rolled her eyes. "Well, get to the point, why don't you? Yeah, according to the law we still man and wife."

"But?"

Ivy curled a delicate hand around the glass of soda water she'd ordered. "He done run off with some tackhead." She brought the glass to her lips and sipped.

Harlan's eyes rolled over her. "His loss."

"That's what I said," Ivy clucked.

Lizard stretched his arm over Harlan's shoulder, presenting his hand. "This dude ain't got much in the manners department," he said. "I'm Leo, but you can call me Lizard."

Ivy grabbed hold of his index and middle fingers. "Ivy," she replied. "Nice to meet you."

Shrugging Lizard off, Harlan rested his chin on the heel of his hand and gazed intently into Ivy's eyes.

"Why you looking at me like that?"

"You still sing?"

Ivy squared her shoulders and beamed. "Like a lark."

Chapter 47

They called themselves the Harlem World Band, played small venues—house parties and dinner clubs located in and around the city.

Emma appointed herself as booking agent; after all, she knew everyone Lucille knew—which was anyone who was anyone in the music business. Within a few months, the Harlem World Band was playing coveted venues in the Hamptons and Martha's Vineyard.

The money was garbage, but they were having too much fun to notice. Eventually, Emma managed to secure a twelve-week spot at the Bamboo Inn.

Upon hearing the news, Harlan swept Emma into his arms and twirled her through the air. "That's great, Mama! What night?"

"Tuesdays."

"Tuesday night?" Disappointed, Harlan set her down and stepped away. "It's deader than dead on Tuesdays."

"Well, you gotta start somewhere," Emma said.

Wednesdays through Saturdays, the Bamboo Inn on Seventh Avenue catered to the High Harlem crowd of professional black men, their stylish female companions, wealthy white college kids, Park Avenue snobs, and curious Europeans on holiday.

On Tuesday evenings, the Bamboo Inn was frequented by porters, janitors, and doormen, accompanied by their wives who made their living as maids, washerwomen, and hairdressers. And while the High Harlem crowd threw paper money at the band, the Tuesday-night crowd could only afford to toss coins.

The only night of the week that bread was placed on the tables was Tuesday. This because the Chinese waiters knew that the common colored folk were partial to sopping up the tangy brown sauces that accompanied the egg foo yong that was so popular with that crowd.

Every evening, excluding Tuesdays, the blue-black behemoth of a bouncer wore a monkey suit, top hat, and tails. On Tuesdays, however, he was attired in simple black slacks and a gray or navy-blue dress coat.

The only dazzle on Tuesday nights came from the colored spotlights bouncing off the rotating mirrored ball that hung from the ceiling. That and the occasional well-known musician who stopped in for a Singapore sling before heading someplace livelier.

Lucille Hegamin and her husband were occasional Tuesday-night patrons.

The thing between Harlan and Lucille had left Emma salty toward her childhood friend. For months, Emma had refused to take Lucille's phone calls and would stealthily ignore her if they happened upon each other at a house party or nightclub. Eventually, though, Emma's ruffled feathers smoothed, and she and Lucille mended their relationship. Albeit, at the beginning the stitching was loose and sloppy. So for a time, the friends badgered each other with insults camouflaged as compliments.

"Girl, that gray hair suits you!"

"Don't you worry about those few extra pounds; you carry

them well!"

When Lucille looked up from her plate of egg foo yong and spotted Emma and Sam coming through the door, she waved them over to her table.

Emma nodded at the bottle in the center of the table. "Champagne?"

"We celebrating!" Lucille chirped.

Emma's eyebrows arched. "Oh?"

Bill wrapped his arm around Lucille's shoulders and proudly announced that Lucille had finished her first full year of nursing school.

"Well, that is cause for celebration," Sam said. "Congrats, Lucille!"

"Thank you, Sam."

Emma picked up a pair of chopsticks from the table and twirled them between her fingers like batons. "Has it been a year already?"

"Yep."

"Where does the time go?" Emma wondered aloud.

"I ask that question every goddamn day," Lucille laughed.

The friends looked at each other and smiled.

Bill caught the cuff of a passing waiter. "Two more champagne glasses here, please."

"It went quick," Emma muttered, shaking her head.

"Maybe for you, but it was an eternity for me."

"All them books and reading. I couldn't have done it," Emma conceded. "You were always smart."

Lucille gushed at the compliment.

Emma raised her champagne flute. "To Lucille!"

"To Lucille!" the men cheered.

"To time!" Emma added jubilantly.

"The bitch!" Lucille chuckled.

When the Harlem World Band took the stage, Lucille leaned over the table and whispered, "Harlan looks good."

"Sound good too," Sam said.

The band serenaded the audience with "Strange Fruit," "Moonlight Serenade," "If I Didn't Care," and "Body and Soul."

Lucille was so impressed with their renditions, with Harlan's professionalism and showmanship, that she braved the shower of nickels and dimes so that she could lay a crisp ten-dollar bill at his feet.

Chapter 48

WESTERN UNION TELEGRAM
FEB 9/1940
MRS. SAM ELLIOTT
MR. HARLAN ELLIOTT
17 E. 133RD STREET
NEW YORK CITY

Word has reached me here in Paris that the Harlem World Band is a treasure that should be shared with the French. I would like to extend an invitation for your band to come to Paris, specifically to my establishment L'Escadrille in Montmartre. I am proposing a two-month engagement beginning in late March. In exchange, I will provide passage to Paris, hotel accommodations, and a salary that will not make you rich, but will keep you in food and libations for the entirety of your engagement. Of course, there are ample opportunities here to make money, and I would certainly encourage you to take advantage of those prospects. I look forward to your favorable response.

Eugene James Bullard
rue Fontaine, 5
Paris, France

Harlan was out and Sam was at work, so the only other person who could appreciate Emma's excitement was Lucille.

"Hello—" Lucille barely got her greeting out before Emma was off and running, chattering excitedly about Paris and Harlan and the band.

"Whoa, whoa, Emma," Lucille laughed, as she lifted the black phone into the crook of her arm and carried it over to the sofa. "I heard Paris," she said, reaching for her silver cigarette case.

Emma began again, slower this time.

Lucille lit her cigarette and inhaled, her eyes moving from the window to the snaking telephone cord.

Emma ended her ramblings with a shuddering sigh.

Lucille said, "Well, it took him long enough."

"W-what?" Emma stammered.

"Eugene... Gene, well, he asked if I would bring the band to Paris, to his club for a month-long run, but I told him I was all done with that." Lucille knocked a long ash into the ashtray.

"Oh?" Emma responded from East Harlem.

"So I suggested Harlan and his band."

"You did?"

"Anyway," Lucille continued, "I told him that the Harlem World Band would be just as good as having me and mine."

Emma giggled, "So you lied? The musicians are one thing, but the girl—"

"Oh please, she can't touch me with a ten-foot pole—"

"Though she tries—"

"Every. Single. Time!"

They laughed.

"So what does Harlan have to say about all this?"

"He ain't home, so he don't know yet."

In Lucille's kitchen, the kettle on the stove began to screech.

"Well, I thought I was calling to give you good news, but I guess I need to thank you."

Lucille stubbed out her cigarette and stood. "No need for that."

"I-I just want you to know that Harlan has grown," Emma babbled nervously. "He's matured a lot. That Lizard, well, he's been a real good influence on him and—"

"Emma, Harlan has the job. You don't have to sell him. I was sold when I saw him at the Bamboo, and besides, the talk in the streets is all positive. That's why I recommended him to Gene."

"Well, thank you anyway."

"Like I said, Harlan earned it."

Chapter 49

On February 20, 1940, 17 East 133rd Street exploded in jubilant celebration—a bon voyage party that started at eight o'clock Saturday night and stretched to Sunday noon. Catered food, champagne, balloons, and party streamers.

It seemed all of Harlem had come out to wish Harlan farewell.

At midnight, Emma's surprise arrived wearing a brown Stevedore low over his face. Before anyone could see who he was, she grabbed his hand and whisked him through the unsuspecting revelers, up the stairs, and into her bedroom.

"Wait here," she whispered. "Sam will come and get you when it's time."

"And?" he said, smiling coyly.

Emma cocked her head. "And what?"

"And?" he repeated, rubbing his belly, his face lit brightly with his million-volt smile.

"Oh yes," Emma laughed, "and when Sam comes up, he'll have a plate of red beans and rice."

At half past the witching hour, Emma found Harlan propped up against the parlor wall staring down the blouse of a slant-eyed girl with greasy curls. As she hooked her arm around Harlan's waist, she shot the girl a look so sharp it nearly sliced her in two.

"He's here," Emma whispered, dragging Harlan across the

floor. Harlan scanned the crowd. "Where?"

"In my bedroom."

"Did you hide him in the closet like you do my Christmas and birthday gifts?"

Emma popped him playfully upside the head. "Boy, go and find Lizard."

Harlan pushed his way through the throng of well-wishers. Each step brought him face-to-face with someone who wanted to shake his hand, slap his back, or convey some critical piece of information Harlan would need on his trip across the Atlantic.

By the time he found Lizard in the cellar, puffing on a cigarette, it was nearly one o'clock.

"What you doing down here?"

"Aww, it's a lot of people up there. I just needed some air." Harlan glanced around the cellar. Fanning his arms, he said, "You need air, so you came down here?"

Lizard shrugged his shoulders.

"My mama and daddy threw this party for us, you better come on and enjoy it."

Lizard dropped the cigarette into the dirt and mashed it with the toe of his shoe, following Harlan up the wooden staircase into the soggy smoke-and-perfume-choked heat of the house.

"Mama wants you to play," Harlan called over his shoulder as they made their way toward the group of musicians Emma had hired for the party.

"My horn is up in your room," Lizard shouted back.

"Nah it ain't, Mama brought it down."

Emma, smiling like a cat with a mouse, stood at the front of the parlor clutching Lizard's strawberry-colored trumpet case to her chest.

"Anything special you want to hear, Mrs. Elliott?" Lizard asked, carefully removing his horn.

"Whatever you play is fine by me."

Lizard started with "Potato Head Blues," a Louis Armstrong classic. He expertly mimicked Satchmo's rapid notes—nailing the D chord, toggling the G, flying into a quarter E note, hitting it so hard it took his breath away. He stopped. He didn't really feel like playing. His mind was on other things and his heart was elsewhere.

Lizard nodded apologetically to the crowd, swabbed his brow, and gulped air. Just as he pressed his mouth back to the lip of the trumpet—three horn blasts, perfectly pitched E notes, rattled his left eardrum.

Lizard turned toward the sound, his fingers still dancing over the valve pistons, all Es, all Es—building, building—and at the moment when he was supposed to drop back to D and bear down in a sort of dazzling placidity, his gray-green eyes clashed with Louis Armstrong's brown ones and Lizard lost his breath a second time.

Buoyed by cheers and applause, Louis swaggered into the parlor, retrieved the note Lizard had dropped, and went on to remind everyone why he was the king.

They performed three songs together, Louis nodding approvingly, patting Lizard on the back like a proud father.

Later, in the backyard, beneath an ever-brightening sky, seemingly oblivious to the February morning bite, Lizard found Louis Armstrong perched on a rusty lawn chair holding court. His black-and-gray-checkered dress shirt was unbuttoned to the navel, revealing a white cotton undershirt. Dangling from the gold chain around his neck was a hexagram the size of a half-dollar fashioned from the same precious metal.

When Louis waved Lizard over, the cluster of men parted. Lizard grabbed a milk crate and edged into the space they'd made for him. He sat quietly, reveling in their stories of music, women, and the ups and downs of life, until one by one the men began to drift away, eventually leaving Lizard and Louis alone.

"Call me Pops," Louis said when Lizard started yet another question with, "Mr. Armstrong..."

"This?" Louis pointed to the hexagram resting on his chest. He cupped it in his hand and stroked it lovingly with his thumb, explaining to Lizard that the pendant was a Jewish symbol known as the Star of David.

"You're Jewish?" Lizard asked, stunned.

Louis snickered. "No, no, I'm not."

"Then why do you wear it?"

Louis folded his arms. "Well, when I was growing up in New Orleans, there was this family called the Karnofskys who had a junk business. I needed a job to help support my family, and they gave me one. I was seven years old."

Lizard's head bobbed. "Seven?"

Louis held up seven fingers. "Anyway, them Karnofskys were different from most of the other white folk I'd come across."

"Different how?"

Louis leaned forward and rubbed his knees. "Well, ya see, son, they ain't never—not once—called me a nigger, ape, tar baby, or any of them other horrible names they call us black folk." He waved his hands at Lizard. "'Course, you so light, you probably haven't suffered that type of humiliation. They were a different kind of white folk; so different that they treated me like family. They fed me. Not at the back door neither. I ate right at the table with them! In fact, when things got too hot at my house, they took me in."

Lizard's eyes shone with astonishment.

"I thought white folk stuck together, so I was confused when I saw the treatment the family got from people who were white like them."

Lizard leaned in. "What d'you mean? How'd they treat 'em?"

Louis shrugged. "Like niggers."

"Why was that?"

"Because they were Jewish," Louis said pointedly.

Lizard cast his eyes down to his shoes and frowned.

"That family was real good to me. When I left New Orleans for Chicago, Mrs. Karnofsky gave me this pendant." He tapped the hexagram with his index finger. "And I've kept it with me ever since."

Suddenly aware of the cold, Louis stood and raked his hands up and down his arms. "Son, I don't hate anyone. That's not to say that I don't have it in me. I believe we all got it in us—but whenever I feel it trying to climb out, I look at this here pendant and am reminded that love is more powerful than hate will ever be." He slowly buttoned his shirt. "I think I smell bacon. What about you? You ready for some breakfast?"

"Yes, sir, Mr.—"

"Pops," Louis said gently. "Call me Pops."

"Yes, sir, Pops."

Lizard followed his icon to the door. Louis reached for the handle, turned his head, and asked, "So, why they call you Lizard?"

Lizard grinned. "Because Satchmo was already taken."

Chapter 50

They met up three more times to fuck. The last being just four days before Harlan's bon voyage celebration. But Gwen wouldn't receive an invitation, nor would she be informed of his imminent departure. Harlan didn't feel obligated to share anything with Gwen, other than his sex.

Gwen, naive and unseasoned, assumed that Harlan's desire to sleep with her was the very underpinning of true love—no matter what her mother said.

The final time she and Harlan were together, Gwen, writhing in ecstasy beneath him, sunk her fingernails into his back and declared her undying love for him over and over again like a broken record.

Harlan didn't return the affection; he just grunted, rolled off her, and reached for the pack of smokes on the nightstand.

Afterward, he accompanied Gwen as far as his front door and pecked her on the lips. "I'll come up to the fairgrounds on Wednesday."

"Okay," Gwen bubbled, leaning in to steal another kiss.

Wednesday came and went, and Harlan failed to show. Nor did he appear at Grand Central Station where he sometimes met Gwen as she exited one train to board another.

She phoned his home numerous times only to be informed by whichever parent answered that Harlan was out, but they'd be sure to let him know she called. Again.

While Harlan's absence was disappointing, it was tolerable because Gwen had the memory of their lovemaking to feast on. But when the warmth he'd fired between her legs cooled, giving rise to an ache in her heart, she had no choice but to take matters into her own hands.

She went to Harlem, marched up the steps of Sam and Emma's brownstone, and lay hard and long on their doorbell as bold as a scorned woman twice her age.

Emma angrily wrenched open the door. "So where's the fire?"

Gwen blushed beneath the woman's hot glare. "I'm sorry, um... Good afternoon," she stammered, suddenly remembering her manners. "I was wondering if Harlan was home."

Emma rolled her eyes in exasperation. What had become of these young women? Calling her house at any hour, day or night, and showing up on her stoop—unannounced, no less—puppy dog–eyed, barely able to keep the begging out of their voices. Obviously, their mamas had raised them wrong.

"What's your name, girl?"

"Gwendolyn. Gwen," she whispered.

"Well, Gwendolyn, Gwen, Harlan ain't here. He should be halfway to France by now."

Flabbergasted, Gwen leaned back and took a long hard look at the house. Surely she was at the wrong address, talking to some mother who also had a son named Harlan.

Emma stepped onto the stoop and followed Gwen's searching eyes with her own.

"What you looking for?"

"I-I'm sorry, miss," Gwen uttered uneasily, "but I'm looking for Harlan *Elliott*."

Emma's eyes narrowed. When she spoke again, her voice was slow and deliberate. "Yes, that's my son. Harlan Elliott."

Gwen's face went dark. "France?"

"Yes, chile, France," Emma sighed. "He'll be back in two months or so. I'll tell him you stopped by."

And with that, Emma backed into the house and shut the door.

Part VII

Montmartre

Chapter 51

Harlan and his band arrived in France on a clammy March morning. Eugene Bullard met them at the pier, embraced them one by one, and pressed hard kisses onto each of their cheeks.

Georgia born and bred, tall, dark, and handsome, Bullard had fled the oppressive racial atmosphere of the South as a teenager by stowing away on a ship bound for Scotland. From there he made his way to Paris where he supported himself as a boxer.

At the onset of the First World War, Bullard enlisted in the Foreign Legion and became a machine-gunner. In time, he joined the French Air Force, where he took part in more than twenty combat missions before being promoted to the rank of sergeant. His heroism earned him the Croix de Guerre and he would go down in history as being the world's first black fighter pilot.

After the war, Bullard, a skilled drummer, returned to Paris to pursue his love of music. He eventually became the manager of the famous Le Grand Duc located in the Parisian neighborhood of Montmartre before going on to open his own cabaret, L'Escadrille.

In the sedan, the group exchanged few words, struck silent by the sights of pigeon-filled squares, narrow streets lined with cafés, pastry shops, and Parisian dames strutting along the cobblestone boulevards in peep-toe high heels and jaunty hats.

On their arrival in Montmartre—the Mount of Martyrs, the Harlem of Paris—Ivy pressed her forehead against the window and pointed at a white-domed building perched on a high hill. "What's that?"

"It's a church called Sacré-Coeur," Eugene explained.

"Ugh," Ivy responded. "It looks like a giant birthday cake!"

"Looks to me like some big ole white titties," Harlan commented loudly.

The observation raised a chorus of raucous of laughter.

Eugene rolled down the window, flooding the car with a staggering bouquet of strong coffee, freshly baked croissants, and heady perfume. Reaching his hand out, he indicated the Moulin Rouge, saying, "Josephine Baker performed there. And you see that hotel over there? That's where Langston Hughes stayed when he first came to Paris. There, to the left, is the American Express office. You can receive and send letters and telegrams from there. That club over there is Le Grand Duc. I used to manage it back in the day when Bricktop was the main attraction. Do y'all know her? Oh, look, that's where Pablo Picasso once lived, and right over there is my club: L'Escadrille."

Their heads swiveled with the dizzying commentary. They'd recognized some of the names, but not all. Nevertheless, they nodded and hummed interestedly in their throats.

"W.E.B. Du Bois used to sit in that café and hold court for hours." The sedan slowed to a stop.

"Ah! *That* is Florence. It used to be called Chez Florence, named after Florence Jones. Phenomenal talent and a pistol! One night she dragged Prince Henry onto the floor and coaxed him into participating in a Black Bottom dance contest. He wasn't very good."

Eugene fell quiet as the car rolled forward again. When it reached the corner, he added with mournful reverence, "Florence is dead now."

They would stay in the Lyceum Hotel—a slender, daisy-colored building sandwiched between a garden on the verge of bloom and a café so small it could only accommodate one customer at a time. They followed Eugene through a vestibule covered in aqua-colored tiles, into a lobby no bigger than a box. There, Eugene spoke a few quick words of French to the young towhead at the front desk. She replied with a gracious smile and slid three brass keys across the counter.

The rooms were tiny and plain: radiator, window, a set of twin beds, no closet. Guests either kept their clothing in their luggage or hung the articles on the row of nails that had been driven into the wall for just that purpose.

"The toilet is down the hall," Eugene told them. "There are plenty of places to eat cheap. Get some rest and be at the club no later than nine." With that, he trotted down the stairs and was gone.

Outside, the residue of an early-morning shower glimmered on chimney pots and slanted terra-cotta rooftops.

Harlan opened the window, stuck his head out, and bellowed, "Paris, I'm here!"

Behind him, Lizard collapsed onto the bed and kicked off his shoes, which clattered to the floor. Harlan whipped around. When his eyes met Lizard's miserable gaze, he asked, "What's with you?"

Lizard shook his head. "Nothing, man. Nothing at all."

Chapter 52

With the arrival of Harlan's band and others, Montmartre came alive again. For a while, the threat of war between Germany and Great Britain had scattered the musicians like ants. The cabarets had closed down and overnight Montmartre was transformed into a ghost town, leaving the Zazous without a place to revel in the American swing music that had come to define them.

The Zazous took their name after Cab Calloway's hit "Zaz Zuh Zaz." They'd thoroughly immersed themselves in swing culture, going so far as adopting Calloway's style of dress, gliding back-step dance moves, and hep language.

During those grim days of September 1939 and the months that followed, Zazous could be spotted wandering the quiet streets, the men adorned in brightly colored zoot suits, broad brim hats, and suede shoes. The women slathered their lips in red chili pepper–colored lipstick, regaled themselves in short skirts and ridiculously wide-shouldered blazers. They wandered hooked-armed in groups or alone through Montmartre's streets, stopping at the shuttered cabarets, peering mournfully into the dark structures.

For a time, Parisian bands had tried to fill the void, but they were little more than tragic substitutes.

When the New Year dawned, and not a shot had been fired from Germany or England, Eugene Bullard and the other cabaret owners decided it was time to reverse the tides, to rekindle the soul of Montmartre, and set out to woo the musicians back.

The response was quick or none at all. Many had secured work in other countries, in other venues, or had returned home—to Harlem, Chicago, and St. Louis. One trumpeter explained in his telegram, *It may be quiet now, but that don't mean there ain't a cotton mouth in the tall grass.* He knew without consulting a map, globe, or atlas just how dangerously close Germany was to France, and it made him uneasy.

Lizard harbored similar misgivings, so when Harlan had first come to him with the opportunity, he had flat-out declined. Eventually, of course, Harlan wore Lizard down, and he got his way, just like always.

Chapter 53

The weeks stumbled through March, April, and into May, and still Harlan and the rest of his group hadn't acquired a sense of Paris beyond her mirth-filled nights.

After playing L'Escadrille until three a.m., they spent the rest of the morning wandering from one cabaret to the next, dancing with patrons, flirting, and draining champagne from bottles left in silver ice buckets.

When the cabarets closed at eight a.m., all of the musicians gathered at various cafés for breakfast. Over eggs fried in olive oil, flaky croissants, and coffee, they recounted the evening's events and shared news from back home. By eleven, most returned to their flats and hotel rooms, climbed into bed, and slept until twilight.

Being in Montmartre was like attending one long party, but even the best parties had to come to an end.

On the morning of May 10, 1940, German forces sank their fangs into France's west coast. Panicked, all of the musicians who had been lured to Paris to sate the natives' thirst for black music rushed the homes of their sponsors, demanding immediate passage back to America.

In his rose-colored sitting room, Eugene nervously tugged the lobe of his left ear.

"Listen," he said, presenting his palms like a gift. "I've already checked, and all of the ships are booked solid into July.

You could all take a train into one of the bordering countries and try your luck from there, but from what I've been told, there's no guarantee you'll get on a ship before June."

Ivy broke into sobs, and both Lincoln and Bruno leaped to comfort her. Lizard shot Harlan an accusatory look.

"This thing can go either way," Eugene offered bitterly. "Let's just hope it goes the right way."

***

Those who stayed in Paris because they had nowhere to go, or simply no inclination to leave, flocked to Montmartre to escape the dark drift of their anxiety. To get lost in the music, numb themselves with alcohol, reefer, and opium, engage in carnal pleasure with strangers, to sin through the last days.

God cried. The dry bones of the devout crackled in the cemeteries, skies split, bled pink, and the devil wailed: *Don't worry tomorrow, live for today. Don't just dip your toe, wade in. Discard your scarves, welcome the wind against your neck; let it rake its airy fingers through your hair. Leave your umbrellas at home, step out into the rain and get wet. Let the children have cake for breakfast, tell strangers you love them. Fuck, drink. Feed the pigeons fresh bread. These are the last days; there will be no weeping here because Montmartre is not a place of sadness or regrets, it's a haven of art, freedom, and celebration, so revel, revel!*

On the afternoon of June 14, Harlan woke to a fan of brunette hair across his face. He brushed it away, stirring the woman beside him. She sighed sleepily, wiggled her behind against his groin, and murmured, "*Bonjour, mon chéri.*"

Peering into the muted darkness of the room, Harlan's eyes seized on a towering, ornate pier mirror, not two feet from the bed. He lay very still, anticipating the moment his memory would race forward, informing him of those things that he presently could not recall. Specifically, where he was and the name of the woman lying next to him.

He was just four days away from boarding a steamer bound for New York. Eugene had delivered the news a few days earlier. Everyone was happy to hear it, everyone except Harlan.

Paris had been a revelation. Not once had he been called out of his name. Not once had he been denied entry into a restaurant or hotel.

Back in New York, none of the white girls he'd bedded ever invited him home for dinner. If he ran into them beyond Harlem's clearly dened borders, his *Hey, how you been?* was usually met with an empty gaze. There had been none of that ugliness in Paris.

A deafening blast of a bullhorn wrecked his musings and startled the woman erect. In that instant, her name flew onto Harlan's tongue; he opened his mouth and it fluttered out on a winged question: "Astrid?"

Astrid cast a brief glance at him before tumbling out of bed and racing across the room to the window. She pulled back the drapes and sunlight stormed the room, setting her alabaster skin ablaze. She pulled open the window and the clamor of hundreds of marching feet, shod in jackboots, echoed up from the street.

Harlan sat up. "What's that? A parade?"

Astrid's lips moved, but he was unable to hear her words over the din; but then again, he didn't need to because the alarm in her eyes was earsplitting.

He joined her at the window and peered down at a sea of goose-stepping soldiers. An enormous swastika had been draped over the Arc de Triomphe, smaller versions flapped from apartment-building windows, waved as flags by toddlers.

Beneath the rain of confetti, hundreds of people cheered and threw kisses at the procession. Others stood tight-lipped, faces stiff with disbelief.

"What are they saying?"

"They say," she whimpered, "this is the end as we know it."

The great dragon was hurled down—that ancient serpent called the devil, or Satan, who leads the whole world astray. He was hurled to the earth, and his angels with him.
—Revelation 12:9

Chapter 54

In the cabarets that night, Nazis outnumbered the Parisians— sitting three to a table, visor caps balanced on their knees, standing against the walls, and lurking in doorways and the shadowy halls near the toilets.

Onstage at L'Escadrille, a terrified Ivy tried to engage them—gesturing with her hips and fingers as she sang. She did her best to treat them as if they were any other paying customer out to have a good time, but her movements were clumsy and the smile she offered was more terrified grin than cheerful beam. Behind her, the musicians stumbled through songs, fell off tempo, stalled, and had to start from the top.

At the end of their second set, a disgusted Eugene told them it was best they call it a night instead of continuing to stink up the place.

At the word go, Ivy, Lincoln, and Bruno hurried toward the door. "Hey, where y'all going?" Harlan cried.

"Back to the hotel," Ivy threw over her shoulder before stepping hastily into the night.

Harlan looked at Lizard. "You gonna run and hide too?"

Lizard made a face.

"Aww, c'mon, man, we only have three days left, let's enjoy it."

Lizard glanced at the stone-faced soldiers. "Can't you see things have changed?" he mumbled.

"Aww, fuck 'em."

They ended up at the Flea Pit, a bistro frequented by black musicians and their flunkies. Lizard was relieved to find the place free of Nazis.

Whiskey-and-soda in hand, Harlan invited himself into a game of darts while Lizard sat at an empty table facing the door.

A buxom redhead who had been ogling Harlan from across the room downed her whiskey, swaggered over, and whispered a lewd proposal in his ear. Harlan threw back his head and laughed until he coughed.

After some back and forth, the woman grabbed his hand and strolled him toward the door.

"Don't be jealous," Harlan chided Lizard as they walked by, "some women just prefer chocolate over milk."

Lizard rolled his eyes.

"Is he your friend?" the woman asked in her broken English.

"That's my brother," Harlan proudly replied.

"Your brother?" The woman's eyes glowed with amusement.

She turned and called out to a leggy blonde huddled over a table of polka-playing saxophonists. "*Viens içi*, Janet."

The blonde tottered over.

"This is my sister Janet," the red-haired woman spouted in her crippled English.

Just like Harlan and Lizard, the women looked nothing alike. They joined Lizard's table and ordered a round of drinks.

After a while, Lizard, who had always prided himself on being able to hold his liquor, realized that the room was spinning and the wooden floor was buckling beneath his feet. He pressed his hands to his head, closed his eyes, and groaned, "I think I'm drunk."

Janet ran her tongue along his jawline. "Me too," she whispered. Lizard squirmed, giggled like a toddler.

Harlan slipped a cigarette between his lips, rapped his knuckles on the table, and announced that it was time to go.

Under the moonless sky, the couples stumbled down winding streets, their laughter rising like smoke, sailing through open windows, stealing into dreams.

A block before they reached the main avenue, a figure stepped from the shadows and asked for a light.

The women fell silent. Lizard fought the urge to run. Only Harlan seemed oblivious to the threat—he continued to reel with laughter over a joke that had dropped dead with fright.

The redhead yanked his arm. "He asked for a light. Do you have one?" she sputtered nervously.

"Did he? Well, how would I know, I don't speak French!" Laughter hooked him again as he patted his pockets in search of his matches.

The women rummaged nervously through their small dinner purses. Lizard stood frozen—more mannequin than man.

"Sorry, I guess I left my matches back at the... at the um..." Harlan struggled to conjure the word. He jerked his thumb over his shoulder. "Back there." Rocking forward, he squinted at the man before him, finally noticing the uniform and the swastika bound to his forearm. Harlan's high dripped away. "Sorry, buddy, I guess you're out of luck," he said, and then looked at the redhead. "Translate that fer him."

The soldier smiled menacingly. "*Buddy*? What does this *buddy* mean?" he growled in English.

Harlan's head bobbed. "It means pal. Friend."

"Friend?" The soldier spat a wad of phlegm at Harlan's feet.

"You and I could never be friends."

Harlan threw his shoulders back. "Whatever." He grabbed the redhead's hand. "'Scuse us."

The soldier stealthily blocked their path. He eyed Lizard and the women with disgust, and they withered.

"Consorting with Negroes?" he snorted disgustedly. "You three should be ashamed of yourselves."

"You *three*?" Harlan grunted. "He ain't white."

The soldier cocked his head and gaped at Lizard. "Humph, race mixing." He shuddered. "It fills the world with mongrels like yourself." Harlan mumbled something and the soldier stepped boldly to him. "What did you say?"

Harlan held his gaze. "I said, he ain't no mongrel."

The two men glared at each other.

Three more soldiers approached from down the street, their heavy footsteps echoing ominously. The first soldier waved them over. When they were within earshot, he spoke to them in rapid-fire German.

Lizard clenched his jaw and balled his fists in anticipation of what was to follow.

The soldiers surrounded them, barring all possible exits.

Harlan's head spun left and right. "Okay," he shouted, "what the fuck is this?"

"We think you should maybe come with us," the first soldier stated coolly. "*Buddy*."

Lizard dropped his trumpet and threw a wild punch that hit nothing but air. Harlan used his guitar case as a battering ram, charging the soldier closest to him, knocking him down.

The victory was fleeting—within seconds both Harlan and Lizard were on the ground, flailing against a torrent of fists and boot heels.

The women ran screaming from the scene.

In the apartments above, lamps were turned on, curtains parted—the brave ones opened their windows, flung their heads out to get a full-on look at the brawl. But no one called for the police or drenched the assailants in cold water. When the annoyed and the awakened saw the swastikas, they hastily closed their windows and climbed back into bed.

Harlan floated out of a fog of unconsciousness to find himself slumped over in the backseat of a speeding military jeep. His body throbbed with pain, and he could taste blood in his mouth. Alongside him was Lizard, head flung back on his neck and mouth ajar; he was snoring like a drunkard. Miraculously, the soldiers had beaten Lizard into slumber. If the situation hadn't been so grim, so terrifying, Harlan would have laughed at the comedy of it.

The soldier in the passenger seat barked something that prompted the driver to shift gears, slowing the vehicle to a leisurely sightseeing pace.

Mind racing, but giving no indication that he was awake, Harlan remained slouched and still as the jeep rolled unhurriedly past brick apartment buildings and the linden trees that lined the streets and avenues. From the corner of his eye, he spied the Eiffel Tower and held it in his sights until the jeep made a sharp left, down a narrow street.

Minutes later, Lizard's snoring came to an abrupt halt, his body tensed, and his eyelids began to flutter. Before Harlan could rest a bracing hand on his thigh, Lizard lurched forward, hollering and swinging his fists.

The jeep swerved wildly, sideswiping two parked cars. After

the driver regained control and brought the vehicle to a halt, both soldiers wrangled Lizard back into the seat. They pulled their batons and beat him about his head and ribs until he cowered in submission. Then they turned their aggression on Harlan, even though he had done nothing other than tremble with fear.

Chapter 55

The sky was blush with morning when the jeep rolled to a stop before a dome-shaped building crowned in thick gray rubber. Harlan and Lizard were dragged by their collars from the jeep, thrown to the ground, kicked, ordered back on their feet, and then shoved through the guarded entryway into the building.

The American musicians stumbled down the corridor, past vacant concession stands pushed up against walls with posters depicting smiling, cherry-cheeked men, women, and children engaged in ice-skating, roller-skating, and cycling.

At the dome's brightly lit epicenter, Harlan and Lizard were muscled down the steps and abandoned in the rink which was crowded with more than a hundred people. They stood, shoulders touching, gazing at the mass of anguished and confused faces.

"*Içi, içi!*"

Harlan and Lizard turned toward the beckoning voice.

"*Içi, içi,*" the short black man cried again, frantically waving both of his hands.

They started toward him, stepping carefully along the zigzag paths made by the rows upon rows of sleeping pallets covering the floor.

The man urged them on, his eyes fluttering nervously from Harlan and Lizard to the armed guards who watched from the rows of red stadium seats. When they reached him, the man pointed at two vacant pallets. "*Asseyez-vous.*"

Harlan sat down, but Lizard remained standing, his head tilted, staring at the massive swastikas that dangled from the arched metal support beams.

The man hunched down beside Harlan. "*Je m'appelle Meher Feki.*" Harlan nodded.

"*Votre nom?*"

"Harlan."

Meher nodded. "Harlan," he repeated, and then looked at Lizard. "*Son nom?*"

"His name is Lizard," Harlan said.

"Li-zard?" Meher murmured, before jabbering on in French, exceeding Harlan's rudimentary comprehension of the language.

Harlan raised a halting hand. "I'm American. I speak English."

"Ah!" Meher said. "Me, I too speak English." He went on to explain that he'd been born in Tunisia but had been living in France for twenty-eight years, employed as a chauffeur for a wealthy Swiss family in Belleville. "Two days ago, the German soldiers stop the car, order me out. I come out. I ask them what is the problem. They no give an answer. They hit me in the head until I fall to the ground, where they kick and kick."

Meher pointed to the knots on his head and raised his shirt, exposing his bruised rib cage. "My madam, she is screaming. Tears on her face. Her husband pull her back, cover her mouth with his hands. Don't try to save me." As he relived the scene, Meher's eyes turned damp. "They bring me here. I don't know what I have done. What crime I have committed. I ask and ask, and they say nothing, just beat me."

Once again, Meher pointed to the knots on his head. "I have a wife, two kids. Where they think I am? They must think I am dead."

Chapter 56

Under the hot, glaring lights of the dome, sleep was impossible for anyone other than the young innocents and the elderly who were closing in on their last days. This wasn't to say that their slumber was easy—twitching limbs, clenched fists, and whimpering was evidence that it was far from serene.

The rest of them, Harlan included, lay awake with their eyes as wide as half-dollars and hearts drumming with dread. The women clasped their hands over their mouths to keep their screams captive, while their eyes implored the men to turn their reticence into revolt. The men looked at the soldiers, at their guns. When they once again met the women's urging eyes, their faces were dark with shame.

Harlan didn't know what to make of the situation. If he possessed more than an ounce of naïveté, if the bruises to his body didn't ache so, if the stench of fear wasn't so potent it made him want to gag, Harlan might have convinced himself that this was nothing more than a Scotch-and-reefer-induced nightmare.

The next day, Harlan and the other detainees were loaded onto dozens of buses, transported two hours outside of Paris, and unloaded at a sleepy train station. They were ordered to lace their fingers over their heads and then hustled past a group of yawning French soldiers and one lone ticket clerk pretending to read his newspaper.

In cattle cars still reeking of livestock there were loaves of bread and pails of water. Spotting the treasure, the prisoners raced recklessly forward, consuming every crumb and drop.

A French soldier climbed into the car and pointed at a burly man sporting a lush brown beard. "*Vous êtes en charge. Si quelqu'un s'échappe, nous vous fusillerons.*"

The man's jaw dropped. He pressed a trembling index finger into his chest. "*M-m-moi?*"

The soldier pulled out his sidearm, pressed the nozzle against the man's temple, and repeated his demand.

"What did he say?" Harlan whispered to Meher.

"The soldier told the man he is in charge. If anyone gets away, he will be shot."

On the hay-scattered floor, Harlan sat between Meher and a grizzled, olive-colored man with bulging knuckles. Across the car, Lizard, who hadn't spoken one word to Harlan or anyone else, turned over an empty water pail, sat down, leaned against the wall, and closed his eyes. Two more men did the same. Mothers lifted their children up to the box-shaped windows; others stood at the openings and wept into the sunlight.

In one corner of the car, a small albino boy sat curled in his mother's lap, his arms coiled like ropes around her neck. Huddled in another corner were two very slim, dark-haired men who appeared to be in their twenties. Their eyebrows had been plucked away to stripes. They spoke in whispers behind their palms, gesturing gracefully with their shoulders.

If it weren't for the shadow of new growth insulting their beautiful faces, Harlan would have mistaken them for women. As his eyes drifted from their faces, he wondered about Ivy,

Bruno, and Lincoln. Had they made it safely back to the hotel or had they suffered a similar fate?

By noon, the heat in the car was unbearable.

Modesty tossed aside, the women unbuttoned their blouses and rolled up the hems of their skirts and dresses.

The men shrugged off their shirts and used them to wipe perspiration from their faces and armpits or wound them around their heads like turbans.

The young children fussed and complained, setting off a wave of despair that the burly, bearded man tried to squash with a song. Clapping his meaty hands, he hopped around the children, imploring them with his smile, manipulating their hands with his own, thundering: "*Chantez! Chantez!*"

Soon, everyone was clapping and singing so loudly that they didn't notice as the train came to a stop. When the doors slid open, the song faded and smiles dropped away.

Peering in at them were a German officer and a frail, humpbacked man wearing wire-framed glasses. The officer commanded the crowd in German, and an interpreter translated the orders into French.

Slowly, cautiously, the people began to exit the car.

Meher turned to Harlan. "*Voici où se dégourdir les jambes et utiliser les toilettes.*"

Harlan shot him a quizzical look.

Meher responded with a sheepish smile. "My apologies, I forget. American. English. We use the toilet now and pull our legs."

"Pull our legs?"

Meher rolled his eyes with amusement. "We do this for our

legs," he said, reaching his hands high above his head.

"Oh," Harlan sighed, "stretch."

"*Oui*, stretch."

They were corralled into the center of a field dotted with wild flowers and ordered to quickly relieve themselves.

"Together?" one man protested. "Please, the women and children should have their privacy." He begged until the soldiers, tired of his lament, aimed their rifles at his heart.

They remained there for an hour. Enough time to collect bunches of flowers, to lie down on the soft grass and gaze at the clouds, to pretend that this was the beautiful end to a horrible dream.

If not for the presence of the soldiers, a passerby would have looked on the scene and thought they were viewing a group of people enjoying a relaxing day in the countryside.

When it came time, the captives, distracted by thoughts of escape, moved grudgingly toward the cattle cars.

But where would they run? Where were they? As far as they knew, it was the end of the world. There wasn't a signpost or structure for as far as they could see.

As Harlan hoisted himself into the car, a woman behind him screamed, "No!"

He looked around to see Meher streaking across the field, his dark head shimmering in the sunlight, short legs and arms pumping hard with determination.

An officer pulled his gun, aimed, and fired. Meher swerved, and the bullet cut through the dirt a yard from him. The second shot missed as well.

"Stop running, Meher," Harlan whispered to himself. "Stop.

Running."

The third bullet struck Meher in the back, and he fell dead onto the grass.

The officer holstered his gun and strolled over to a group of soldiers standing in the shade of the train cars. After they saluted him, there was a brief exchange, which ended with the officer looking at the fifth car.

Lizard, who was watching from the doorway of the car, backed slowly into the shadows.

The officer marched up to the man who had been charged as sentry. He pulled his weapon and pressed it against the man's nose.

The man dropped to his knees, clasped his hands at his chin, begging, "*S'il vous plait, je vous en supplie, monsieur!*"

But there was no mercy given.

The shot sent him pitching like a rocking chair. He seemed to sway forever before finally, thankfully, keeling over dead.

When the train stopped again, it was dark. All eyes turned to the doors in terrified anticipation.

Outside, the voices of the patrolling soldiers rose and fell, faded and swelled. The night air seeped into the cars, carrying scents of burning tobacco and fragrant trees.

The doors remained closed and locked. The night sky gave birth to flickering silver stars. The prisoners lay down on the hay-strewn floor and closed their eyes.

Chapter 57

How they woke them.

As if they were the most reviled creatures on the earth. As if they were criminals. Whacking them across their heads and feet with batons, shouting, yelling, spitting in their faces, dragging them up by their hair and tossing them out of the cars onto their faces.

"Line up!"

Holding their stomachs, clutching their backs, wiping the soldiers' foaming foulness from their faces, the prisoners fell into a queue so ragged, it inflamed the already incensed militia, and the captives fell under a second assault.

They were led down a cratered and pocked road fringed with trees and the occasional cottage. A few kilometers along, the group came upon an odd sight: a barely worn pair of men's brown leather shoes, laces tied into perfect bows, sat abandoned in the center of the road as if their owner had simply disintegrated into thin air. Gawking, the prisoners stepped gingerly around the peculiarity.

Continuing on, they wrestled with the onslaught of words raging in their heads—prayers mostly, but also questions, bits of monologue, explanations, apologies, and the preambles of letters that would never reach paper.

A mockingbird perched on a weathered signpost caught Lizard's attention. He raised his eyes and squinted at the fading marker: *Weimar 2KM*.

Lizard stopped hard and Harlan, who was just steps behind him and lost in his own thoughts, walked right into his back. A third man stumbled into Harlan and a fourth into the third.

The bird ranged its black eyes over its audience, made a big show of fanning its tail, and flew off into the treetops.

Now Lizard's shoulders slumped as if he had taken on a heavy load.

The group trudged on. The sun climbed higher, burned hotter.

Small children were passed from the shoulders of weary parents to the shoulders of stronger strangers. A man guiding a mule carting hay clomped past without a glance.

A structure emerged in the distance. It appeared to be a grand estate, complete with a stone security wall, towering wrought-iron entry gates, railed terraces, and a clock tower. Up close revealed barbed wire coiled along the walls and fence; beyond that, rows of barracks that stretched for acres.

Glinting in the sun above the entrance, fashioned from the same sturdy metal of the entry gates, was an insignia that read: *Jedem das Seine.*

A young girl with tight black curls aimed her finger at the words, looked at her mother, and asked, "*Qu'est-ce qu'il est marqué?*"

The woman slapped her daughter's finger back down to her side.

Lizard, who had not uttered a word since he and Harlan were snatched from the streets of Montmartre, finally spoke: "It means, *Everyone gets what they deserve.*"

A surprised Harlan caught Lizard by the arm. "Hey, how'd

you know that?"

Lizard's mouth twitched. The irony of the situation, the downright improbability, had formed a scream in his throat that he had suppressed for two long days and nights. Now it was inching across his tongue, prying at his lips. Grimacing, he successfully forced the scream back down his trachea and looked Harlan dead in the eye. "My father used to say, *You can't go home again*, but he was wrong."

"What?"

Lizard smiled unevenly. "Never mind, man," he said, waving his hand. "It don't even matter."

Part VIII

The Bitch of Buchenwald

Chapter 58

The soldiers took the abstract things first: name, date of birth, country of origin. Then the concrete possessions: money, jewelry, family photographs, the pretty hair clip clasped onto the ponytail of a doe-eyed six-year-old, the children themselves.

After that, the prisoners were ordered to strip out of their clothing. With every stitch discarded, scraps of dignity followed. Later, the hair clippers would relieve them of their vanity.

In the bathhouses, doused in dark disinfectant that reeked and stung like battery acid, they washed themselves under the pounding spray of cold water. After that, physicians poked, prodded, and plunged gloved fingers into all of their orifices—promptly ridding them of any remaining pride they might have secreted away.

Between the medical bunker and the uniform bunker, the soldiers used fists, curses, batons, and boot heels to break their will.

Dressed in blue-and-white-striped prison uniforms, the captives trotted into a massive open-air space known as Roll Call Square. They were made to stand with their arms crossed behind their heads as they listened to the commandant recite the rules, regulations, and penalties associated with life in Buchenwald Concentration Camp.

Later, they ate a meal of stale bread, potato soup, and coffee.

It was the worst food they'd ever tasted, the saddest feast they'd ever been unlucky enough to attend.

Lizard was assigned to a barracks that housed fifty-three men. Within months, the occupants would swell to two hundred. For now, though, Lizard had his pick of beds.

He chose a lower bunk, opposite the window, sat down on the lumpy straw mattress, and gazed out at the star-freckled sky. Hushed conversation hummed all around him. Soon, however, the talk died as people drifted off to sleep or retreated into the chaos of their worried minds.

Lizard remained awake long into the night, contemplating the choices he'd made, the lies he'd told, and the roads he'd wandered that had now delivered him back to the very place his parents had fled so many years earlier.

He supposed it had all begun with his birth, an innocent enough event that was no different from anyone else's. He was the youngest of three, the last child to be born to Moise and Rachel Rubenstein—Jews who had fled Weimar after Germany was defeated in the Great War.

"You think we wanted to leave our home?" Lizard's father often lamented. "We had to go because the Germans put their defeat squarely on the shoulders of Jews."

"And the Communists," Rachel always reminded him.

"Yes, the Communists. They accused us of working for foreign interests. They called us traitors, treated us like criminals. This," Moise blared, pounding his fist on the dinner table, "after Jews fought loyally in the war!"

They'd arrived at Ellis Island in September of 1920 and were met by a cousin who had been as close as a brother to Moise.

The family traveled by train to St. Louis, where for over twenty years the cousin had lived, worked, and built a life for himself.

"And now you will do the same," he told Moise.

The first years were lean. The family of five shared one bedroom at the back of the cousin's small home. Leo (he'd not yet christened himself Lizard) and his sisters shared a double bed and their parents slept on the floor.

Moise, a gifted tailor, took any and all menial jobs that came his way to supplement the scant income from his stock and trade.

In time, though, his business grew and prospered, and within three years the family moved into a two-bedroom cold-water flat. Four years after that, Moise was solvent enough to purchase a modest three-bedroom home.

"Here in America," Moise reminded his children daily, "you can become anything you want to be."

Lizard would take his father's words to lengths he would have never imagined.

Chapter 59

A fighter from the time he was ensconced in his mother's womb, Lizard burst into the world with fists coiled as tight as rosebuds.

Moise looked at his infant son and exclaimed, "Look at that! I think we have the next Young Barney Aaron on our hands!"

They named him Leo Benjamin Rubenstein.

Lizard grew up to be fearless and stubborn—refusing to walk blocks out of his way in order to avoid the young Polish and Irish Catholic immigrants who harassed Jewish kids as they made their way to and from school each day.

Go back to Jewland, kike!

You ain't wanted here, you dirty money-grubbing Jew!

Jesus killer!

Steely-eyed, Lizard would cock his kippah to the side and walk brazenly through the melee of insults, silently challenging anyone to touch him. More often than not, he made it home unscathed. But every once in a while someone would force his hand, leaving him no choice but to stand and fight.

On one occasion, Lizard found himself cornered by a gang of bat-wielding bigots. He charged directly into the trouble and, catching hold of the lead instigator's bat, turned the wooden weapon violently against him, nearly beating the youngster to death.

The boy, one David O'Malley, suffered a broken nose,

cracked jaw, and fractured collarbone. For his infraction, the fourteen-year-old Lizard spent sixty days at the Daniel Dodge Reform School for Boys.

It was there that Leo Benjamin Rubenstein discovered who and what he was meant to be.

Similar to traditional prisons, the Daniel Dodge Reform School had barred windows and towering brick walls. It housed boys in cell blocks according to their racial category and age group.

The boys rose at six o'clock and sat for breakfast at seven. From seven thirty until noon, they attended traditional school courses. After lunch, they were immersed in trade classes that focused on plumbing, masonry, and tailoring. At four o'clock the boys were sent to the yard to engage in an hour of physical activity. After dinner, they were left to their own devices until eight thirty when the guards announced lights-out. Punishments were dealt out in the form of cold-water baths, flogging, and solitary confinement.

Upon Lizard's arrival, he was immediately absorbed by a group of Jewish delinquents who happily schooled him about life on the inside.

In the yard, Abraham, the skinny but fierce leader of the young Jewish clan, tilted his chin at the throng of black boys perched on a nearby bench, harmonizing over the strum of a battered guitar.

"Those *schvartzes*," he spat, "always with the singing. If they worked as hard as they sang, they would be wealthier than us Jews!"

Lizard didn't know much about black people. Had never had any direct dealings with Negroes. He'd seen them, of course—the maids and chauffeurs, coming and going from the homes of his neighbors.

Lizard's father had wanted to hire a maid, but his mother wouldn't hear of it. She didn't think there was anyone on this earth—black or white—who could cook and clean for her family as well as she could. His parents thought that Negroes were basically good people who made bad decisions.

"A little slow upstairs," Moise would say, tapping his fountain pen to his temple. "God was not as kind to them as He was to the Jews. They're one step below human, which is just one step above ape." Lizard never quite understood the rationale, but he knew better than to challenge his father's philosophy.

Abraham jumped up, awkwardly swiveling his hips. "And the way they dance? Ha! Like circus dogs. All that's missing is a pink tutu."

The boys dissolved with laughter. But Lizard wished Abraham and the others would shut up so he could hear the lyrics of the song.

Abraham aimed a finger at a dark-haired, olive-skinned boy passing the group. "Hey you, calzone, come here!" he screamed.

The boy lowered his head and quickened his pace.

"You don't hear me? You got mozzarella in your ears?"

The boy threw a nervous glance over his shoulder and then sprinted away.

"Whatever," Abraham huffed, puffing his chest out like a rooster. One of the other boys poked Abraham's shoulder. "Hey, where's Leo going?"

Abraham turned around to see Lizard sauntering across the yard toward the black boys.

"Leo! Hey, Leo, where ya going?" Abraham cried, flinging

his arms in the air.

The boys stopped singing when they saw Lizard approaching. The three who were seated stood. Two of them pounded their fists against their palms.

"Look, white boy, you need to go back to your section of the yard."

Lizard's feet shuffled to a stop. He looked stupidly around as if he'd just awakened from a trance.

"Go on now," another boy added with a flick of his fingers.

Lizard raised his hands. "I just want to ask a question."

The black boys glared at him.

"That music. What do you call it?"

The boys exchanged amused glances. When they looked at Lizard again, the menace had vanished from their eyes.

"That there is what we black folk call the blues."

Lizard pondered this. It made perfect sense. "I feel it here," he said, thumping his chest.

"Do you now?"

Another threw out, "That's where you supposed to feel it."

"Well, you *should* feel it. Negroes got the blues 'cause of crackers like you."

Lizard backed away. "I just wanted you to know that I like the way it sounds."

When Lizard returned, Abraham sunk his fingers into his shoulders.

"Are you *meshuggener*? Do you know you could have been killed?"

Lizard wriggled free. "Come on, Abraham. Killed?"

"Listen, we're in here for petty crimes—shoplifting, joyriding.Maybe our mothers think we yank our wieners a little too much—but them," Abraham jabbed his index finger in the direction of the black boys, "they've killed people."

Lizard smirked. "If they're murderers, Abraham, why aren't they in a real jail?"

Abraham's cheeks warmed. The bell sounded, saving him from any further humiliation.

Back in his cell, the song looped in Lizard's mind, lullabying him to sleep. The next morning, he hummed it over the sink while brushing his teeth.

At dinner, Lizard scoffed down his meal and rushed out to the yard so that he wouldn't miss a note.

Far away from Abraham and his cohorts, perched alone on a bench in earshot of the music, Lizard marveled about this life they sang of, so very different from his own, and wondered how it could be so foreign yet feel remarkably like home. He closed his eyes. His arms turned to goose flesh.

Abraham walked over and clapped him upside the head. "What's wrong with you?"

Lizard's eyes flew open. "Nothing. Why?" He had never felt more right in his life.

Chapter 60

At dinner the following evening, tray of food in hand, Lizard strolled right past Abraham. Stopping at the table of colored boys, he asked the lead one, Joe Brown, "Can I eat with you?"

The lanky, square-jawed guitar player side-eyed him. "Here?" Lizard nodded.

"You want to sit with *us*?"

"Yeah."

Joe glanced over at Abraham, who was sneering at him. Joe grinned and shoved the boy next to him. "Sure, sit on down," he said, loud enough for the entire dining hall to hear.

Over creamed corn, green beans, and mystery meat, they talked baseball, girls, and music. Afterward, Lizard followed them out to the yard, happy to be close to the music, to experience it under his skin.

The next day, Lizard joined Joe and his friends for lunch; the day after that he invited himself to their table for breakfast. After a week, he completely abandoned Abraham and his clique, choosing to not only take his meals with the Negroes, but spend his free time with them too.

"You ever play before?" Joe held out his instrument. He didn't allow just anyone to touch his guitar, to touch Sweetness— so named because she was long, brown, and sweet to the touch.

Lizard eyed it hesitantly.

"I see the way you look at her, I know you want to. So go on," Joe pressed.

Lizard took the guitar and cradled it in his arms like a newborn. "I studied the violin," he offered timidly as he raked his fingers over the strings.

"Violin?" Joe coughed, thrusting his pinky finger out and tipping an imaginary teacup to his lips. "Looka here, lemme show you how to play a real man's instrument."

Within days, Lizard was picking as if he'd been playing for years.

"Hey, you doing real good," Joe commented proudly. "Maybe you got some black in you."

"Could be," another member of the group chimed, pointing, "look at his hair. More nigger naps than a little bit."

Lizard ran his hands over his crown of tightly coiled curls. "Yeah, my mother hates it, she says I got hair like wool."

Joe plunged his hands into Lizard's crown of hair. "Yep, it feels just like mine."

Maybe he did have some black in him, Lizard mused. The idea thrilled him.

Of course, his choice to associate with the colored boys made him unpopular with inmates as well as guards. He was labeled a traitor and nigger lover.

Abraham told Lizard that race mixing was a sin of the highest caliber, right up there with adultery and murder.

The guards expressed their disdain for Lizard by tossing his room. Someone took a dump in his shoes; another person soaked his bed in urine.

It was a rough time, but Lizard was thick-skinned, resilient, even good-humored about the situation. Instead of cracking skulls, he channeled his frustration into music, penning a song about his woes, which he called "Reform School Blues."

He shared it with his new friends. It was the corniest thing any of them had ever heard and they told him so.

Chapter 61

The day Lizard was packing to head home, Joe came to his cell and shoved a torn piece of paper at him. "Come look for me when I get out."

"When's that?"

"Thirty days."

"I will."

"All right then," Joe mumbled and hurried away.

On Lizard's first day back home, his eldest sister cornered him, pressed him for details about brawls and shanks.

Lizard balked. "Shanks? Where in the world did you learn that word?" He assured her that he didn't have any stories like that to share. And the ones he did have, well, he knew his sister would just gaze at him like a stranger.

"So," she ventured, socking him gently on the shoulder, "are you a hardened criminal now?"

Lizard shook his head. He wasn't hardened at all, and no more a criminal than he was before he'd gone in. The truth was, the experience had split him in two and laid him wide open.

Thirty-one days later, Lizard boarded the first of two streetcars that would take him to Joe's home located in the northwest section of the city in a neighborhood known as the Ville.

On the second streetcar, a woman, the last white person

(besides Lizard), rose from her seat and looked expectantly over at him. "Aren't you getting off here, young man?"

"No ma'am, I'm riding this till the end of the line." The woman gawked at him in bewilderment.

He got off on St. Louis Avenue, a treelined street with modest homes and respectable front yards. As he walked along, children stopped their games to stare. One young mother called to him from her doorway, "Hello? Hello, are you lost?"

"Yes, ma'am, I believe I am. I'm looking for 304 Sarah Street."

"You are?"

"Yes, ma'am."

"Who you going to see at 304?"

"Joe Brown."

The woman knew the Browns. After a moment she pointed up the street. "Well, uh, just keep straight another three or so blocks and you'll walk right into Sarah."

"Thank you."

Lizard could feel a hundred eyes watching him.

When Ella Brown opened her door and found Lizard standing there with that black kippah on his head, she was stunned. She looked over his shoulder, down the street, and then back at Lizard. Her eyes slanted suspiciously. "Yes?"

"Hello," Lizard waved, "I'm here to see Joe."

Ella folded her arms and arched her left eyebrow. "Joe who?"

"Joe Brown," Lizard said confidently.

"And who are you?"

"Leo Rubenstein."

She tilted her head back and groaned. "Wait here a minute." Before the door closed completely, Ella's voice boomed: "Frank, there's a Jew on my porch!"

When the door opened again, Joe was standing there with a huge grin plastered on his face. "Hey, Leo!"

Lizard raised his hand in greeting. "Told you I'd come looking for you."

"Come on in."

Inside, Frank and Ella Brown stood shoulder to shoulder at the center of their tidy living room. A pair of matching eight-year-old boys were seated on the powder-blue sofa, bug-eyed, mouths agape.

"Leo, these are my parents. Mom, Dad, this is Leo."

"Hello, sir, ma'am."

"Hello," they chimed together.

Joe pointed at the boys. "And these here are the twins, Hal and Clement."

"Your brothers?" Lizard said.

"Yep."

Lizard offered the gobsmacked boys a cheerful "Hey!"

"Hey," Hal and Clement chirped back in stereo.

Joe looked at his parents. "This is the guy I told you about. Remember, the one who picked up on the guitar real quick?"

Frank and Ella nodded like wooden puppets. The twins continued to stare.

"Is it okay if we go up to my room for a while?"

Again, Frank and Ella bobbed their heads. Clement and Hal looked at each other and then over their shoulders at their parents.

Halfway up the stairs, Joe chuckled. "S'cuse them. They ain't never had no white people in the house before."

Lizard continued to make weekly visits to Joe's home, and by the time his parents realized that he had been lying about his whereabouts—playing baseball, at the Jewish Community Center, the library, down the street reading the Torah to old, blind Mr. Horowitz—Lizard had become a part of the Brown family.

It was at 304 Sarah Street that Lizard first experienced barbecued ribs, fried shrimp, grits, collard greens, and candied yams.

Turned out, every member of the Brown family was musically inclined. Ella's voice was her instrument, Hal and Clement played piano and guitar, and Frank was a master on the trumpet and clarinet.

The family encouraged Lizard to try his hand at each. He was an easy study, a natural musician, and it seemed there was no instrument he couldn't play. In the end, though, the trumpet stole his heart.

When Lizard wasn't playing the trumpet, he was thinking about playing the trumpet, dreaming about playing the trumpet, closed up in his room playing the air like a trumpet.

Lizard wasn't just smitten with the trumpet; he was downright sick with love.

Chapter 62

His nickname came about like this: Lizard was at the Brown's home (as usual), up in Joe's room playing the trumpet (like always). Ella Brown called the boys down for a meal (peanut butter and jelly sandwiches, tall, cold glasses of milk). The twins were at the table, hovering over a schoolbook.

"What's that y'all looking at?"

"Snakes," Clement said.

"And lizards," Hal added.

"Oh," Lizard said, biting into his sandwich.

"They cold-blooded," Hal informed him.

Lizard nodded, took another bite of his sandwich and swallow of milk.

"Like white folk," Clement cackled.

Ella went stiff. Lizard stopped chewing. Joe lowered his eyes and chuckled.

Lizard swallowed hard. "W-what? No, we're not. We're mammals too, you know. Warm-blooded just like you."

The twins looked at Ella. Hal cried, "But Mama, you always say—"

Ella rushed to him, fanning her hands. "Hush now. You talk too much," she warned through clenched teeth.

Hal's mouth snapped shut. But the words rattled top speed from Clement's mouth: "Mamayoualwayssaythatwhitepeopleiscoldblooded!"

Ella's face burned with shame as Joe doubled over with laughter.

"Well," she contended boisterously, "Leo ain't like most white folk." With that, she gave Lizard's shoulder an affectionate squeeze.

Clement looked at Lizard real hard. "I think I'ma call you Lizard any old ways."

"Me too," Hal said.

"Me three," Joe giggled.

It certainly wasn't a name Lizard would have chosen for himself. He supposed he could shed it somewhere down the line, exchange it for something with a bit more flourish. But the nickname grew on him, and he grew into it.

Chapter 63

One overcast summer Sunday, Moise folded a brown tweed suit into a box and handed it to Lizard, along with the address to which he was to deliver the package.

"Don't dally," Moise cautioned. "I expect you back here within the hour."

"Yes, Papa."

Lizard delivered the suit to the address, which just happened to be in a neighborhood that bordered the Ville. He couldn't come all the way across town and not drop in to see his adopted family. Besides, it was Sunday. Ella always made a spread of food on Sundays.

So there he was, seated at the Browns' dining room table, halfway through a plate of fried chicken, turnip greens, and potato salad, when the doorbell rang.

Frank started to rise from his chair, but Ella patted his hand. "Sit down, baby, and eat your food before it gets cold." She went to the door and opened it. Street sounds sailed into the house, that and fragrant honeysuckle.

"Lizard," she squeaked. "I m-mean Leo."

At the strangled sound of Ella's voice, they all looked up from their plates. She was standing in the doorway flanked by Moise and a police officer.

Frank stood abruptly, toppling his chair. The officer reacted to the clamor by seizing the butt of his pistol.

Joe held his breath; the twins locked hands.

"I don't want any trouble," Moise said. "I just want to take my son back home, back where he belongs."

"It's not like we holding your boy hostage," Frank croaked angrily.

"Like I said, I don't want any trouble."

"And neither do I."

The police officer walked over to Lizard. "You okay, son? Did these people hurt you?"

Ella went gray.

Lizard looked past the cop and addressed his father: "You followed me?"

"You gave me no other choice."

He rose slowly on trembling legs and looked at Frank. "I'm sorry for—"

"No need for all of that," the officer scolded, cutting him off. "You don't have anything to apologize for. Let's just get you back home."

Lizard pulled the cloth napkin from his collar and dropped it onto the table.

On the front porch, Frank handed Lizard his trumpet. "I can't, Mr. Brown—"

"You will," Frank said.

Lizard looked at Moise for approval.

"Okay already," Moise sputtered. "Let's go."

Clutching Frank's trumpet to his chest, Lizard climbed into the passenger seat of the green Packard.

In his cruiser, the policeman turned the ignition key and stepped on the accelerator, revving the engine until the racket brought people to their windows. When he was satisfied with the spectacle he'd created, he sped off, siren wailing.

Just as the Packard pulled away from the curb, Joe bounded down to the sidewalk, cupped his hands around his mouth, and shouted, "Lizard, stay black, man!"

Chapter 64

"I've apologized, what more can I do?"

Red-eyed and sniffing, Lizard's mother stomped from the living room into the kitchen. She returned holding a white dinner plate. "Take it and throw it down to the ground."

Groaning, Lizard took the plate and hurled it to the floor, shattering it into a dozen pieces.

"Now apologize to it," his mother demanded.

"What? Ma!"

"Do it!" Moise ordered.

Lizard looked at the shards and mumbled, "Sorry."

"Tell me, Leo," Rachel said, "did it go back to the way it was?"

"N-no, of course not."

"Exactly. I am the plate, Leo. Your father, sisters—we are all the plate. Do you see now?"

Home no longer felt like home to Lizard.

Everything seemed bland—the walls, the food his mother poured all of her love into preparing, the air he breathed. All of it.

Lizard couldn't blame his family; he knew it was he who was different, and they knew it too. He had a new walk and a new way of speaking. Sometimes he would look up from his meal, from his textbook, and catch one or all of them staring at him as if he was an uninvited dinner guest at their Passover table.

And the music, the way he played now, improvising the masters, denigrating them, ghettoizing Bach, Strauss, and Beethoven—effectively coloring the classics Negro.

"What did they do to you?" his mother wailed, wringing her hands.

"I won't have that type of music played in my house," Moise declared.

So Lizard left. With a satchel filled with clothing, his trumpet, his violin, and a few dollars, he set off for Kansas City. He chose Kansas City because Frank Brown was fond of saying—when Mrs. Brown was out of earshot—"Jazz may have been born in New Orleans, but it got its dick wet in Kansas City!"

Chapter 65

When Lizard stepped off the train in Kansas City, he spotted a short, plump man sporting a lavender-colored bowler and carrying a shiny saxophone. The man's short limbs and wide girth did little to impede his speed; he loped down the platform as if someone was chasing him. Lizard raced to catch up, cornering him at a newsstand where the man had stopped to purchase an afternoon paper.

"'Scuse me, sir, where can I make use of these?"

The man looked him up and down. "That fiddle and them bones?"

"Yes, sir."

"You wanna pawn 'em?"

"Nah, play 'em."

"Well then, follow me."

Eighteenth and Vine. The jazz district of Kansas City, the heartbeat of the Negro community, was comprised of nightclubs, rib shacks, and dreary-looking flats all squashed together on dirty streets. Even on sunny days, 18th and Vine swarmed with shadows.

But at night the neighborhood burst to life. Rivers of people streamed along the sidewalks, music piped out from the clubs, prostitutes pedaled their flesh from windows.

The plump man told Lizard his name was Ozzie and directed

him to a dilapidated row house where he could rent a room on the cheap. Lizard paid the woman for two nights, climbed the rickety steps to his bedroom, and lay on the bed in his clothes, waiting for the sun to set.

Later, under a blue-black sky, Lizard hurried excitedly from one nightclub to the next, drowning himself in music, barbecue, and beer. Three days later, he secured a job washing dishes at the Peacock Palace. The pay was criminal, barely enough to cover Lizard's rent, hardly a dime leftover for food. But that didn't matter to him—the music was more than gratifying. So he kept his gut quiet with a daily diet of toast, coffee, and water for breakfast, lunch, and dinner.

At first he played for change in the busy alleys behind the clubs and competed in cutting contests. He barely won a round, but the experience—playing in front of a crowd, alongside veterans—was worth more to him than winning.

After a month, he sent a letter home to his parents, letting them know that he missed them, loved them dearly, and although things were hard, he was happy.

A response came a week later. When Lizard unfolded the page, he was grateful to see a worn five-dollar bill, but saddened that there were no words accompanying it.

Three months in, he found himself at Milton's, mesmerized by a pudgy trumpeter who played with a white handkerchief clutched in one hand.

"Who is that?" he whispered aloud.

The man standing beside him whispered back, "That's Louis Armstrong. Where you from, Mars?"

Lizard turned to look at the wisecracker. He recognized him as a popular clarinet player who hustled reefer on the side.

"You could say that," he laughed. "I'm from St. Louis."

The man eyed him. "I've seen you before."

Lizard cleared his throat. "Could be. I been here a few months, working at the Peacock and gigging at the clubs."

The man extended his hand. "Mezz Mezzrow."

"Lizard."

"I knew a Lizard once; he got shot dead in Chicago over a piece of ass."

Lizard didn't know what to say to that, and for a while they stood quiet, entranced by the wizard Louis and his magical horn.

"So what do you play?" Mezz ventured when the applause died.

"Trumpet."

"Ah, well, you've just witnessed the best trumpet player in the world."

"I believe that," Lizard said, his eyes dancing with wonderment. "I've never heard anything like it. I wish I could play like that one day."

Mezz doubled over with laughter. "Keep wishing, white boy. You need soul to play like Armstrong—or any other black musician, for that matter."

Lizard looked Mezz up and down. "I've heard *you* play. Sounds to me like you got plenty of soul."

Mezz's eyes bulged. "Wait... you... you think *I'm* white?"

To Lizard, Mezz looked as white as he did. "You saying you're not?"

Grinning, Mezz slid a joint from behind his ear and slipped it between his lips. After two tokes he held it out to Lizard.

"No thanks."

"Lemme tell you something, young blood." Mezz coughed

from behind a cloud of expelled smoke. "As a man thinks, so he is."

Lizard's face clouded with bewilderment. He started to question Mezz but was interrupted when a reed-thin black man plowed between them and caught Mezz by the shoulder.

"Man, where you been? I been looking all over fer your black ass!"

"Been around, you know," Mezz chuckled, "here and there." He looked at Lizard. "I'll see you, okay?"

Lizard nodded.

Mezz shot him a sly wink and trotted off with his friend.

As a man thinks, so he is.

As a man thinks, so he is.

As a man thinks, so he is.

The words echoed in Lizard's mind. It couldn't possibly be that simple, could it?

Chapter 66

Lizard had been in Kansas City for six years when Moise fell ill. On the train to St. Louis, Lizard took a seat in the segregated car. He was approached by a young black porter who skillfully avoided looking directly at his face. Eyes fixed on the buttons of Lizard's shirt, the porter said, "'Scuse me, sir, but this here car is for colored folk. White folks section is two cars up."

"Yes, I'm in the right place," Lizard replied.

"Oh." The porter's shoulders relaxed, his brown eyes met Lizard's gray-green ones. When he spoke again, the formality in his voice was tempered. "Well, you have a pleasant trip."

"Thank you."

Yes, it was as easy as that.

His father died, and Lizard returned to Kansas City, swapped out his surname for the less-Jewish-sounding Robbins, pawned his violin, and used the money to buy a secondhand gramophone along with any record he could find that had Louis Armstrong's name on the label.

Over the years, Lizard continued to grow into the persona he'd created—passing himself off as Negro, playing in their bands, steadily mastering their music, living in their communities, absorbing their culture, their nuanced language (verbal and otherwise), adopting the way they talked, walked, and danced. He made love to their women on Friday and Saturday nights and attended their churches on Sunday mornings.

For a long time, Lizard thought he and Mezz Mezzrow were the only ones living their white lives as black men. But as he burrowed deeper into his lie, he became increasingly aware that he and Mezz were far from lone wolves. Indeed, they were part of an expansive clan that had willingly migrated to the dark side of the color line.

***

Lizard would have stayed in Kansas City for the rest of his life had he not lost his cool after a less-than-ethical nightclub owner named Brady refused to pay him for a gig. He had tried reasoning with the man, and when he still refused to cough up the money, Lizard felt he was left with no choice. He pulled out his pistol and whipped Brady until he was unrecognizable, even to his own mama.

Not only were the police looking for Lizard, but a host of Brady's friends and family were too. Kansas City was no longer safe, so he fled home to St. Louis.

His family never pretended to understand the life he'd chosen for himself.

"A jazz and blues musician? Really, Leo?"

And if that wasn't confounding enough, they couldn't make sense of the hep clothing, lingo, and swaggering gait he'd adopted.

"Yellow? That color is kind of... well, loud for a suit, don't you think?"

"Beat up the chops? What does that mean? Well, why can't

you just say she talks a lot? Geez."

"Son, did you hurt your foot? No? Then why are you limping around like that?"

It was all so embarrassing for them.

That said, Lizard wasn't the most shameful member of his family—there was a cousin rumored to be wearing women's underclothes beneath his tailored suits, and another who had conceived a child out of wedlock.

Of course, his mother and sisters had no idea Lizard was living his life as a black man. That news would certainly have trumped any humiliation that came along with having a cross-dressing businessman and a bastard offspring in the family.

Chapter 67

Legendary. Mythical.

Lizard knew Harlem would be a revelation even before he arrived. Majestic brownstones, elegant brick buildings filled with apartments as spacious as country homes. And there was music everywhere—cascading out of open windows, sailing from cars, being performed on corners, hummed by children skipping to school.

Lizard couldn't imagine Harlem being anything other than what it was when he arrived in the spring of '37. He rented a room at the Woodside Hotel on 147th Street and Lenox—the place almost all the colored musicians called home when visiting Harlem.

He wasn't in town a full week before Harlan Elliott walked into that bar and changed the course of his life. Lizard might have avoided the mess he was currently in in Germany had he taken up an offer to stay with a friend in Greenwich Village, walked into some other Harlem dive, or simply blown Harlan off when he struck up a conversation.

Lizard could blame his circumstances on one of those things or all of them. In the end, though, his fate was sealed by the only other possession he cherished more than his trumpet.

Just before Lizard walked into the blistering shower, a soldier pressed the end of his baton into his chest; his eyes dropped down to the damning, dangling, circumcised thing between Lizard's legs.

When the soldier's eyes once again met Lizard's, he was grinning. "Jew, eh?"

Later that same night, Lizard rose from the bed, went to the window, and looked out at the paling night sky.

What a life I've lived, he thought to himself. *Born twice. Once as a Jew and then as a black man. How many people can make that claim? And haven't I played alongside my idol, my muse? My life has been magical. Really, what more could any man ever hope for?*

Floating an imaginary trumpet to his lips, Lizard filled his cheeks with air and blew.

Chapter 68

Across the Atlantic, in Brooklyn, Gwen was in the bathroom, crouched over the toilet, eyes closed, fingers gripping the elastic band of her underwear.

"Please, please, please," she chanted before pushing the underwear down to her knees, bowing her head, peeking at the seat. Not a drop, smear, smudge, or hint of blood. The pristinely clean, cotton-panel seat mocked her.

When her menstrual cycle had arrived at age eleven, Gwen hadn't known what it was, so for two days she walked around with her underwear packed with toilet paper, convinced she was dying.

It was her sister Irene who spotted the rust-colored blotch on Gwen's skirt, took her aside, and explained things. Later, she brought Gwen to their mother. At the news, Ethel became annoyed, as if Gwen's entry into womanhood was a burden she alone would have to bear. Ethel wagged her finger in her daughter's face, spouting threats and spinning metaphors. "You better keep that purse latched until you're married!"

Now, Gwen wished she had heeded her mother's warning. She pulled her underwear to her waist, flushed the toilet, and ran her clean hands under a spray of hot water.

Pregnant.

The word made her dizzy.

As hard-handed as her sister could be with her, Gwen knew

that Irene was the only one she could confide in. But Irene was sick, having spent the better part of the spring cycling in and out Kings County Hospital's female ward.

Irene was being treated for endometriosis, which the attending physician assured her was a condition entirely nonfatal and curable. Even so, Gwen felt it would be highly inappropriate and selfish to burden Irene with her problems as she was grappling with her own.

***

Uptown, at 17 East 133rd Street, sandwiched between the oval oak frame and the looking glass on the wall above Emma's dresser were two postcards, two telegrams, and a single black-and-white photo.

The first telegram had arrived the day after Harlan reached Montmartre: *Mom, Dad. Here safe. Love, your son*

The first postcard, a watercolor painting of the Eiffel Tower, arrived two weeks later: *Hi! I'm having so much fun. I want to stay here forever. Harlan*

A week after that, an envelope arrived, containing a photo of the entire group poised in front of the L'Escadrille. Harlan, showing all of his teeth, was leaning on Lizard like a crutch. Lizard looked solemn, his eyes focused on something beyond the photographer's shoulder. Ivy and the other guys were grinning, bodies slightly tilted, arms splayed as if they'd just finished an elaborate dance routine. Eugene Bullard stood at the edge of the frame, hands on his hips, looking very pleased with himself.

The front of the second postcard was an incredibly detailed montage of a train crossing over a bridge, the Arc de Triomphe, a country house, the Eiffel Tower, the Seine, and a pigtailed little girl holding a bouquet of flowers. Emma remembered wondering just how in the world the artist managed to put all of that in one place and not have it look tacky? *Dear Mom and Dad, still having fun. Wish you were here. Harlan*

When Germany took the coast of France, Emma panicked, sent a telegram begging Harlan to come home. Now. When she didn't receive an immediate response, she placed a call to Eugene Bullard, not giving a damn about the time difference—it was four o'clock on Sunday morning in France when Bullard's wife yawned hello into the receiver.

She explained to Emma that Eugene never came home before seven and that she would have him call her as soon as he arrived. And Emma wasn't to worry, the American newspapers always made things sound worse than they were.

As promised, Eugene phoned back, but the connection was choppy. Emma spent most of the call yelling, "What? What?" until the line went dead.

Sam asked, "Well, what did he say?"

"I think he said he was trying to get Harlan and the others on the next ship out."

Days later, the second telegram from Harlan arrived: *Sailing on the 14th. Will arrive on the 28th of June. Harlan*

That was the last she'd heard from her son.

It was now the middle of July and Eugene, his wife, and the rest of Harlan's band were huddled on her stoop, bearing gifts from France, as if presents could replace her missing child.

She led them into the parlor.

Eugene said he'd filed reports with the French authorities.

"But now that the Germans are in charge, who knows—"

His wife stabbed the top of his hand with her fingernail.

Eugene groaned. "Um, I mean to say, I'm sure they'll turn up."

Emma smirked.

Bruno leaned forward. "Mrs. Elliott, do you know where Lizard's people are?"

Emma pressed her palms against her cheeks. "St. Louis, I think, but I'm not sure. I'm not sure of anything anymore."

She was so tired. Sick of crying, of waiting for news that never came, tired of thinking the worst.

Eugene folded his hands. "You been in touch with the State Department?"

"Every day," Sam said.

"Three times a day," Emma added.

"And what they say?"

"They don't know any more than the day before."

"And what's that?"

"Nothing. They don't know shit."

Emma chewed the inside of her cheek, fought the tears that were threatening to come. "Lucille reached out to some friends in Paris. They say they'll ask around, see what they can find out."

Sam squeezed her hand.

"Oh, that's good," Eugene breathed. "How long that been?"

"What? Since Lucille reached out?"

"Uh-huh."

"A few weeks."

"And no word yet?"

"Nah."

The truth was, Lucille had heard back from her friends, but

their responses had been less than uplifting.

They too had friends and family who'd gone missing.

Poof! Vanished without a trace.

There were rumors about people being abducted from their homes, snatched right off the streets. Not just Jews, but anyone who didn't fit into Hitler's master race.

That's all they would say. In fact, they'd probably said too much. The Gestapo had eyes and ears everywhere.

Chapter 69

As if Emma and Sam weren't going through enough, the New York City Department of Buildings came along and made things worse.

The letter was hand-delivered by a young, terrified-looking, pimply faced white man. After Sam signed for it, he carried it into the house and handed it to Emma.

"What's this?"

"I dunno."

Emma tore open the envelope and read the letter. Her lips moved silently with the words. When she was done, she crushed it into a ball and threw it angrily across the room. Sam followed the flight of the paper ball.

"What's it say?"

Emma fell back into the sofa. "These motherfuckers wanna take our house for $13,000!"

Sam wasn't a scholar, but he knew there was a difference between take and buy.

"What, why?"

"It don't say why, all it say is that they have a legal right to do so."

"Force us to sell? I don't understand."

Emma sighed. "Gimme the damn paper."

Sam got up and retrieved the crumpled notice. He smoothed the paper as best he could and handed it to Emma.

After looking it over she said, "They call it eminent domain."

"What's that?"

"It means that white folk can do whatever they want, whenever they want, to colored folk!"

The next day, letter in hand, Emma went to the Department of Buildings and sat for three hours in a room crammed with angry Harlemites who had also received notices.

This is some bullshit!

Fair market value my ass! My house is worth more than what they're offering.

Where are we supposed to go?

Emma was shown to a small office that stank of cigarettes and aftershave. The walls were lined with metal file cabinets. On the windowsill, next to a mountain of manila folders, was a ficus, dying a slow death.

Emma sat across the desk from an old, balding man with soupy green eyes and teeth so crooked and brown, she could barely stand to look him in the face.

"As the homeowner," he said in his raspy voice, "you have the right to refuse the offer. But lemme tell you, the city wants what the city wants, and they will get it." He fell into a coughing fit, opened his desk drawer, and removed a wilted pack of cigarettes. "If I were you," he continued, lighting a smoke and inhaling deeply, "I would take the money while the offer is still on the table."

"Still on the table?"

He nodded, "Yeah, the city can take your house without giving you one single dime."

Emma stiffened. "How is that possible?"

"Not only is it possible, it's also legal," he coughed.

Emma glanced anxiously around the room. "You say the city's going to build tenement housing, right? Well, why can't they just build someplace else?"

"I can't answer that, ma'am," he said with a shrug of his shoulders. "That's a question for someone above my pay grade."

Emma perked up. "Well, I'd like to speak to him, then."

The man released a long, weary sigh. "You and the hundreds of other people who've received this letter. But I'll tell you right now, it's never gonna happen."

Emma chewed thoughtfully on her bottom lip. "Then I'll get a lawyer," she announced triumphantly.

"Again, Mrs. Elliott, that is your prerogative, but keep in mind that the city has a team of lawyers that are hell-bent on making sure you don't win. And believe me, you won't."

On the train ride home, Emma was despondent and grim-faced. Her world was falling apart, piece by jagged, painful piece.

Emma sat lost in her misery for most of the journey, only vaguely aware of the other commuters around her. That is, until the train pulled out of the 23rd Street station when she suddenly realized that she was being watched. She turned her head toward the offending eyes of the white man seated next her.

"What? What is it?" she snapped.

The man's face burned red. He aimed his rolled newspaper at her lap.

Emma looked down to see a roach scuttling across the green fabric of her dress.

He raised the newspaper to swat it, but Emma snagged it with her hand.

"Leave it be," she snarled. "It's *my* roach! You white people always tryin' to take everything from colored folk!"

Chapter 70

That morning, at the same time Emma was preparing to head downtown to the Department of Buildings, news came via telegram from Kings County Hospital that Irene had passed away at 4:14 a.m.

Ethel doubled over and screamed.

Aubrey, who was seated at the table eating breakfast, sprang from his chair, rushed to his wife, catching her by the shoulders just as she sank to the floor.

"Ethel, what's happened?"

"She gone, she gone, she gone!" Ethel wailed, beating the telegram against her forehead. "Why, God, why!"

Gwen appeared in the doorway. "Mummy?"

Aubrey gently pried the telegram from Ethel's grip. After he read it, his face seemed to cave in on itself. The look he gave Gwen was the saddest expression she'd ever seen on her father's face. It terrified her, and without knowing what had happened, she began to cry.

They did what any family does after losing a loved one: they shouldered the hurt as best they could, well aware that the pain could and probably would linger on for years.

Nearly every night, Gwen would burst into tears when she climbed into bed and glanced across the room at her sister's empty bed. She so missed seeing her propped up on a pillow, her head covered in rollers, her face buried in the pages of her Bible.

Mealtime was hard too. If not for the radio and the scraping of silverware against the porcelain plates, there would have been no sound at all around that table.

During one of those silent meals, Ethel asked Gwen to pass the dish of roasted yams. When Ethel reached for the platter, her eyes fell on her daughter's fingers which were fat as sausages. The platter slipped from Ethel's hand and clattered onto the table, scattering the sliced yams across the blue eyelet tablecloth.

Aubrey sucked his teeth.

"Mummy!" Gwen exclaimed, rising from her chair, already cleaning up the mess.

Ethel's hand hovered over the table, her fingers eternally reaching. "What a mess," Aubrey muttered disgustedly.

Gwen said, "Mummy, you okay?"

Aubrey's eyes swung to his wife's astonished face and then to the reaching fingers. "Ethel?"

"Right in my face, right under my nose. How could I have been so blind? You..." Ethel fell back into her chair, the rest of the words dissolving on her tongue.

Gwen backed away from the table, lips trembling, wringing her hands.

Ethel swallowed. "Who breed you?"

Aubrey straightened his back and frowned. "What's that you said, Ethel?"

Gwen's eyes began to water.

Ethel stood, planted her palms on the table, and hissed, "I *said*, who breed you?"

Chapter 71

Beyond the barbed-wire fence of Buchenwald, nestled on a slope dotted with spruce trees, sat a brown and redbrick house with crowstepped gables and a wooden front door.

Twice a day, when the sun made its ascent and descent, its rays struck the door's brass hardware, creating shards of multi-colored light. The moment was always magical, reminding even the most disheartened that anything was possible, even the creation of rainbows without the benefit of water.

The first time Harlan saw the woman who lived in that house, he was trudging to the latrines, having been ordered there along with six others. He stopped to watch her gallop across the property atop a white mare, mesmerized by her bouncing blond hair. The black leather crop she held was fitted with a red glass bauble shaped like an Asscher-cut diamond. It looked more like a scepter than a jockey whip.

The scene was both breathtaking and bewildering. Harlan gawked until someone behind him warned in a hushed and panicked voice, "Don't look, drop your eyes!"

He realized then that she was the one the prisoners whispered about: Ilse Koch, the commandant's wife, the Bitch of Buchenwald. Heart-shaped face, intense blue eyes—an attractive woman who didn't look like she had an ounce of devil in her.

Harlan lowered his eyes and continued to the latrines where

a sewage pipe had ruptured, creating a sinkhole large enough to hold eight men. The stench was ungodly. His stomach lurched; he bent over and emptied his guts. Four other men did the same.

"Dig!" one soldier barked from behind the handkerchief he had pressed over his nose and mouth.

Harlan righted himself, dragged the sleeve of his uniform over his mouth, and looked stupidly around for a shovel. The other men jumped obediently into the hole and began clawing at the filth with their hands. After a moment, Harlan reluctantly joined them.

Someone gasped. Harlan looked into the horrified face of the man standing beside him and followed his eyes down to a point just inches from their feet. Jutting from the broken pipe were human bones sagging with burned flesh that bore an eerie resemblance to scorched, scalloped lace.

Chapter 72

October swooped down on Buchenwald like a famished crow, gobbling up all the summer flowers. Within weeks, the green leaves of the red beech trees faded to brown, curled, and drifted to the ground.

Every day more prisoners were killed or died. Every day new ones arrived. Every day Harlan wondered why he hadn't yet gone mad.

By then the soldiers were calling him Jesse Owens, after the black American track-and-field athlete who'd gone to Berlin in 1936 and had embarrassed Hitler by winning four Olympic gold medals.

Harlan hadn't seen Lizard since the day they'd first arrived. He feared Lizard might be dead, prayed that he wasn't. When Lizard shuffled past him in the mess hall one afternoon, Harlan couldn't hide his joy. He leaped off the ration line, caught Lizard by the arm, and pulled him to his chest in an awkward hug. "It's so good to see you."

Sapling thin, Lizard's complexion had taken on a gray tint. Not only that, it was if he had molted—his skin was so thin, it seemed transparent.

Lizard blinked at him.

"Hey, man, it's me, Harlan."

Lizard swayed, blinking again. "Oh, yeah, yeah," he mumbled sluggishly.

Harlan cast a puzzled glance at the yellow star on Lizard's shirt.

As the question formed on his tongue, a soldier came charging toward them.

"*Weitergehen!*" His demand soared above the din of metal spoons scraping the bottoms of metal bowls.

Harlan shook his friend's arm. "Lizard, you gotta hold it together, man. You hear me? You gotta hang on, brother, you hear me?"

Lizard's head bounced. "Uh-huh. Hold it together."

Watching the swiftly approaching soldier, Harlan pushed Lizard toward the door and rejoined the line.

One morning Harlan woke, glanced out the window, and spied a large object at the center of the square covered with a black tarp.

What is that? Where did it come from?

No one had answers.

They lined up as usual, waiting for the day's cruelty to begin. After two hours, the wind picked up, thrashing the tarp. The sound was annoying, but the sight of it—black canvas flailing like the devil's cape—was even more unnerving.

Three hours later, an officer ordered the tarp removed. The four prisoners charged with the duty did fierce battle with the weight of the covering and the wind. Just when Harlan thought Mother Nature would win, the tarp came flying off, revealing the horror beneath.

He'd seen it in Westerns and depicted in comic strips. Just looking at it made him gasp for air: the gallows was large enough to hang four men at one time.

Ilse, astride her horse, appeared just after noon. The prisoners had had neither breakfast nor lunch. Waving away the helping hands of soldiers who rushed to assist her, Ilse skillfully dismounted the beast in one fluid move.

She circled the gallows, admiring the workmanship, head nodding with satisfaction, her fingers stroking the red bauble on the end of her riding crop like a good luck charm.

On the platform, her boots clomped across the wooden floor, reverberating inside the prisoners' rib cages. Ilse gave each beam a sturdy shake and tugged roughly on the looped ropes. She did all of this with a cheerful smile on her face.

Ilse summoned a soldier and spoke to him in a whisper. The prisoners strained to hear but were unable to catch a word.

The soldier then turned and signaled to the guard in the watchtower. A second later the sirens began to wail.

Back on the ground, Ilse strolled casually from one prisoner to the next, whacking her jockey whip against her thigh.

The sirens continued to howl.

Twenty minutes, thirty, forty-five.

Finally, Ilse raised her whip into the air, and the sirens fell silent. "That one," she said, aiming her whip at the unlucky soul.

Harlan craned to see who it was, but from his vantage the man's face was unrecognizable.

The prisoner was dragged from the line and thrown onto the gallows' steps. He lay there, still as death, until a soldier brought his boot heel down on his head. Shrieking, the prisoner grabbed his head and flopped around like a fish until the soldier pulled him onto the platform and ordered him to stand behind the middle noose.

Ilse calmly followed, her jockey whip tucked securely beneath her arm. Sliding her free hand through the noose, she splayed her fingers, waggled them at the prisoner, and then laughed in a high-pitched titter that raised the hairs on Harlan's neck.

Another soldier, carrying a chair, jogged up the stairs and placed it before the poor soul.

Harlan held his breath, waiting for the man to spring up and fight for his life. But the man did nothing. He just stood there, shoulders hunched, head lolling like a weight on his neck.

The soldier grabbed his chin, forcing him to look at his fellow inmates.

It was Lizard.

"No, no, no," trickled from Harlan's mouth.

"*Eins... zwei... drei!*"

The soldiers lifted Lizard onto the chair, slipped the noose over his head, and pulled the knot. Lizard's knees buckled, the rope cut into his Adam's apple. His eyes bulged—gagging, he clawed savagely at the rope, locked his knees, and held his weight on his tiptoes.

Ilse circled, smiling, pleased with his struggle to survive. Minutes later, she hopped off the platform, mounted her horse, and rode away.

One hour. Two. Three.

"Hold on, Lizard, hold on," Harlan chanted.

The sun moved west, dragging long, dark shadows across the prison grounds. The temperature plunged; prisoners rubbed their arms, shivering.

Lizard held on.

A woman crumpled to the ground; her husband threw himself protectively over her unconscious body. The soldiers beat them both and dragged them away.

At six o'clock Ilse returned on foot, adorned in a sweeping burgundy dress embroidered with purple running vines.

On the platform, she rounded the chair, gripped the backrest, and gave it a little shake.

Lizard wobbled. Harlan inhaled so abruptly the air made a whistling sound down his throat.

Laughing with childish glee, she shook the chair again, this time with vigor. Lizard rocked forward, wheezing. The arteries in his neck bulged, his face reddened, and his eyes dripped water.

With each rattle, the chair slid backward a little bit more, until his toes balanced on the edge of the seat, his eyes looking as if they might explode from their sockets. Harlan wrapped his arms around his shoulders, dropped his chin onto his chest, and closed his eyes.

Ilse pulled the chair away. Lizard's feet paddled the air and then wilted.

They left his body there for weeks, rotting away in full sight.

The birds roosted on his head, night animals gorged themselves on his flesh, insects laid eggs in his ears.

Finally, in late November, when the chilly north winds rolled over the hills, undressing the trees, scattering leaves, the prisoners were ordered to take down what remained of Lizard.

Days later, December arrived bearing soft snow.

Chapter 73

On Christmas Eve morning, scents of roasted goose, carp, and sour cabbage mingled with fragrant Obatzda and marzipan wafted down from the Koch home, into the yard of the teeth-clattering prisoners turning blue from the gnawing cold.

At four o' clock, before the sun faded away, Ilse came down to the yard in a chauffeured black Mercedes-Benz, bearing baskets of cookies, as if she were St. Nick. Wrapped in fur, puffing on a cigarette, she watched from the warmth of the car as the soldiers distributed the treats amongst the prisoners.

The cookies, shaped like swastikas, were as large as a man's palm. Harlan brought the treat to his nose and sniffed. He hadn't smelled anything that appetizing in a long time. His stomach groaned with longing, but he was already thinking about throwing the cookie to the ground and stomping it to crumbs. She had, after all, murdered his best friend and brother. Eating the cookie would be like an act of forgiveness and Harlan could never forgive her.

But still...

It wasn't just Christmas Eve; it was also his birthday. After all he'd been through—all he continued to suffer—didn't he deserve a gift? Even one molded into this heinous image?

Harlan shook his head. Held the cookie in the air, released one finger and then another. In his mind, he saw the cookie hurtling to the frozen ground. But his body refused to comply. His thumb and index finger remained tightly clamped to the pastry.

Harlan looked down at himself; he was so emaciated that he could press his hands into his back and feel his grumbling stomach. And he wasn't sleeping; his dreams were filled with nightmares of Lizard—more than a hundred of him, swinging from ropes dangling from oblivion. On top of that, Darlene had returned, flocking through the darkness of his sleep, batting wings bright with flames.

He raised his head, mumbled an apology to the heavens, and devoured the cookie in two bites.

The sweet taste still in his mouth, Harlan broke into sobs.

Chapter 74

No one was more surprised than Gwen when she went into the maternity ward on December 28, 1940 and delivered not one baby, but two.

A set of twin boys.

Gwen didn't even have one boy's name, let alone two. She looked pitifully at her mother who was seated beside her hospital bed. "What do you think I should name them?"

Ethel was, at that moment, rifling through her purse in search of the bottle of nerve pills prescribed by the family doctor. It had all been too much—Irene's death and Gwen's pregnancy. Ethel had developed a twitching eye and then her hair began to shed. Other people drop weight, but not Ethel—she put on twenty pounds and was diagnosed with hypertension and diabetes. Her emotions swung between episodes of wailing grief and raging anger.

"What?" Ethel hummed absently as she emptied the contents of the purse onto her lap. Two quarters, a stick of gum, a wallet, and a prayer card. No pills. "I must have left them at home," she mumbled to herself, shoveling the items back into her purse.

"Mummy?" Gwen called softly.

"Yes."

"I was asking what you think I should name them."

Ethel tapped her finger against the silver clasp of her purse. "Well, the Bible has some very good names."

"Yes, I guess."

"Um, your father always wanted a son. It would be nice to name one after him."

Gwen smiled. "I like that idea."

"The other one, you could name after his father."

Gwen's face turned to stone. She had refused to divulge the name of the father, not even when Ethel flew at her with her fists, lashed her with the iron's cord, or threw her and her clothes into the hallway, shrieking that she never wanted to see her again. Not even then would Gwen give Harlan's name, and she wouldn't give it now.

Ethel sucked her teeth. "Anyway, it was just a suggestion."

Gwen rolled the bedsheet in her hands. "What's the name of that man who lives in apartment 3C?"

Ethel thought for a moment. "Mr. Henderson?"

"Yes, Henderson. That's a nice name."

Ethel shrugged. "I guess it's okay. His first name is better, though."

"What's that?"

"Robert."

"Robert? Hmmm. Bobby for short."

"I guess."

Mother and daughter continued to mull over possible names until the nurse wheeled the babies in for their afternoon feeding.

"Aubrey and Robert," Ethel cooed.

"Bre and Bobby," Gwen sang.

Uptown, amidst boxes filled with a lifetime of memories, Emma took to her bed, sick with grief for her missing son.

Outside, the December wind tore up and down the Harlem streets, howling Emma's anguish.

Chapter 75

In '41 America entered the war, dragging her allies along with her. Buchenwald's population swelled exponentially with daily arrivals of captures of all ethnicities: Jews, Gypsies, cripples, accused spies, Poles, blacks, and mixed-race people.

One man, Sebastian Abel, with his white-blond hair and sapphire eyes, could have been a poster boy for Hitler's master race campaign. But alas, Sebastian did not fit the *führer*'s bill, because he was a man who loved men.

German father, Dutch mother, Sebastian had spent the first twenty years of his life in German Southwest Africa before he and his family moved to England. A smart fellow, versed in four languages including Afrikaans, Sebastian loved the classics—both music and literature. He had a sweet tooth that had, at times so he claimed, been more of an inconvenience than his so-called homosexual sickness.

Sebastian talked the entire time he was at Buchenwald, which was less than a week. He talked while he ate, while he moved stones from one end of the quarry to the other, and even while he slept. More annoying than his insistent babble was the sunny smile that almost always graced his face.

The prisoners thought he was crazy. No sane man would behave as if Buchenwald was a day in the park instead of hell on earth.

Why are you so happy? Don't you know what this place is?

Sebastian said he was well aware of what Buchenwald was and what purpose it was built to serve. He confessed that his father had worked at a similar institution in German Southwest Africa called Shark Island, where Germans had spent half a decade exterminating Africans.

"I am very ashamed of the German half of me," he announced sadly.

That was one of only two times that Harlan saw Sebastian without his smile; the other was the night before he catwalked his way into eternity.

Rape. It was a common occurrence at Buchenwald—a blight on an already blighted life. Nightly, the soldiers pulled women from beds, dragged them behind the barracks, and demoralized them in the worst possible ways. Sometimes they did the same to the men. Sebastian's delicate manner made him an easy target, and one night they drove a baton into his anus.

At roll call the following morning, Sebastian strolled calmly off the line, sashaying his way past amused soldiers, toward the front gates.

"Halt!" was shouted numerous times, but Sebastian kept walking, his hip sway growing more seductive, more mesmerizing, with every step.

No need for a runway, the slats of sunlight on the ground substituted just fine. One hand perched on his waist, his free arm whipping like a tail, Sebastian continued high-stepping.

"Halt!" It was the final warning. Pistols were drawn, aimed.

Even though his blond tresses were lying in some dusty pile, Sebastian summoned the spirit of each and every chopped strand and whipped his head so forcefully, the prisoners nearest him felt the draft.

One bullet to the heart.

Sebastian, ever smiling, gave the queen's signature wave and fell dead.

Years later, especially on dark days, Harlan would find himself thinking about Sebastian in the same way one longed for water during drought.

Chapter 76

On a crisp Saturday in September of 1944, a few months before the twins' fourth birthday, Gwen dressed the boys in matching gray sweaters and red caps. Her intention was to take them to the Prospect Park Zoo and then for a whirl on the merry-go-round, but when she got outside, instead of walking toward the park, she headed in the opposite direction.

The boys tugged her hands. Bobby, the smaller of the two, wailed, "Mother, the park is the other way!"

They weren't identical in looks or character. Bre was tall, dark, and gregarious. Bobby was an inch shorter than his brother and shy; a mama's boy early on, he stuck to Gwen like a tight panty—so said Ethel. Gwen marveled at how different they looked from each other while both still being the spitting images of Harlan.

She quickened her pace. "I know that but I've changed my mind about the park. I think we should ride the trains instead."

The boys cheered. They loved riding the trains. Sometimes the trio would spend an entire day switching between lines, getting off at random stations to explore unfamiliar neighborhoods.

Their subway journeys had been confined to Brooklyn, but on that Saturday, Gwen made up her mind to take them all the way to Harlem and introduce her sons to their father.

In Harlem, they tunneled their way through the flock of Saturday shoppers. Gwen's heart skipped and jumped in her chest like that of an elated child on the last day of school.

"Stay close to Mother," she warned, crushing their hands in her own.

Gwen had no idea what she would say to Harlan. Maybe she wouldn't say a word, maybe when he opened the door she would just shove the boys at him and flee.

Motherhood had been difficult enough to get used to without Ethel's relentless criticisms about her parenting skills. Gwen couldn't do anything right where those boys were concerned.

How many times do I have to show you how to properly wash a diaper?

Aww, your nipples hurt? Well, they were feeling damn good when you were making those babies, right? Stop your bellyaching and stick that bubby in his mouth before he wakes the other one.

She was doing her best, but her best would never be good enough for Ethel Gill.

Sometimes Gwen fantasized about taking the twins to Eastern Parkway and leaving them on one of the many benches that lined the promenade. Other times she imagined smothering them in their sleep. The previous winter, Gwen had bundled the boys in wool coats, knit scarves, and hats, and had taken them to Prospect Park. It was the middle of the workweek; it was cold, the park was empty and white with day-old snow.

The boys snapped icicles off low branches and licked them to water, made snowballs and snow angels. When she asked if they were cold, if they were ready to head home, the boys dragged mittened hands over their runny red noses and said no.

When she'd stopped to adjust her pink earmuffs, Gwen

realized that they had ventured farther into the park than she had intended. Just ahead was the boathouse and behind that, the frozen lake.

Her feet safely planted on solid ground, Gwen had sent her sons out onto the ice. *A little farther, go on. It's just like ice-skating*, she urged.

The boys clasped hands and spun. "Mother, come play with us!"

Gwen strained to hear the crack and splinter of the ice above their squeals and laughter. She was smiling so hard, her teeth ached from the cold.

And then came the patrolling police car.

The officer stumbled through the snow, waving his hands and shouting: "Get those kids off the ice! Lady, don't you know that's dangerous? They could fall through and drown."

No, she didn't know, Gwen had lied. "Stupid me," she said, wiping away fake tears. She thanked him a hundred times.

On the way back home, she threatened the boys to keep quiet about the lake and the policeman. "If you say one word about it, just one, I'll make you eat pepper sauce… again."

***

She'd met a man. A nice older gentleman named Edgar who felt as trapped and suffocated in his marriage as Gwen felt in motherhood. The two had exchanged vows of love and had fantasized about walking away from everyone and everything, starting afresh in California. They'd even toyed with the idea of changing their names.

But for now it was all just talk.

"You can't leave your kids," he'd said. "And nothing against your boys, but I been there and done that. I raised four with my wife, and I ain't interested in raising any more."

"And if I didn't have children?"

"Well, that would be an entirely different story."

From the 135th Street station, Gwen and her sons made their way south on Lenox Avenue, walking a wide circle around hopscotch boxes chalked in blue on the sidewalk, toward 133rd Street.

Past dog walkers and people lounging on their stoops, they turned left onto 133rd Street, and continued quickly up the street. When they reached the corner of Fifth Avenue and 133rd Street, Gwen's mouth formed a large *O*.

The crossing light changed and changed again, and still Gwen just stood there, stuck.

The boys looked at each other. "Mother?" they chimed in harmony.

Without a word, she stepped off the sidewalk, against the light, and dragged the children across the busy avenue. Amidst the blare of angry car horns and curse words thrown from the motorists she'd nearly turned into vehicular murderers, Gwen shouted, "Where are the houses? Where are the goddamn houses?"

She questioned the utter desolation.

The boys pulled away from her grip and went running toward a flock of sun-basking seagulls. On their approach, the birds took flight, lit silver by the sun; they glided toward the smattering of rain clouds looming over the Harlem River.

Gwen walked to the corner to check the street sign, to make

sure this bareness was indeed East 133rd Street.

It was.

That was it. East 133rd Street was no longer there. All of the houses were gone and so was Harlan. And as long as Gwen was stuck with those boys, Edgar wasn't going to leave his wife. At least not to be with Gwen.

"Bre! Bobby!" she screeched.

"Can we get some ice cream, Mother?" Bre asked, falling into step alongside her.

Gwen stopped walking, raised her hand, and brought it down across Bre's face. Bobby jumped back, trembling.

"Shut your nasty mouth. Always begging, always taking," she snarled.

Eyes flaming with hatred, Bre rubbed his cheek, but said nothing.

Head high, back straight, Gwen courageously blinked back the water in her eyes and marched swiftly toward the subway station with Mary Bruce's voice blaring in her head.

Smile, Gwenie!

Smile!

Smile!

Chapter 77

Harlan had given up counting days, sunsets, and the number of people he'd seen die, since doing so had nearly sent him to the brink of insanity. He needed to keep his mind intact because that's where his memories were stored, and he couldn't risk losing them. When the hell that was Buchenwald became too much to bear, he could retreat into his mind and relive good times.

Friends?

Real friendship required months, sometimes years of nurturing—a luxury the prisoners of Buchenwald simply did not have. Time was a constant worry that hung over their heads like an anvil. *Acquaintances* would be a more appropriate word, though Harlan had very few of them.

Losing Lizard had mangled his heart in a way he never wanted to experience again. So while some people took others into their hearts, Harlan kept them at arm's length.

Why Harlan's life had been spared for all these years was a question for the ages. He was far from special and served no significant purpose within Buchenwald, yet he continued to cheat death, even though he often longed for its bloody sickle.

By late March of 1945, it seemed that Harlan might get his wish.

The prisoners hadn't had a scrap of food in ten days and were weak with hunger. Starvation wasted no time cutting down the feeble, littering the barracks with silent and stinking emaciated bodies.

Rumors raged.

I hear Germany is losing the war.

The Second Coming is at hand!

Hitler is dead.

Chapter 78

Crouched beneath a window, Bulger, a wiry, copper-colored man, whispered to anyone who cared to listen: "This is the fourth day in a row I seen a bunch of men marched through them gates."

Harlan was lying in bed with his eyes closed.

"I must have counted two thousand men."

"Which gates?" Harlan questioned. "The rear ones?"

"Yeah, the back gates. I think they might be letting people go," Bulger offered hopefully.

"Not likely," Harlan responded.

The rear gates led to a dense forest of beech trees known as the Singing Forest.

What they did to prisoners back there, out of sight, was worse than the public lynchings Ilse Koch was so fond of. In the thick of the woods—where no one could see but the birds— the soldiers ordered prisoners out of their clothing, shackled their wrists behind their backs, and hanged them on industrial-strength nails that had been driven into the trees. The prisoners dangled for hours or days. Arm joints popping, bones slipping. Sometimes, just for sport, Ilse would come down to whip the prisoners' legs and genitals with her riding crop. Her laughter mingled with the prisoners' agonizing screams and drifted, thin and haunting, into the prison yard. It touched the ear like a balladeer's melancholy refrain—hence the name.

"The front is moving closer!" came a hiss from the shadows.

Harlan opened his eyes and turned onto his side. He'd been hearing that claim for years.

"Maybe." Bulger's voice was riddled with excitement.

Harlan closed his eyes again.

"Three days and no roll call. What do you think that means?" someone asked.

"There aren't many soldiers in the yard," Bulger whispered. "I count..." His lips moved soundlessly for a moment. "Ten. Just ten. We can take ten."

The voice in the shadows quipped, "I'm sure there are more than ten. They're like ghosts. You don't see them, but they see you."

Bulger scurried to another window, insisting, "I tell you we can take them. We can."

Harlan had noticed the dwindling number of soldiers and officers. Ilse hadn't been seen for weeks, nor had the white smoke curling from the chimney of her fairy-tale house. Sometimes, in the well of the night, prisoners could hear scuttling in the darkness outside the barracks—no doubt the sound of soldiers fleeing like rats from a sinking ship.

Harlan turned over again, trying to find a comfortable position, but every which way hurt. Frustrated, he sat up; the effort left him winded. He surveyed the barracks and then lay back down. Soon he was asleep.

Hours later, he awakened to find the barracks drenched in shadows and silence so still, he thought he was alone.

"Hey, is anyone—"

"Shhhhhh."

Harlan sat up, peered into the darkness, spotted a group of men crowded around the doorway. "What's going on?"

"Shhhhh!"

Harlan weakly climbed from his bunk and limped toward the cluster of bodies. Halfway there, the bunch turned, rushed him, and hurled him down to the floor.

With not a drop of strength left, Harlan lay there, motionless.

Outside an explosion went off, and then another, followed by sprays of machine-gun fire, panicked cries, and the rumble of scattering feet.

The battle was short-lived.

Within minutes, American tanks, the avenging angels flying stars and stripes, leveled the front and rear gates and rolled triumphantly into the prison yard. The air exploded with whoops and cheers.

Harlan's frail heart and weak legs prevented him from moving beyond the doorway of the barracks, so he watched from the shadows, unsure if what he was seeing was real or imagined.

When a smiling soldier bounded up to him, Harlan reached out and touched his arm.

Indeed, he was real.

Overwhelmed, Harlan sank to the floor and wept.

Part IX

Home

Chapter 79

When the letter from the State Department arrived, notifying them that their son, Harlan Samuel Elliott, had been found, Emma dropped to her knees and screamed with joy.

Three weeks later, she and Sam were standing at a Midtown pier, huddled beneath a black umbrella, anxiously awaiting the arrival of their one and only child. The passengers spilled down the gangplank dodging raindrops, as stevedores hurriedly unloaded suitcases, steamer trunks, barrels, and boxes.

When the drizzle stopped, Sam closed the umbrella, removed his hat, and loosened his tie. Emma shrugged off her trench coat and looked at her watch.

"What's taking so long?"

"He's on this boat, baby, don't you worry. He's here."

They'd waited five years, but those last few minutes were the most agonizing.

A jumbo-sized man with shoulders as broad as an avenue started down the gangplank, pushing a wheelchair. Sam and Emma stepped aside, clearing space for the attendant and his patient. The burly man rolled the wheelchair to a halt and looked impatiently around. There were very few people left on the dock, save for Emma, Sam, and the stevedores.

The man looked directly at Sam. "Mr. Elliott?"

Emma's and Sam's heads snapped up.

"Y-Yes," Sam stammered, nervously rolling the rim of his

hat between his fingers.

"Hello, sir." The man extended his hand. "I'm Frank."

Sam looked at the hand and then at Emma. A long awkward moment passed before he finally shook Frank's hand. "This is my wife, Emma."

Emma glanced at the blanket-shrouded person in the chair.

"This sleepyhead," Frank chuckled in an accent neither one of them had ever heard before, "I believe is your son, Harlan."

They stared down at the fedora and dark glasses and then up the gangplank. Surely this man was mistaken. This was not their son.

Frank gave Harlan's shoulder a gentle shake.

Harlan lurched awake, head wobbling; the fedora rocked on his crown, the cocoon of blankets slipping from his frail shoulders. He peered over the rim of his dark glasses. "Mom? Dad?"

Frank leaned over and tucked the layers of cloth back into place. Emma and Sam stared in disbelief.

"It must be so nice to have your son home again, huh?" Frank's voice was hesitant.

With an unsteady hand, Emma reached down and slipped the glasses from Harlan's recessed face.

Harlan grinned. "Hey, Ma."

Tears flowed down Emma's cheeks. "Oh my God, Harlan, Harlan," she moaned, covering his face with kisses.

Swallowing his own tears, Sam threw his arms around Harlan's shoulders and planted a kiss on his forehead.

In the taxi home, Harlan sat between his parents, just as he had so many years earlier, when he'd first come to New York as a young boy. They rode in silence with their hands tightly clasped.

The streets and sidewalks were busy with people window-shopping and standing on corners laughing, children skipping rope and riding bicycles. Sunlight bore down on the wet streets, creating rainbows in puddles; raindrops dangled from telephone lines.

Harlan stared out at the scene with all the wonder and delight of a child.

When the cab came to a stop at 200 West 119 Street, Harlan looked up at the five-story building and asked, "What's this place?"

"Oh, um..." Emma stammered.

"We sold the house," Sam quickly interjected. "A lot has changed since you've been away." He said "away" as if Harlan had spent the last five years on holiday, frolicking on a sugar-white beach.

The apartment was on the third floor, and the building did not have an elevator. The walk from the cab into the building taxed Harlan of the little strength he had; no way could he climb three flights of stairs.

After some contemplation, Sam handed his hat and coat to Emma and crouched down alongside Harlan. "I'll just have to carry you." Sam had never been a big man and age had chiseled some of him away.

Emma didn't think it was a good idea and said so. "I can run up and see if JoJo is home. I'm sure he'd be happy to help."

Their neighbor JoJo Clark moved furniture for a living, so for him, hoisting Harlan up the flights of stairs would be as easy as carrying a five-pound bag of flour.

"It'll be fine," Sam assured her. "Get on, Harlan."

Up they went, Harlan clamped to his father's back like a

knapsack; Emma close behind, hands braced out ahead of her as if beaming an invisible force to help them along.

By the time they reached the third floor, Sam was perspiring and panting. He set Harlan down and promptly fell against the wall, exhausted. But seeing the shame pulsing in Harlan's face, Sam swiftly made light of the situation. "I bet you didn't think your old man had it in him, huh?" he grinned. "Next time you carry *me* up, okay?"

Harlan nodded.

The apartment was spacious and cheery with a generous amount of windows. Three bedrooms, two bathrooms, and a kitchen half the size of the one they'd had in the brownstone.

Except for a few new pieces, the furniture was all the same.

Harlan flopped down onto the couch and pointed at the piano in the corner of the room. "That new?"

"Yes," Emma said.

Sam turned on the radio. Count Basie's popular tune "Jumpin' at the Woodside" blared in the air.

Harlan winced, asked his father if he wouldn't mind finding another station.

"Sure, sure," Sam said, "whatever you want."

Emma clapped her hands together. "I bet you're hungry, huh?" She rushed into the kitchen. "I was cooking all day yesterday. Fried chicken, deviled eggs, collard greens, candied yams, tater salad, mac and cheese..."

How many times over the years had Harlan dreamed about eating his mother's cooking? He couldn't even begin to count.

"...and Mrs. Atkins sent over an apple pie. You remember her, don't you? I sent your father out to get some ice cream. The fool came back with rum raisin. I told him, *You know Harlan don't like no rum raisin, Harlan likes vanilla!* You still like vanilla, don'tcha?" Emma ducked her head around the doorway, her eyes sparkling with something approaching happiness.

"Mama, I haven't had ice cream in five years. I don't remember if I like vanilla or rum raisin."

Emma didn't know why, but this broke her heart. She moved to the stove and turned the flame on beneath the pot of greens.

Harlan asked, "So, are we expecting company?"

Sam smirked. "Nope."

"That's a lot of food for just us three, don't you think?"

"Well, you know how your mother is." Sam clasped his hands on top of his head and rolled his eyes to the ceiling.

Emma appeared, blushing with shame. "I just wanted you to have all of your favorites."

Just as they sat down to eat, the phone started ringing.

He get in okay?

How he look?

Can we come by?

Aww, yeah, I understand, maybe in a few days, after he's settled in.

Tell him I asked about him, okay?

I told you, God is good all the time.

Eventually, Sam took the phone off the hook.

They talked around the pressing questions.

Harlan didn't bring up the last five years, and Sam and Emma didn't either. Instead, they spoke about the changes in Harlem; the end of its golden era, the climbing crime rate, Lucille's new husband, and her career as a nurse at Harlem Hospital.

Harlan listened, head bobbing, eyebrows climbing and falling, barely touching his food.

They tried not to stare, but it was difficult because Harlan looked like death walking. He hadn't eaten enough to fill the belly of a field mouse when he rubbed his eyes and yawned, "I think I'd like to go to bed now."

It was barely five o'clock.

When the sun went down, Harlan turned on the light and kept it on through the night. He lay in bed, keenly aware of every opening and closing door, the clacking of shoes, car horns, and conversations had in the neighboring apartments.

He must have opened and closed his eyes a thousand times, fully expecting to awake from this dream to find himself back at Buchenwald, standing in the prison yard, legs numb.

And then, for one wild moment, Harlan thought that maybe he was dead, and Buchenwald hadn't been hell after all, but purgatory, and now he had finally ascended into heaven.

Heaven? An apartment on West 119th Street was God's idea of nirvana? The idea was ludicrous—probably the most ridiculous notion he'd had since those last days in Buchenwald when he'd seriously considered chewing off his thumbs.

In the living room, Emma placed a call to Martin Carter, a family friend and doctor. "He looks real bad," she whispered into the receiver. "Will you come and give him a look?"

"Of course, I'll be there tomorrow 'round eleven."

Chapter 80

Dr. Carter was in the bedroom with Harlan for nearly two hours. When he came out, his toffee-colored face was clouded with concern. "He's very dehydrated. Don't worry about his appetite; it'll get better over time. Give him lots of milk, that'll open it up. He needs vitamins too. Iron."

The doctor paused, looked at Emma and then down at his hands. Her pulse quickened.

Meeting her anxious gaze, he blurted, "What happened to him? I asked, but he wouldn't say. What he tell you?"

Emma shrugged her shoulders. "We didn't ask. It seems too soon, and he ain't say. So for now, all we know is what the State Department's letter said."

"What was that?"

"That he was found in a German prison."

The doctor shook his head. "Prison?" He glanced at Harlan's closed door. "Have you seen him? I mean, under his clothes?"

Emma wrung her hands. "N-no. Why?"

Dr. Carter sighed. "He's all scarred up. I ain't seen nothing like it since I was in Virginia, treating them old slaves."

Emma's eyes bulged. "W-what?"

He removed the stethoscope from his neck and threw it angrily into his black satchel. "I think he was in one them camps."

"Camps?"

317

"Yeah, them camps they killed all them Jews in."

Emma shook her head. "Nah, Dr. Carter, I don't think so. Harlan ain't no Jew, why would they put him in one of those?"

Dr. Carter's eyes darkened. "Y'all music people. Do you know Valaida?"

"Valaida Snow? Sure, I know her some. Not well, but we get along okay."

"So you know what happened to her over in Europe, right?"

"I read something in the paper, heard talk."

"She was in Denmark and them Nazis snatched her right off the street and threw her into one of them camps—them concentration camps. Kept her there for over a year and nearly beat the pretty off her."

Emma shot a nervous glance at Harlan's door.

"White folks," the doctor mumbled disgustedly, "they just ain't no good, no matter where they are. By the time they let her go, she was damn near dead. Skinnier than your boy in there. Just seventy pounds. Now you know that ain't no kinda weight for a black woman."

Emma folded her arms over her breasts. A dull thud beat at her temples. "But they say she lied," she uttered, so unwilling to believe the unbelievable. "The *Daily News* claimed she was over there smoking dope. That's why they put her in jail. Only the black papers said otherwise."

Dr. Carter shot her a sickened look. "I ain't take you for a woman who swallowed white lies."

Embarrassed, Emma lowered her eyes.

Dr. Carter pressed: "Why would she tell a story like that?"

Emma shook her head. "I don't know, people lie."

The doctor snatched his bag up and started toward the door.

"Well, I believe her," he said, reaching for the doorknob. "And I say Harlan was in the same sort of place."

After Dr. Carter left, Emma made a cup of tea and sat down at the kitchen table to fret.

What if what the doctor said was true? She'd read about what the Jews had gone through in those camps; she'd seen the devastation for herself in a black-and-white newsreel that screened before the main feature of a movie she could no longer recall.

She didn't remember seeing any black people in the footage, so Dr. Carter must be mistaken. It was just Jews who were interned and murdered in those camps. Wasn't it? She hadn't heard any different. Every time the news reported on the Holocaust, they talked about the Jews and no one else. There was certainly no mention of Negroes—she would have remembered that. Yes, Dr. Carter must have his facts wrong.

Emma finished her tea, went to the cabinet, removed a glass from the shelf, and filled it with milk. She carried it down the hall to Harlan's bedroom, knocked once, and pushed the door open before he could answer.

Even though it was late May and people had already started running their fans, Harlan's bedroom windows were closed and he was buried beneath two blankets.

"I brought you some milk." She set the glass on the nightstand, tiptoed to the window, and pulled it open. "Harlan, you awake?"

"Yeah."

Emma didn't miss the annoyance in his muffled response. "I said I brought you milk. Dr. Carter said it'll open up your appetite."

"Okay."

Emma grabbed her elbows. "He also said that you need to take vitamins, 'specially iron. I'm going to go to the pharmacy in a few. You wanna come along and get some fresh air?"

"No thanks."

She cleared her throat. "Um. Dr. Carter also said that... well, you got some scars on your body that look... well, he said they look real bad."

Harlan didn't say a word.

"You wanna talk about it?"

"No."

Emma moved her hands from her elbows to her shoulders.

"Well, maybe you'd prefer to talk to your father about what... um... happened to you over there?"

She waited for Harlan to respond. When he said nothing, she sat down on the corner of the bed and rested her hand on his leg.

"For God's sake, won't you even look at me?" Looking at her was the least he could do; after all, she was his mother, a mother who had spent five years in turmoil. Five years of praying, crying, and writing letters to the president, not to mention the small fortune she'd spent on overseas phone calls.

After the city bought the house, Emma had gone there every day and sat on the stoop for hours, just in case by some miracle Harlan showed up. Even after the city razed the entire area, she still went and waited in the vast nothingness.

Emma had done everything short of going to Europe to find him herself. And if she could have done that, she would have. So why couldn't he just give her the little bit she was asking for?

Harlan pushed back the blankets. The corners of his eyes

were crusty; his breath was rank. "Mama," he breathed tiredly, "no sense in both of us walking around with broken hearts."

Emma gazed at him. Moments later, she rose quietly from the bed and left the room.

Chapter 81

That July, a kind of madness seized Harlem. Place the blame where you want—oppressive summer heat, American hubris gone wild (they'd won the war, after all), or the nuclear bomb the government detonated in the New Mexico desert. Pick one or all—your choice—but the fact remains, Harlem was raging.

In an apartment in the building across the street, a man came home from work, sat down to dinner with his family, and then shot them all dead. The newspapers said that before he killed himself, he ate a dessert of fresh peaches and whipped cream at the very dinner table his wife and children were bleeding out on.

One starry Saturday night, Betty Brown, a single woman, down on her luck and pregnant with her fourth child, took her babies to the Third Avenue Bridge and flung them, and then herself, into the river.

A returning war veteran stripped naked and proceeded to march down 125th Street, blowing a whistle, brandishing his freakishly long penis at astonished onlookers.

Harlan hadn't washed in weeks and was drinking heavily. He'd drained all the alcohol in the apartment and bloodied his fist against the wall when he demanded that Sam buy more and Sam refused. Afraid that father and son would come to blows, Emma ran out and purchased two bottles of Scotch. If the look Sam gave her had been a bullet, Emma would have been dead.

When Harlan wasn't drinking, he was sleeping, sitting in bed staring at the walls, or pacing in his room, chain-smoking. Sometimes his parents could hear him sobbing through the walls.

Emma brought him meals because he rarely left his bedroom, except to relieve himself and sometimes not even then. A neighbor reported that she had seen Harlan urinating out the window.

Sam threatened to have him committed, and Emma promised to kill Sam if he did.

Once Emma made the mistake of mentioning Lizard's name, and for that offense Harlan didn't speak to her for a week.

Aware of Emma and Sam's difficulties, Lucille and other close friends sent flowers and notes of encouragement. The religious amongst them lit candles for Harlan and added his name to the church catalogs of the sick and shut-in.

Harlan didn't know it, but he had entire congregations praying for his recovery.

One steamy Tuesday afternoon, Emma opened the apartment door to find John Smith standing there in his army duds.

"How long has it been?"

"Too long, Mrs. Elliott."

After Darlene died and Mayremma moved with John to New Jersey, John had only come back to visit a handful of times in just as many years. However, he had kept in touch by phone, calling on birthdays and holidays.

"You are looking so good. Tall and as handsome as you wanna be."

John blushed. "It's the uniform."

"You make that uniform look good. I will say this: you brave to be wearing it out in public."

"Why's that?"

Emma cocked her head. "Ain't you heard? White boys stringing up Negro soldiers, saying they deserve to die for killing white men, even if those white men were Germans."

"Oh, yeah, I did hear 'bout that. That's them crackers down south though."

"And the crackers up north too." Emma swept a piece of lint off his lapel. "Sit down. Get you something cold to drink?"

"No thank you, I'm good."

John studied the dark halos around her eyes and the silver edging her hairline.

"How's your mother doing?"

"Aww, she's all right." His eyes roamed around the apartment. "You miss the house?"

Emma shrugged. "Yes, I do. Living in a building is plenty noisy though."

"You should come out to New Jersey, it's nice and quiet."

"Don't think it hasn't crossed my mind."

John tilted his chin at the piano. "You still giving lessons?"

"Here and there. Not like I used to."

John glanced at his watch.

Emma got the hint. "Well, I know you didn't come to jabber with me. How'd you hear he was back?"

"Word gets around."

"That it does." Emma smoothed her hands over her skirt. "He hasn't felt much like company. I'll tell him you're here, but I doubt he'll see you."

John stood. "No need to announce me, just point the way."

Emma twisted her lips. "The thing is, John, Harlan ain't

the same person you used to know, and sometimes he gets real irritable—"

John raised a halting hand. "Does he have a gun in there? 'Cause I can handle a little irritability. I spent the war dodging bullets, but I don't wanna have to dodge any here at home." He chuckled.

"Nah," Emma shook her head, "he don't have a gun."

"You sure?"

"You still a fool. Go on now, Harlan's room is down the hall, second door on your left."

John didn't bother to knock; he walked right in and snatched the blankets away. "Get up, nigga!"

Harlan shot up, eyelids flapping. He stared, face contorting, shoulders jumping. "John?"

"The one and only!"

Harlan made an attempt to smile, but his lips refused to cooperate.

"John, wow," he mumbled, pulling the covers over his scarred thighs. "Been years, right? Look at you, an army man." Harlan reached for the pack of smokes resting on the night table.

"Geez, man, it smells like ass and armpits in here." John pinched his nose. "Open a fucking window. It's ninety damn degrees outside, and you closed up in here like it's winter."

Harlan slipped a cigarette between his lips. "Aww, shut up, you sound like my mother."

John sat on the windowsill. "So, how you been?"

"You know," Harlan raked his fingers across the wild hair on his cheeks, "surviving. H-how 'bout you? And your moms? How's she doing?"

"Can't complain. She's doing okay. I'm driving a cab now."

"Really? Out there in Jersey?"

"Yep. Just part-time, you know, in between gigs."

"Oh, you still playing?"

"Of course, ain't you?"

"Nah, gave it up," Harlan sniffed.

"Sorry to hear that."

With the unlit cigarette dangling from his mouth, Harlan said, "No need to sound like somebody died. It's just music."

John grunted. "Just music? Was a time when music was your life."

"Well, things change." Harlan's eyes carefully avoided John's penetrating gaze. "Hey, so how's your mother?"

John folded his arms. "You already asked me that."

"Did I?" Harlan laughed. "My mind, it goes in and out sometimes. You got a light?"

"Sure." John handed him a silver-plated lighter embossed with the initials *JS*.

Harlan ran his thumb over the letters. "Nice," he breathed. Cigarette smoke mushroomed. John opened the window, removed a pack of cigarettes from his jacket pocket, and shook a joint into the palm of his hand. "Hey, look what I got."

Harlan eyed it, licking his lips. "Is that what I think it is? I haven't had one of those in five years."

"Well then, it looks like I came at the right damn time."

"Fire it up."

"I'm not smoking in your mama's house. You know she hates this shit. Let's take a drive, maybe go see the old neighborhood."

"You got a car?"

"Negro, didn't I tell you I was driving a cab?"

Harlan scratched his head. "Yeah, but you said you was

driving a cab in New Jersey."

John shot him an exasperated look. "What you think, the cab turns into a pumpkin if I drive it to New York? Man, you been shut up in this funky-ass room too long, the bad air in here is fucking with your mind."

Harlan smashed his cigarette into an ashtray overflowing with butts and peanut shells. "Yeah, well, the old neighborhood ain't nothing but dirt now. Mama said the city bought up all the houses and then tore them down; that's why we had to move here."

John nodded. "Don't mean we can't roll through, just for old time's sake. We'll go down to the water, burn this beauty over the river."

"I-I don't know."

"Or, " John suggested lightly, "we can drop in at Abyssinian."

Harlan frowned. "The church?"

"Yeah."

"You kidding? You went to war and came back religious?"

John gave him a sober look. "And you didn't? Out in those trenches, me and God became the best of friends. He kept me safe and sent me back home to my mama, intact."

"Well, I wasn't in the war," Harlan mumbled, dropping his head a bit.

"Them scars on your legs say different."

Harlan lit a new cigarette and pulled hard.

"Look here, I got friends and you got friends who came back in bags with tags on their toes and some who didn't come back at all, like your man Lizard. We the lucky ones. God brought us home for a reason. You think this all an accident? Nah, man, this is God's plan."

John pushed himself up from the sill, walked over to Harlan, and crouched down by the bed. "I know you been through some bad shit, and you dealing with some pain that you think no one understands. But I'm here to tell you that God understands, and because He loves you, He is willing to take all that pain and anger from you; all you got to do is give it to Him."

Harlan's mouth twitched. He pushed the heels of his hands into his eyes; tears trickled down his forearms. "You full of shit," he gurgled.

"Nah, man, not about this." John patted Harlan's knee. "You go on ahead and cry, ain't nothing wrong with crying. It's cleansing."

After Harlan mopped his face with the edge of the blanket, he said, "You think God's all right with us smoking weed?"

"Why wouldn't He be? He the one created it. It grows outta the ground just like the flowers and the trees, don't it?"

Chapter 82

It wasn't a thing Harlan could tell people. Not his mother, father, or John Smith. If he even hinted at what he was seeing, the things he thought about doing to himself and others—well, it would mean a straitjacket and rubber room for him.

Sometimes Harlan looked at his mother and saw the image of that bitch who killed Lizard rippling like water over Emma's sweet face. The first time it happened, he was sitting at the dinner table, blinking and blinking. Emma asked if there was anything wrong, if he'd gotten something in his eye. Harlan just kept blinking at the rice that was squirming on his plate like maggots. He shoved the plate away and stood. When he looked at Emma, the bitch was looking back at him. He cried out, his intestines knotted and then unraveled, and Harlan soiled himself right there in the dining room. Sam jumped up, hollering, but then fell quiet. He took Harlan by the arm. "Let's get you cleaned up, son." Whimpering like a child, Harlan pressed his face into Sam's shoulder to hide his eyes from Emma's startled ones.

That wasn't something you worked into casual conversation.

And the ghosts? Who could he tell about the ghosts? Even with the lights on, the dead haunted him, crowding his room, wounds open and letting so much blood, it covered his floor like an ocean.

Harlan couldn't tell a soul about that.

Outside of his window, the Harlem streets disappeared, the

children, the cars—all vanished, replaced by the Buchenwald prison yard and the gallows and the guards glaring up at him, guns aimed.

No, that wasn't anything he could talk about.

So he suffered, and not necessarily in silence. The haggard appearance of his parents was proof of that.

Harlan remained in that apartment for four straight years, rarely venturing out into the hallway or down onto the street.

Even if he hadn't climbed onto the fire escape in the dead of winter, naked and screaming in German, they still would have had to move because the landlord had had it up to here with tenants' complaints about Harlan's screeching in the middle of the night; and so he was left with no other choice but to evict them.

Emma and Sam didn't want to tell Harlan they were planning to move. When he questioned them about the boxes filled with family heirlooms, records, and such, Emma said that she was putting them in storage for safekeeping.

"From what?"

To that she replied, "Safe from paint splatter."

So the apartment getting a fresh coat of paint was the first lie. The second dilemma was how exactly they planned on getting Harlan out of the old apartment and into the new one.

Dr. Carter presented a viable solution: "Drug him."

He came the day of the move, and shifted his eyes away from Harlan's marble stare when he lied, "This will help with those rashes," referring to the scarlet bumps—eerily resembling rope burns—that sometimes appeared around Harlan's wrists.

Dr. Martin stuck the needle in Harlan's arm and the sedative took hold within minutes. When the movers arrived, Harlan was sprawled on the sofa, snoring.

Sam pointed at his son. "Y'all gotta move him too."

Sure that he was yanking their chains, the trio of muscled, bald-headed brothers laughed.

"Nah, I ain't joking, I need one of you to carry him down to the taxi and then up to the new apartment." Sam gave his watch a nervous glance. "We got 'bout four hours before he wakes up, so get the hominy grits out your asses."

Chapter 83

Three more years of life swinging between chaos and calm. Emma's nerves were shot to hell, and her husband who did not drink was now spooning Scotch into his evening cup of coffee, instead of sugar.

Electric shock treatment had come up numerous times, but Emma quickly tabled the idea, claiming that she didn't have the heart to plunge Harlan into that type of hell even though he was dragging them through his own.

The thing that finally saved their sanity was isoniazid.

Sam shook the bottle of pills at Dr. Carter. "You said this is used to treat TB? But Harlan don't have that, so how's it going to help him?"

"Sometimes," Dr. Carter explained, "medicine is developed for one thing and ends up being just as good for another."

Emma took the bottle from Sam and studied the label. "But will taking these pills *give* Harlan TB?"

"No, of course not."

Harlan was sitting between his parents, lacing and unlacing his fingers. Emma looked at him and touched the bottle of pills to his thigh.

"What do you think, son? You think you want to give these a try?"

Not that he had a choice. Even if Harlan had said no, Emma would have ground the pills to powder and sprinkled them into his glass of morning orange juice or onto his plate of hot grits.

And the pills really did seem to help. So after years of feeling unhinged, Emma started to feel more grounded, more hopeful for Harlan's future.

"The money from the house is just sitting in the bank, collecting dust," she pointed out one morning over breakfast.

"It's called interest, Emma," Sam replied.

"Whatever. It ain't doing us no good."

"What you wanna do with it?"

"Buy a house."

"Another one? Where?"

"Jersey."

"New Jersey?"

"It's nice and quiet over there."

"Far, though."

"Far from what?"

"Far from here, where I make my living."

"You think you can't find work out there?"

"I can find work anywhere," Sam said.

"So what's the problem?"

"Ain't no problem."

"I think we need a change. It'd be nice to get away from these trifling Harlem niggers."

"Trifling?"

"Uh-hum. 'Sides, I think it would do Harlan a world of good."

"Well, he's doing good right here. Them pills have worked wonders—he's getting out some, back to playing his guitar.

What more moving to Jersey gonna do?"

"Didn't I already explain myself?"

"Trifling Harlem niggers?"

"Yes."

"You don't think they got those type of folk in New Jersey?"

"Sam, please!"

"Okay."

"Maybe out there he'll meet a decent girl, not like these hussies he running with here. He can get married and give us some grandbabies. Don't you want some grands?"

"Sure."

"I don't wanna be a grandmother here in the city. I want a house with a porch and backyard where my grands can romp and play."

"Well, why not go back to Macon?" Sam asked.

"And have to step off the sidewalk to 'low white people to pass? Can't look 'em in the eye, gotta look at their shoes? No thank you. New Jersey is as far south as I am willing to go."

"So, New Jersey then?"

"That's what I said."

"Well, you the boss, baby."

"And don't you forget it."

Chapter 84

In the early 1950s, white people were fleeing Trenton, New Jersey for the quaint seaside towns along the shore. Those who hadn't posted a *For Sale* sign in their yard were planning to do so.

For decades, Trenton residents had flat-out refused to sell to blacks. Those who did were ostracized and the new families terrorized. But by the '50s, Trenton's sister city, Newark, was growing blacker by the day. And anyone with an ounce of sense could see that Trenton was slowly succumbing to the same fate.

Seventeen Fountain Avenue. A two-story, pink-red brick house, three bedrooms, one bathroom, combined living and dining areas, and a rickety front porch slung over a patch of grass. Square in the middle of the yard grew an old, fat tree with thick, sloping branches.

"It's a nice little house."

"Need work though." Sam scratched thoughtfully at his chin.

"Well, you the person for it."

"You sure about this, Emma?"

She grabbed his hand. "It feels right. Don't you feel it?"

"Yeah, I guess."

"You think Harlan will like it?"

"Do he got a choice?"

"I think this is a good place to stay for a while."

"A while? Woman, you planning on moving us again?"

"Not with boxes and moving men."

"What you saying then?"

"I'm saying we gonna grow old here."

"We already old, baby."

"I mean *older*. The next time we move, it'll be on up to heaven."

Chapter 85

Surrendering to the lullaby and goodnight of autumn, the flowers threw down their petals and wilted. The trees, as if ashamed, waited till night fell before dropping their golden leaves.

The fire department locked off the hydrants, barbecue grills were stored away, white shoes and purses moved to the shadowy corners of closets, children returned to school.

Labor Day was a month-old memory by the time the moving truck, followed by Sam, Emma, and Harlan (in their sun-yellow Chevrolet Fleetmaster), along with Lucille and her new husband Gomez Allen (in their powder-blue Ford De Luxe convertible coupe), pulled up to 17 Fountain Avenue and wrecked the doleful quiet of the dying season.

Car doors opened, radios on, the shriek of violin strings that prefaced Nat King Cole's velvet voice caught the warm autumn breeze and sailed across the street into Patsy Harris's sitting room.

Patricia "Patsy" Harris, a thirty-year-old fading prom queen and reluctant mother of three, had few luxuries in her life. Listening to *Queen for a Day* was one of them.

Glued to the radio, Patsy swatted at her ears as if the music was a bothersome fly. During the commercial break she stood to close the window, but spotting the spectacle, she reached for the phone instead.

"Hello?"

"Hey, Jill?"

"Patsy? Let me call you back after *Queen for a Day* goes off."

"This is important."

"Oh. The baby okay?"

"It's not the baby. We just got some new neighbors."

"Oh?"

"Niggers."

"Oh!"

An hour later, Patsy, bouncing her four-month-old on her shoulder, was still at the window, phone fixed to her ear, rattling off descriptions of the people, their cars, and their furniture.

"Um, wait a minute, Jill. A Newark Checker cab just pulled up."

"A cab, huh?"

"Another nigger."

"A passenger?"

"No, the driver."

John Smith leapt from the taxi, nodded at the moving men, strolled up the steps, and disappeared into the house.

"They unpack any watermelon?" Jill snickered from her house around the corner on Sweets Avenue.

"Not yet, but I expect to smell some fried chicken any second now."

Minutes after he arrived, John left. He returned an hour later with Mayemma sitting in the passenger seat.

Before stepping from the car, Mayemma checked her lipstick and adjusted her wig. She was tilting the scales at three hundred pounds and Emma, who was waiting on the porch, couldn't hide her surprise when Mayemma began ambling toward her.

"Oh my goodness," Patsy breathed. "The taxi driver just came back with a hog!"

"You lying, Patsy. A real, live hog?"

They tried not to get teary-eyed, but it was hard. They'd both endured so much.

"Guuuurrl," Emma crooned, grinning.

Mayemma tucked her chin into her chest and walked into Emma's open arms.

"Well," Jill sighed, "that makes four colored families in the neighborhood."

"Six," Patsy corrected.

"Six? Are you sure?"

"Yep. Donna called me a few days back and said she spotted coloreds moving into a house on Wayne Avenue."

"Wayne Avenue? Wow."

"And remember last February, that white man and his black wife bought that yellow house on New Rose Street?"

"Oh yeah, I forgot about them. You're right, Patsy. Six."

"I've gotta go, Jill. The baby needs to be changed and I want to catch Frank Agostino before he goes home for the day."

"Something wrong with your pipes?"

"No, not the plumber, his cousin, the locksmith. I want him to put dead bolts on the door. I don't really feel safe living around all these type of people."

"I know what you mean. Me and Charlie feel the same way, that's why we bought a gun."

Chapter 86

Unwelcomed. Incriminated by their dark skin—the white residents charged the Elliotts with wretchedness. Without benefit of judge or jury, they were found guilty and condemned to years of harassment.

At night, while they slept, garbage was dumped onto their little porch, bags of feces (canine and human) set ablaze on their neatly cut lawn, house keys were used to mutilate their car.

Yes, Harlan had a heavy foot and had been known on occasion to push the Fleetmaster beyond the speed limit, but even on those days when he was perfectly law-abiding, the cops still harassed him. Following those incidents, Harlan would be despondent for days, having developed a fear of white men in uniform; police officers, firemen, the security guard at Woolworth's, and the postman—all made him shudder.

As tough as it was on him—on all of them—Emma refused to leave. She had made that house a home, had a flourishing vegetable garden and rosebushes that were the envy of the block.

"Fuck them," she snarled whenever Sam suggested they go back to Harlem. "I ain't gonna let them crackers drive me out. They want me gone, they gonna have to kill me."

That first year, they had to have the car repainted three times. Sam bought a Doberman pinscher and tied it up in the yard to deter those night-creeping predators. A month later, the dog was dead from cyanide-laced meatballs.

"It wasn't even this bad down south," Sam complained.

Emma wasn't going to talk about it again. She smiled at her husband, patted his hand, and gently changed the subject. "Did you meet the new family that moved in across the street? Aww, they such a good-looking couple. They remind me of us when we were young. And they got a little boy who is sweet enough to eat!"

Shaking his head, Sam returned to the backyard to finish digging the dog's grave.

It took a few years and two more murdered dogs, but white flight had swooped in and one day the brown and black residents of Trenton, New Jersey woke to find that there was nary a white person around.

Relieved that his property was now relatively safe from racist vandalism, Sam set to work renovating the basement. He moisture-sealed the stone walls, installed overhead lighting, and covered the dirt floor in hardwood.

On the weekends, if the weather was foul, friends crowded into the basement to play spades and dominoes, and bid whist. Emma and Mayemma cooked pots of food and John and Harlan accompanied Lucille, in town from Harlem, through her repertoire of songs.

The gatherings swelled, and soon Emma was hosting a bi-monthly fish fry, which quickly became the best place to be two Fridays a month that side of the Holland Tunnel.

Eventually, it was almost like old times in that new place across the Hudson River.

Chapter 87

Even with the pills, Harlan still slept with the bedroom lights on. Sometimes, of course, he didn't sleep at all, and Emma would lay awake counting his footsteps as he wandered through the house mumbling to himself.

Every morning, she half expected to discover her son dead by his own hands, and every morning that she found Harlan asleep on the sofa or sitting at the kitchen table hunched over a bowl of Cheerios, her knees went weak with relief.

His night terrors came and went with the seasons and thunderstorms left him trembling for days. Emma and Sam did their best to comfort him through those harrowing times, resigned now to the fact that whatever he had suffered over in Germany couldn't be eradicated with a pill, reefer, Scotch, or a mother's unrelenting love. The fear and rage living inside of Harlan was a virus, creeping and latent, springing unexpectedly—much like a jack-in-the-box or a stalking cat.

In '54, Sam began working as a janitor at the Tilton General Hospital in Fort Dix, New Jersey. He got Harlan hired on as a floater, who sometimes mopped floors, sometimes emptied bedpans, and other times worked as a server in the mess hall.

It was the end of the Korean War, and the three-hundred-bed hospital had become a temporary home for returning veterans.

Harlan felt right at home amongst those limbless, body-ravaged, mentally scarred men. He listened to their stories and shared a few of his own. He treated the patients with the same compassion and empathy that his parents had showed him day in and day out.

At Emma's prodding, Harlan began bringing his guitar to work. "I hear it's therapeutic," she remarked with a sly smile. Harlan knew she was speaking more about his own healing than that of the strangers she would never meet.

After his obligations were done, Harlan often stayed on to jam with those patients who were also musically inclined. They were a comical bunch to watch—blind, bandaged, and amputated—but the music they made consistently belied their physical disabilities.

It was at Tilton General Hospital that Harlan, quite by accident, made his first narcotics transaction as a dealer.

Every morning before leaving for work, he would slip a joint into his pack of cigarettes. At lunchtime, he'd steal away to the boiler room for a few puffs and then again at quitting time if he'd planned on staying around to jam or play cards with the patients.

One day, a vet who'd had his right cheek and eye blown off by a grenade pointed at the pack of smokes nestled in the breast pocket of Harlan's shirt. "Can I have one?" he mumbled through his ruined mouth.

At that moment Harlan was chatting up a doe-eyed nurse's aide and hastily handed the pack of cigarettes to the man. "You can keep it," he said, unwilling to pull his eyes from the woman's full lips.

The man tottered off.

Harlan realized much too late exactly what he'd given away.

The loss, however, was worth it because he had bedded the pretty aide in an empty room on the floor of the hospital occupied by the mentally unstable.

The next day, the man approached Harlan, his one eye rolling happily in its socket. "That was some good weed," he whispered.

Concerned about losing his job, Harlan played foolish: "Weed? I don't know what you're talking about, man."

The vet was persistent: "I let some of the other guys hit it and they want more. So how much you selling it for?"

"Selling?"

"Yeah."

Although Harlan had been a tried and true customer, it had never crossed his mind to become a dealer. But as he stood there looking at the broken man, it occurred to him that Tilton General Hospital might possibly be his personal gold mine. The realization rose in him like the sun. "Let me get back to you on that."

Chapter 88

Being financially independent for the first time in years, Harlan spent most of his money on women and Scotch. He bought himself a used convertible—red with white racing stripes along the sides—and took a girl he'd met waiting for the Trenton city bus to Atlantic City for the weekend. When he came back, he handed a bag of strawberry taffy to Emma and a gag cigar to Sam. When Emma asked about the young lady, Harlan told her he'd taken her back to her husband where she belonged.

In 1955, two white men were accused of killing a young black boy in Money, Mississippi. They swore to God they didn't do it, got off scot-free, and then later admitted to a journalist that they did indeed kill that nigger and would do it again if they got the chance. Emma said that was why God reached down and snatched away America's golden boy, James Dean—because what goes around always comes around.

Mad or not at white people's ways, they all took a liking to that Elvis Presley, with his colored-sounding music and dance moves. When he appeared on *The Ed Sullivan Show* in '56, Emma pretended to faint into Harlan's arms. He was laughing so hard he almost dropped her.

In the South, black Americans, sick of centuries-long maltreatment from a country built on their backs, launched boycotts, freedom rides, and sit-ins. Across the waters, inspired by their American cousins, South Africans also took to the streets to demand civil rights.

As a result, blood was spilled on both continents. Rivers of it flowed through the gutters, seeped into the core of the earth, and came together in a thick, red knot.

Justice was blind, and God was deaf.

That sexy starlet with the blond hair and bow-shaped hips fell in love with the leader of the free world, and when he didn't leave his wife, she took a handful of pills and went to sleep forever. Not too long after that, a lunatic shot a bullet into the head of that president, scattering his brains all over his prep-schooled wife.

A man named Malcolm Little, who had at one point in his life been a thief, addict, and womanizer, found Allah in a tiny jail cell and changed his name to Malcolm X. He told black people that there was a white man paying Dr. Martin Luther King to keep Negroes defenseless, because wasn't no one asking white folk to turn the other cheek. On top of that, Malcolm X had been smug and flip about the assassinated president with the Hollywood looks and that upset a lot of people, so somebody did to him what had been done to JFK just to see how he liked being killed.

But he never did say, because he was dead.

The black minister called King, who was causing so much trouble for white America, marched on Washington, along with 250,000 supporters. On the steps of the memorial dedicated to the great Negro emancipator, Martin Luther King shared a story about a dream he had for America.

Either President Lyndon B. Johnson liked what he heard, or he was good and tired of hearing Negroes sing "We Shall

Overcome," because he signed Martin's dream into law.

When the president of South Africa got wind of what Johnson had done, he laughed and called him stupid, declaring that there would never be an apartheid-free South Africa. "Not here, not ever!"

The first time Sam and Emma had ever heard the name Nelson Mandela was in 1962, when Harlan came home wearing dark shades, black tam, and dashiki, causing Emma to choke on her Nehi soda.

"Who the hell are you supposed to be?"

Harlan pulled a chair from the dining table and straddled it. "I'm still me, just conscious."

Emma eyed him. "Are you off your medicine again?"

"No, Mama, I—"

Emma shoved a finger in his face. "Didn't I tell you to steer clear of them Black Panther hooligans? They ain't nothing but trouble."

Harlan lowered her finger. "The Black Panther Party is all about the betterment of our race—"

"Seems to me they more about guns and violence!"

"Don't believe everything you hear, Mama. Anyway, the Panthers are planning to protest the imprisonment of Nelson Mandela."

"Nelson who?"

Harlan stood and opened his mouth to explain, but Emma brutally interrupted him.

"And I don't like you wearing that African getup. You need to go and find something decent to put on."

Harlan rolled his eyes. "Mama, you need to start taking

347

some pride in your African roots."

Emma clapped her hands. "African roots? I ain't got no goddamn roots in Africa; my roots right down there in Macon, Georgia!"

Turns out, Harlan wasn't a revolutionary after all, just a pussy hound hell-bent on laying every pretty female who joined the party.

That same year, Lucille came out of retirement to record *A Basket of Blues*, with legends Victoria Spivey and Hannah Sylvester.

Lucille was so proud that she had Gomez drive out to Trenton from Harlem in a rainstorm just so she and Emma could listen to the album together.

When Emma saw the jacket (a black-and-white photo of the three elderly singers posed around a piano), she squinted at it and then smirked at Lucille. "All y'all look like ya got one foot in the grave. You shoulda called the record *A Casket of Blues*!"

The two friends laughed themselves to tears.

One Sunday morning, after many years of defection, Emma announced that she wanted Harlan to drive her and Sam to church.

Harlan gazed at the blue straw hat on Emma's head; she looked like someone's grandmother. It was the first time he truly realized that his mother had grown old. His heart tugged.

"Church?"

"Negro, did I stutter?"

"No, ma'am."

Part X

The Summer of Love

Chapter 89

In that famed city by the bay where Mark Twain once spent an entire summer in his winter coat, a hundred thousand people adorned in bell-bottoms and midriffs, high on everything including life, gathered in Golden Gate Park committed to resurrecting love.

Rebelling against the Vietnam War, oppression, and a social system replete with rigid ideas, the hippies tossed away bras and neckties, grew their hair, stuck flowers behind their ears, hung leis around their necks, flashed peace signs, and liberated sex from its dark closet—renamed it "free love" and flaunted it in the faces of the bourgeoisie.

Black with white, men with men, women with women, young with old. Free love. Love for everyone, with everyone. All of that fucking and freethinking required lots of LSD and marijuana. The demand transformed small-time dope peddlers into low-level tycoons, which is why Harlan had money to burn.

The dice rolled swiftly across the wooden floor, bounced against the baseboard, and displayed seven black dots, prompting a chorus of curse words from the losers.

Grinning, Solomon Hardison, a beady-eyed amateur boxer, swept up the wrinkled bills and shoved them deep into his pants pocket.

Harlan huffed: "Ain't you gonna give me a chance to win my

money back?"

Solomon's grin stretched wider. "You're what I call a glutton for punishment."

"Never mind all of that," Harlan said, peeling off ten five-dollar bills. He waved the money in Solomon's face. "You down or what?"

Solomon shrugged. "Sure, fool. I'll keep taking till you're broke."

They were supposed to be playing music, but a midday downpour had sent them running from the backyard into the clawing heat of the basement. It was July, too warm to play in that poorly ventilated cave. So the musicians waited out the rain with gin, pot, and dice.

"Lemme see." Harlan plucked the dice from the floor and set them in the palm of his hand, testing the weight. He then brought the dice close to his eyeballs to examine the validity of the black dots.

"Ain't nothing wrong with them shakers!" Solomon exclaimed.

"Yep, they brand new. I saw Solomon take them out of the box with my very own eyes," John Smith said.

Harlan shot John a hard look. "I can't trust your eyes," he laughed. "I seen your women!"

"Ug-leeee!" someone railed from the other side of the room.

The basement shook with laughter.

"Aww, later for y'all."

"Roll the fucking dice," Solomon demanded. "Let me get this money real quick. I got things to do."

Harlan curled his fingers around the dice, raising his hand above his head, then turned to Solomon. "Double or nothing?"

"We could do triple or nothing if you want."

The dice skated across the floor.

Snake eyes!

Harlan pounded his fist into his palm. "Shit, shit, shit!"

The door creaked open. "Hey," Emma called from atop the landing, "the rain's stopped."

They played till five, and then one by one the musicians and onlookers headed elsewhere. But John stayed behind, parked himself on the porch steps alongside Harlan, and lit a cigarette.

Beneath a darkening sky, they ogled and grinned at the beautiful things posturing billowy Afros, platform shoes, and miniskirts. Even though Independence Day was eight days gone, the nights continued to erupt with firecrackers, cherry bombs, and the silver sputter of sparklers.

A tall brown beauty, dressed in a psychedelic halter dress, sauntered across the street in her bare feet, waving as she approached. "Hey, y'all." She nodded at John, bent over, and planted a kiss on Harlan's cheek. "The music was good tonight."

"Just tonight?"

"Aww, it's always good." She slid her hands over her curvy hips. "So, um, you got something for me?"

"You got something for me?" Harlan shot back.

She nodded, slipped her hand down the front of her dress, and plucked out a rolled bill.

John gave his head a little shake and peered off down the street.

Harlan took the money, went into the house, and returned with a small bag of marijuana.

"Thanks, baby," she cooed, slipping it from his fingers.

"Thanks is all you got for me?"

"For now," she offered with a wink. "See ya later?"

"Yeah."

John and Harlan watched the hypnotic roll and bounce of her ass beneath the thin dress. When she was out of earshot, John muttered, "I don't think she's wearing any drawers."

Harlan chuckled. "Believe me, she ain't."

John stood, stretched his arms high above his head, and yawned.

"You out?"

"Yeah, man, I gotta go make some bread."

"All right then." Harlan presented his open hand. "Stay tight."

John slapped his palm with his own. "You know it."

Chapter 90

When a phone rings at that time of the morning (1:15 a.m.), it can't be good news. Even those who are welcoming the birth of their first or fifth child have the good sense (and manners) to wait until the sun is up before they start dialing numbers to spread the happy word.

Harlan was snoring on the couch, having fallen asleep in the middle of watching the *Johnny Carson show*. He was dreaming he was playing a trombone. Lizard was alongside him, strumming his trumpet like a banjo. Using a peacock plume to conduct the orchestra of two was Harlan's grandfather, dressed in the suit and brown shoes he was buried in.

The phone jolted Harlan from his dream. He sat up and stared stupidly at the American flag fluttering on the black-and-white Zenith console until the phone rang a second time.

"Yeah, h-hello?"

"Harlan? Harlan? They killed John."

Harlan rubbed mucous from his left eye. "What? Who is this?"

"It's Solomon, man. Did you hear me? The fucking pigs killed John."

Harlan gave his head a hard shake. "John who?" He knew at least six.

"John Smith."

"W-what?"

"Goddamn cracker-ass crackers!" Solomon sobbed. "Harlan? You there?"

"Yeah, I'm here," he whispered in a state of disbelief. "Where you at?"

"In Newark, at the diner across from the Fourth Precinct."

Harlan's knees threatened to buckle.

"You coming, man?"

"Yeah," Harlan croaked, "I'll be there."

***

Six blocks from the diner. That's as close as Harlan got before coming upon the sea of people clogging the streets and sidewalks as if it was a Saturday afternoon and someone was giving away money.

Figuring the cops had more important things to do than write tickets, Harlan parked the car next to a hydrant and walked the rest of the way.

Springfield and Belmont avenues were congested with dozens of taxis from Newark and the surrounding towns. The black drivers of those cabs were shaking their fists and shouting at the riot gear–clad police officers who had formed a human barrier in front of their precinct.

Across the street, residents of the Hayes Homes housing projects streamed from the buildings, shouting obscenities and accusations. The police shouted back through bullhorns. Ordered the crowd to disperse and the area cleared, but their demands fell on dead ears.

Harlan mopped sweat from his brow and elbowed his way through the crowd into the packed diner. He spotted Solomon seated in a booth, surrounded by a group of men who Harlan did not recognize.

"Yo, make room for my man," Solomon said. The guy sitting next to him slid out of the booth and stood.

Harlan sat down, rested one elbow on the table, and curled his fingers around his chin. The heat inside of the diner was even more oppressive than it was outside.

"What's happening? Are all those people out there because of John?"

Solomon nodded. "Story goes, pigs stopped John on Fifteenth Avenue. Who knows why? They exchange words and then the pigs pull John out of his cab and start wailing on him."

Harlan plucked a bunch of napkins from the silver holder and wiped his face. "Who told you that?"

Solomon aimed his index finger at the pudgy Latino sitting across the table. "Guillermo saw the whole thing. Ran down the street to get me. By the time we got back, the pigs and John were gone."

"There was so much fucking blood, man," Guillermo said. "Like someone gutted a cow."

"Puddles of it," Solomon added.

Harlan plunged his fingers into his hair. "Then what happened?"

"So," Solomon continued, "me and G walk down to the police station to see what's what. When we get here, there's these two chicks outside screaming bloody murder..." He trailed off, took a moment to swallow his rage. "The chicks said they saw the pigs drag a dead man from the police car into the station."

"And how do you know it was John?"

"Who else could it be?"

Harlan nodded.

"So these girls ain't shutting up, right? They calling the pigs murderers... talking about their mamas... sayin' straight-up foul shit, right?"

Harlan's head bounced again.

"So the cops laugh it off, call the girls crazy, tell 'em maybe if they put down the reefer and got off their black asses and went to work instead of lying up on welfare making babies every year, they wouldn't have time to be in the streets telling lies."

The men around the table grumbled.

"But the sisters ain't letting up. People start coming 'round, listening, asking them questions. The pigs get real nervous. I say, *Where's that taxi man you beat up on Fifteenth Avenue?* And the pigs just look at each other. They back off, whisper into their walkie-talkies—"

"Next thing you know," Guillermo interrupted with a snap of his fingers, "pigs are everywhere—running out of the station, pulling up in cars, dropping out of the sky. Uniformed, under-cover—the fucking calvary."

Solomon flexed his fingers. "I'm telling you, Harlan, them motherfuckers killed John, and they're going to get away with it again, just like they did with all the others!"

Guillermo called out the names of black men who had been recently killed by police: "Lester Long, Bernard Rich, Walter Mathis..."

Outside, the mob of people was punching the air with their fists, chanting, "*Show us John Smith! Show us John Smith!*"

John Smith. Not the last straw, but certainly the one that broke the camel's back.

Newark's black residents had been harassed and abused by

police for decades. Stopped for driving or walking while black, cars tossed, pockets emptied—all while the cops called them niggers, jungle bunnies, and spooks.

The victims? What could they do but stand there still and silent, taking it all, swallowing it whole, like a rape victim waiting for it to end so they could get home and see their mamas, women, children, or just another fucking day.

Living under those conditions was as difficult as walking a tightrope in high wind.

But they did it. Every single day, they did it.

Recently the police brutality had escalated to murder on a regular basis.

Police officers were picking off black men as if it was open season. The families of the dead brought one wrongful-death lawsuit after another, but it was all to no avail. Not only were the officers always cleared of any wrongdoing, they were commended for their actions.

"No Cause for Indictment" became an all-too-familiar headline in the local and national newspapers. Lady Justice might have been blind, but that didn't disqualify her from being racist.

"Look at them," Solomon growled, jabbing his finger against the glass window. "They're scared as hell."

The police officers had never seen so many black and brown faces in one place. It seemed as if all of the Negroes in America had swooped down on Newark.

"Yeah, crackers, the chickens have come home to roost!" Solomon hollered.

His statement was followed by a burst of applause and barking in the diner.

Outside, the agitated crowd drifted closer and closer to the band of officers: "*Show us John Smith! Show us John Smith!*"

Suddenly, a Molotov cocktail exploded against the side of the police station, sending everyone scattering for cover. Warning shots were fired, another cocktail was thrown, rocks and bottles hurled through the hot night.

The police fired more shots into the dark sky; a trash can was tossed through the window of the diner, and Harlan and the others ran out into the chaos of the streets. The cops raced behind, clobbering anyone in reach of their swinging batons.

Heart laboring in his chest, lungs on fire, Harlan's body threatened to fail him. He broke from the crowd and stumbled down a narrow street into an alley. Hiding behind a row of stinking garbage cans, he sat on the filthy ground, trying to catch his breath. In all directions, the night quaked with sirens, gunshots, and breaking glass. Fires were lit, sending spiraling plumes of black smoke into the black sky.

When he reemerged, it was dawn.

The crowds were gone, but the evidence of their righteous indignation could be spotted everywhere—in busted car windows, slashed tires, and the smoldering guts of vandalized businesses.

When Harlan reached his car, he found the driver's-side mirror dangling. Thankfully, that was the only damage the vehicle had suffered. Hands trembling, he coasted the car slowly down the street, looking out on the dazed faces of the residents left to deal with the wreckage. He hadn't traveled more than three blocks before a police cruiser shot into the street, blocking him.

The white officers jumped from the vehicle and barreled toward him, guns drawn. Harlan cut the engine and threw his hands into the air. Before he could utter a word, they ripped open both front doors.

The taller of the two officers hooked Harlan roughly by the neck, dragged him from the car, and slammed him onto the ground. His foot came down on Harlan's cheek, forcing his face into the hot asphalt. "Where's the guns, nigger!" he screamed while his partner searched frantically beneath the car seats, inside the glove compartment and trunk.

"I-I don't have any guns."

The officer buried his shoe deeper into Harlan's skull.

"I didn't find any guns," the second officer said, "but I did find this."

"Well, look at that. What we got here is a dope-dealing nigger," the first officer cackled. "On your feet!" He yanked Harlan up by his Afro while the other man dangled a wrinkled paper bag in his face. "You know what this is?"

Harlan dropped his eyes. "Nope."

But he knew exactly what it was. It was five-to-ten in the state penitentiary.

Chapter 91

At police headquarters, Harlan was booked and finger-printed before being transferred to the Essex County Penitentiary. There he was placed in a cell with three other prisoners, including the dissident poet and playwright the white people called "the most famous nigger in Newark."

LeRoi Jones greeted Harlan with a toothy smile. "What they pin on you, brother?"

Harlan considered the small, stoop-shouldered man. "I had a bag of reefer in my car."

"You had reefer in the car, or they put reefer in your car?"

"Nah, it was mine."

LeRoi shook his head. "They charged me with illegal possession of two firearms. Two," he repeated bitterly, holding up a pair of slim fingers. "Them sons of bitches put them guns in that car."

Harlan sat down on the wooden bench.

"And," LeRoi continued, "these mofos talking 'bout a $25,000 bond!"

"Shhhhhhiiiiiit," whistled from the mouth of a man seated to the left of Harlan.

Frustrated, LeRoi grabbed hold of the thick metal bars and gave them a good rattling. After loudly condemning the police, the president, and all of white America, his eyes grazed over Harlan and the other two men. Their docility sparked a second wave of rage from him.

"I hope that cabbie appreciates what his brothers and sisters are out there doing for him," LeRoi snapped.

"How could he?" Harlan uttered blandly. "A dead man can't appreciate much of anything, not even the coffin they put him in."

LeRoi frowned. "Oh, you ain't hear?"

"Hear what?"

"He ain't dead."

Harlan's head snapped up. "What?"

"I said, he ain't dead. Banged up some, but John Smith is still amongst the living."

"You sure about that?" Harlan's voice was hopeful.

"Yep, I'm positive. Saw him myself."

That night, the streets erupted in violence once again.

Realizing that the Newark police force was ill-equipped and outnumbered, Governor Richard Hughes called in the National Guard, and the state police declared a state of emergency and instituted a citywide curfew.

Prison had a way of draining people of their hope and humanity. But Harlan didn't have to worry about that because he'd gone in empty.

He spent all of his free time in the library. Reading books helped to pass the time. Jim Thompson became a favorite author. Harlan read *The Killer Inside Me* four times.

He refused to keep track of the days because he'd learned during his imprisonment at Buchenwald that counting time was just another form of torture. He kept mostly to himself, and only spoke when spoken to—preferring to save his words for Sunday when his parents came to visit.

It was during one of those Sunday visits that Harlan first saw the magazine. Emma placed it facedown on the table and pushed it across to him. She leaned back and waited for his reaction.

Sam was sitting next to her, fidgeting. Fearful of being knifed to death, he always spent his visits nervously surveying the room.

Harlan reached for the magazine. "What's this?"

It was the July 21 issue of *Time* magazine; gracing the cover, in all of his glorious blackness, was none other than John Smith.

Harlan read the headline aloud: "*Anatomy of a Race Riot.*" He held the magazine away from his face and beamed. "Wow," he murmured, "*Time* magazine."

"Humph," Emma sounded. "He been here to see you?"

"No, but—"

She snatched the magazine from Harlan's hand and glowered at John's image. "People sure do get funny when they get a little money," she spat.

"Mama, I don't think—"

"I can't imagine how much *Time* magazine paid him for the interview. I'm sure he got double because he's on the cover. You'd think he'd come and visit, maybe even give you a few dollars. After all, if it weren't for him, you wouldn't be in here at all!" Emma flung the magazine onto the table. "Lucky you don't need his *Time* magazine money. Matter fact, even if he offers, don't you take a dime, not one red cent. You know how many people died out there in the name of his black ass? As far as I'm concerned, that there is blood money, and you don't need no blood on your hands."

Emma bit her lip, clutched her pink leather purse to her bosom. Her eyes swept over the faces of the prisoners and their visitors. When she looked back at Harlan, the fire in her eyes had paled. She'd said what was in her heart, and now she could move on.

"So, your father damn near ran us into a truck. He got new glasses, but I think he's just getting too damn old to drive."

Chapter 92

It took six months, but John Smith did visit Harlan, on a frigid January day. The scars on his face had healed and faded. He was sporting a bushy mustache, but that new addition didn't detract from the wounded look in his eyes.

"What took you so long?"

"I thought you were sore at me," John responded sheepishly.

"Why would I be sore?"

"Because you're in here, and I'm not."

Harlan shook a cigarette loose from the pack. "You want one?"

"Nah," John said. "I quit."

"Why would you think a thing like that?"

"What?"

"Why would you think that you should be the one in here instead of me?"

John folded his hands on the table. "I dunno, it seems..." He cast his eyes up to the ceiling as if the words he needed were embedded in the cracks. "I guess I feel responsible for everything."

Harlan turned his head and pushed a plume of smoke into the stagnant air. "Yeah, I get that. I saw the magazine."

"Yeah?"

Harlan took a long drag of his cigarette. "Big stuff."

"Not really. It's not like people want my autograph or

anything." John chuckled. "It might have meant something if I had died, then I would have been a martyr. Martyrs mean something to people."

"Yeah," Harlan breathed. "How's your mom doing?"

"She all right, I guess."

"You guess? Ain't you staying with her?"

"Nah, I got a room at the Esquire Motel."

"Oh," Harlan mumbled. "Still driving a cab?"

"My license was revoked."

"More time for you to do what you love."

John shook his head. "I wish, but the cops jacked up my front teeth. Can't blow with bad teeth, they'll fly right out my head."

They both laughed.

"How about you?" The smile slipped from John's lips.

"Can't complain," said Harlan. "Three squares a day, lots of reading material, lots of time to think. What you gonna do, right? I gotta play the cards I was dealt."

John's smile returned. "Reading?"

Harlan smashed the cigarette butt into the ashtray, shook another from the pack, and lit it. "Yeah, man, I'm reading. I mean, not the shit you read, Oscar Wilde and Ayn Rand, but I'm working my way up to them."

"That's good to hear," John said. "What is it they say? Oh yeah, *Knowledge is power*."

"You got that shit right."

They fell into a thoughtful silence. The hum of conversations enwrapped them like a well-worn quilt.

"Hey," Harlan piped, "you gonna like this." He rolled the cigarette into the right knot of his lip. "So I read *Narrative of the*

Life of Frederick Douglass."

Curiosity warming his face, John leaned in. "That's a good book."

"Yeah, it was. Fred said this thing that stayed with me—"

"Fred? You know him like that?" John teased.

Harlan waved his hand. "Seriously, man, listen, there was this one line in the book that stayed with me for days."

"Uh-huh."

"We keep calling what happened in Newark and all of them other cities riots, but it was more than that," Harlan spouted excitedly. "It was a rebellion." Proud of himself, he leaned back, puffed out his chest, and smashed the second cigarette into the ashtray alongside the first.

"Yeah, I would agree. But what does that have to do with Frederick Douglass?"

Harlan lurched forward. "I figure these white folks keep calling these rebellions riots because Frederick Douglass said, *The thing worse than rebellion is the thing that causes rebellion.* And we all know what—or shall I say, who—that thing is, right?"

John nodded, grinning.

"If they—the newspapers and such—called what happened here and everywhere else what it really was, they would be implicating themselves, right? Revealing themselves as the problem."

John stretched his hand across the table. "Harlan Elliott, you dropping knowledge like a scholar. Gimme some."

Harlan whacked John's palm three times.

Later, when John was preparing to leave, Harlan touched his wrist. "Let me ask you something."

"Yeah?"

"Do you remember that first time you came to 119th Street

to see me?"

"Yeah, I remember."

"You said that God saved us and brought us back home to our families because He had a plan for us."

John nodded.

"Do you think this thing that happened to you was God's plan?"

John touched the tip of his tongue to his loose front teeth. "Maybe. I don't know."

Chapter 93

Emma had given the last bit of the money she and Sam saved from the sale of the Harlem brownstone to an expensive attorney who hadn't been able to get the charges against Harlan dropped but had managed to wrangle his sentence down from ten years to five.

Harlan was an exemplary prisoner, so after serving three years and four months, he was paroled on good behavior. On a wet, blustery morning in November of 1970, he walked out of the Essex County Penitentiary and into his mother's open arms. She hugged him so tight it hurt.

"This the last time white folks gonna take you from me," she murmured into his neck.

In the twenty-year-old Chevrolet Fleetmaster, Emma took the backseat and Harlan sat up front, next to his father. The butter-colored car looked out of place amongst the snazzy Cadillacs and Lincolns traveling the highways.

Harlan pointed at the automobiles that roared past them. "Maybe you should get a new car."

"For what? Ain't a thing wrong with the one I have."

Harlan didn't know how his father did it, but he'd kept the Fleetmaster running as smooth as the day it rolled off the assembly line.

The family, happy to be together again, chattered joyfully above the radio, their voices running in hot competition with

Diana Ross. "*Ain't no mountain high enough, ain't no valley low enough, ain't no river wide enough...*"

"We gonna stop to get something to eat?" Harlan asked, rolling down the window to inhale the damp November air. "I've spent three years and four months dreaming about sinking my teeth into a juicy cheeseburger."

Emma clutched her coat collar and backed away from the cold air. "Cheeseburger? Boy, I got a mess of food back at the house."

"Your mama been cooking for three days," Sam said.

"That's a lie," Emma laughed. "I only been cooking for two days." As they sped along, Sam shivered and said, "Harlan, close that damn window. It ain't summertime."

"Aw, Sam, if the boy wants some air, let him have it." Emma coiled her scarf around her head.

"Okay, okay, just one more gulp." Harlan pushed his entire head out the window. *Yes*, he thought to himself, *freedom not only smells sweet, it tastes sweet too.*

"Boy," Emma cried, slapping him on the shoulder, "get your big head back in this window before it's knocked clean off your shoulders!"

Sam turned to him. "You look like a dog with your head hanging out the window like that. Like an old mangy retriever!"

They were all laughing when Sam shot through the stop sign right into the path of a speeding fire truck, and was killed instantly. Emma's spine, pelvis, and legs were mangled unrecognizable. Harlan was ejected through the window like an arrow.

Miraculously, Harlan only suffered a broken arm and skin lacerations, so he was at Emma's side when, two days after the accident, she let go of this life and slipped into the next.

It took three male nurses to wrench Harlan's hand from hers.

During their long and short careers, the hospital staff had bore witness to many things, but none of them could ever remember hearing a man scream the way Harlan did after his mother died. The gut-wrenching howl he released over Emma's quiet body would haunt them for years.

Chapter 94

While Harlan had been in prison, Gomez developed a cough that turned out to be lung cancer. A week after he was diagnosed, he died at home in Harlem, leaving his wife grief-stricken and alone. Lucille was still battling despair when Emma, her oldest and dearest friend in the whole wide world, passed away.

Lucille wasn't in the best of health, but nothing could keep her from saying a final goodbye to the woman who had been more like a sister to her than her own kin. And besides, Harlan was the son she'd never had.

When Lucille stepped off that Greyhound bus and saw Harlan standing there, looking the epitome of the motherless child he now truly was, her heart broke into pieces. He stared out at her from eyes so dark and recessed, they seemed like black holes. And he was thin, nearly as thin as he'd been when he first came home from Germany.

To be fair, Lucille didn't look much better. Her old eyes were red and puffy, her knees were swollen to the size of cantaloupes, and the wig she wore was dusty and ill-fitting.

They greeted each other with forced smiles and firm hugs.

Harlan reached for the blue cosmetics case Lucille carried. "Is this all you have?"

"No. The suitcase is under the bus."

Sure he could manage the army-green Samsonite with his

one good hand, Harlan pulled on the case's handle, but the weight of it nearly dislocated his arm. "What you got in here, Lucille?"

He had to ask a stranger to place it in the trunk of the borrowed Cadillac.

In the car, a litany of sad songs that neither of them wanted to hear streamed from the radio. Harlan lowered the volume. They had ridden in silence for a few miles before Lucille raised a question.

"You get in touch with your people down in Macon?"

Uncle John had died in '49. As for his uncle James, he'd married, moved to Texas, and that was the last anyone knew. Seth was dead as well, and Emma hadn't kept in touch with his widow or their children, so who knew if they were still in Macon or had moved on to some other city or state. Harlan hadn't bothered to investigate because he didn't know them very well to begin with. As far as he was concerned, the only family he had now was Lucille.

He chewed a sliver of skin from his bottom lip and spat it into the air. "Nah, I didn't."

"Hmmm," Lucille sounded. "Well, I hope you don't mind, but I went ahead and placed an obituary in the *Macon Telegraph*. I think there might be some people left there who still remember your parents."

Once at the house, Harlan called on a neighbor to haul Lucille's suitcase into the living room. Not having received an answer to his first inquiry, Harlan asked again: "What's in this suitcase?"

Lucille sighed, unlatched the case, and flipped it open. Harlan cast a puzzled look over the contents—a jumble of clothes, loaves of bread, cans of beans, tuna fish, and Spam.

Lucille blushed like a caught child. "I don't know what happened. I put my clothes in, but it looked so empty, it didn't feel right. It just wasn't full enough. I know that sounds stupid. I just started throwing things in. Suitcases should always be full..." She let her words trail off, embarrassed.

After a long moment Harlan said, "Well, that's okay." He knew he was supposed to comfort her, but he didn't have it in him.

Eyes glistening, Lucille stood waiting for a hug that never came.

Harlan cleared his throat, crouched over the suitcase, and scooped up three loaves of bread. "I'll put these in the kitchen."

The funeral service was held at the Union Baptist Church on Pennington Avenue, where Sam and Emma had been members.

Although Harlan had never attended the church, or even stepped foot in the building, he had become acquainted with a few of the congregants—people Sam and Emma had had over to the house for dinner or a game of spades.

That day, the pews were filled with men in dark suits and women wearing big black hats touching handkerchiefs to the corners of their eyes.

When Harlan arrived, the familiars swooped in, hugging him, cupping his face in their hands, kissing his wet cheeks.

"They were real good people. Real good."

"Your mama sure did love you."

"If you need anything, anything at all, you just call me."

"Tragic, tragic!"

Harlan must have said thank you a thousand times that day.

With Lucille, John, and Mayemma at his side, he swayed before the matching pearl-colored caskets. He didn't think he had any tears left, but when he looked down into his parents' still and silent faces—sadness flooded his chest and he began to weep.

Chapter 95

In May of '71, Emma's garden burst to life.

Harlan spent an entire day sitting in the backyard, staring at the flowers and sipping Scotch. When the bottle was empty, he went into the house, removed a container of bleach from beneath the kitchen sink, and dumped it all over the delicate blooms.

Back in the house, he hung a noose from the attic rafters, moved the toaster into the bathroom, placed all of his parents' various medications into a jar, and set it on the floor by his bed. Some months earlier, he'd discovered a gun in the hall closet, hidden away in an old hatbox. There was one bullet in the chamber.

Every day Harlan walked to and from the liquor store to buy a bottle of Scotch. Every three days he bought a carton of cigarettes. Sometimes he picked up a chicken or fish dinner, but mostly he survived on canned soup and grilled cheese sandwiches.

Harlan kept the house closed up and dark, rarely answered the door or the telephone. Neighbors and friends finally took the hint and left him alone. He spent sleepless hours gazing at family photos, listening to old records, lying on the couch crucified and drunk, sitting so still he could hear the blood sloshing through his veins.

The days came and went; the dead crowded his dreams. He

knew the only way he could escape the ghosts was to join them.

When June arrived the fire hydrants were opened and young girls kicked off their shoes, slipped dandelions into their braids, and skipped through the spray.

On the night before the day he decided to take his life, Harlan went to a neighborhood bar. Way back by the jukebox, he stood alone savoring the music and drinking beer.

The following morning, he woke to fingers of light curled around the tattered window shades. It was Saturday. The air was fragrant with the scent of cut grass. Children on bicycles and roller skates streaked up and down the sidewalks. In the streets, older kids played stickball and skelly. In the driveways, men washed and waxed their automobiles.

Harlan went down to the kitchen and stood at the window, watching the world churn on despite him. He folded a piece of buttered bread into his mouth and went back to his room.

He sat on the bed and rattled the jar of pills near his ear. On the porch next door, a group of teenagers sang raucous and off-key, while the hum of crickets rose and fell above their sloppy serenade.

After a while, Harlan went into his parents' bedroom and stood on the carpeted floor, trembling like a newborn foal. The room was as they had left it—bed neatly made, curtains parted. A pair of Sam's trousers were draped neatly over the back of the leather armchair. Bottles of perfume lined the dressing table; a Bible sat closed on the nightstand. On the wall hung framed pictures of Harlan as a child, Emma's parents, Sam's mother, and the group photo taken in Montmartre.

When he felt ready, Harlan unscrewed the jar, grabbed a handful of pills, dropped one onto his tongue, and then another.

The closet door squeaked ajar just as the third pill careened down his throat.

That door.

It had been the bane of Emma's existence from the time they'd moved in. No matter what Sam did—oil the hinges, change the knob—the door refused to stay shut.

Harlan set the jar down and crossed the room. A foot from the closet, he spotted a pair of shoes peaking out from the shadows.

His heart quickened. When had the intruder broken in? While he was passed out drunk? He squinted at the shoes and swore he saw them move.

"Hey, man, hey, I don't want no trouble." Harlan scanned the bedroom for a weapon. "I got a gun, man. I will blow you the fuck away!" If he could hear the fright in his own voice, so could the trespasser. "You come out now, and I'll let you be on your way. No cops, I promise."

The telephone blared, and a startled Harlan stumbled backward, toppling the jar of pills, scattering the pink, yellow, and white tablets everywhere. He stood paralyzed with his back against the wall. His eyes remained glued to the threat in the closet. The phone continued to ring. Minutes ticked away and the only thing that changed in the room was the light.

Finally, summoning all of the courage he'd stored away for his suicide, Harlan flew at the closet door, ripped it open, and lunged into the darkness, arms whirling like a propeller.

His knuckles scraped cloth and cold wire hangers.

Harlan laughed at his own foolishness. How the brown shoes had broken rank and found their way to the front of the closet, he did not know. He picked them up and ran his fingers over the stiff chocolate-colored leather before flipping them over, exposing the mildly scuffed soles.

The shoes were laced. Harlan thought that was odd. He couldn't recall ever seeing Sam wear them, yet they looked familiar. So familiar that it triggered a memory he couldn't quite grasp.

The phone blared again.

"Hello?"

Lucille's concerned voice drifted into his ear: "Hey, baby, I'm just calling to check on you..."

Harlan's lips trembled.

"Harlan?"

"Yeah. Hey, Lucille." His voice rose, dipped, and splintered.

"You okay?"

"No. No, I'm not." Tears spilled down his cheeks, landed on the shoes, and tunneled clean tracks through the dust. "I don't want to be here no more," he sobbed.

"Well, baby," Lucille sighed, "you don't have to be there. You can be here, with me."

Harlan left Trenton that very night.

He didn't take much, just a few pieces of clothing, some photos, and his favorite guitar. Initially, he packed the brown shoes, but returned them at the last moment to the closet floor.

Locking the front door, Harlan set off down the street beneath a violet sky. By some divining he didn't understand, he knew he would never pass that way again.

Chapter 96

Lucille still lived in Harlem, but not in the grand home of her hey-day. She had been forced to leave that palace decades ago when her star had faded and she'd stopped making music and started emptying bedpans for a living. Now she lived in a tiny one-bedroom apartment on the sixth floor of a ten-story tenement building.

"It's not much, but it's home."

The apartment was crammed with relics from her former residence—large pieces of furniture, gaudy sculptures, and six-foot-tall vases filled with colorful plumes. Nearly every inch of wall was hidden beneath an array of family photos and framed memorabilia.

She pointed at the floral sofa. "You'll sleep there. It's one of those convertible beds. The bathroom is back there, kitchen over there. I think there's room in the hall closet to hang your clothes. What doesn't fit, you'll just have to leave in your suitcase." Lucille stopped talking, rested her hands on her hips, and considered her surroundings. "So this is it."

She slipped a set of keys from the pocket of her orange housedress and handed them to Harlan. "I think your mama and daddy would be glad to know that you're here."

The convertible bed turned out to be a monster that nightly sought to impale Harlan with its coiled metal springs.

The other problem was this: Every day, Lucille rose before dawn, clomped loudly into the kitchen (which was an extension of the living room), and flicked on the bright overhead lights and the radio. She made her coffee, clipped coupons, and placed telephone calls to various companies that were, according to her, "trying to railroad an old woman."

When she was done with Ma Bell and the others, Lucille spent an hour or so complaining about the rowdy neighbors above her, the president, the mayor, and the skank next door who didn't have the decency to keep her music to a respectable level when she knew good goddamn well there was a senior citizen on the other side of her wall.

Lucille would then march into the living room and stand above Harlan until he opened his eyes.

"Morning, Lucille."

"Well, good morning to you too. You want a cup of coffee? Some eggs? Bacon?"

"Sure."

"Okay. Do you want some eggs? Bacon?" She was also becoming forgetful.

For a time, being back in Harlem was exactly what Harlan needed.

He'd stopped drinking. Cold turkey. Didn't even think about copping a bag of weed. He took up walking—covering miles each day. Sometimes he would just find a shaded park bench and sit for hours people-watching.

For a brief period Harlan would buy a newspaper and read it from cover to cover, but he found the news too depressing.

Twin Boys Found Strangled to Death in Bushwick Apartment Building.

Entire Family Lost in Early-Morning Three-Alarm Fire.

In a case of "mistaken identity," prominent black poet Henry Dumas was shot to death at a Harlem train station by a New York Transit Authority police officer.

Another Nazi War Criminal Found in...

Thoughts of suicide still lingered—coming and going like his desire for alcohol and reefer.

One steamy August day, Harlan walked himself all the way to his old neighborhood and stood in the shadow of the colossal housing tenement that had displaced his and hundreds of other families.

Flooded with memories and despondent, Harlan continued east on 133rd Street, somehow made it across the busy Harlem River Drive, and spent an hour mesmerized by the ebb and flow of the filthy river. He found himself gripped by a melancholy so severe, he had to fight the urge to plunge himself over the railing into the murky waters.

The episode was as unnerving as it was sobering.

Harlem held many memories, but the ghosts that remained were bitter and vengeful. Harlan was fragile, which made him easy prey—he knew he couldn't stay in Harlem, not if he intended to live long enough to figure out what God had planned for him.

Chapter 97

He had been living with Lucille for a year when in the summer of 1972 she decided to rid herself of the awful dusty wig she'd been wearing for a decade. Her intention that day was to chop off her processed hair for a natural cropped style, made popular by the forward-thinking women of the Black Is Beautiful movement.

Harlan tagged along for moral support.

Lucille climbed into the red-leather and chrome chair, snatched the scarf from her head, and said, "Take it all off."

The barber, a young man with silver slats between his teeth, twirled a black comb in his hand like a baton. "You sure that's what you want?" Lucille shot him a lopsided look. "Don't let this gray hair fool you, baby. I still know what I want and when I want it." She was the only woman in the shop that day, the grand dame amongst a bevy of loud-talking men, unused to having to censor themselves in the very place they had always been able to speak freely. More than just a place to get a haircut, the barbershop was a church, meeting hall, classroom, and sanctuary all balled into one.

But all of that changed when the women started wearing their hair like the men. Now they crowded into the barbershops reeking of musk oil and Afro Sheen, wearing dashikis, wooden bracelets stacked clear up their forearms, and ridiculously large hooped earrings.

The women fully expected to be treated like the black queens they claimed their ancestors to be. All of this to say, there was to be no cursing when a lady was in the shop. Even the bull-dagger barbers rolled their eyes when they saw them coming.

After the barber had worked his magic on Lucille, he spun the chair around, bringing her face-to-face with her mirrored image. She sat stupefied, gently fingering her cropped silver hair.

"Lawd," she whispered, looking at Harlan. "Whadya think?"

"I think you look beautiful." He rested his hand on her shoulder. "Now all you need is a pair of those big hoop earrings the sistas wear."

Lucille shook her head. "Nah, I'm fine with my pearls. Those things they wearing look too much like handcuffs."

Above their heads, the bladed fans cycled, shredding the heat into a smooth breeze that swept the fallen tufts of hair across the floor into corners and out onto the sidewalk whenever someone entered or left the shop.

A tall man pulled the door back, mistook the rolling hair for rodents, and did a hop-shuffle that entangled his ankles. He would have fallen flat on his face if Harlan hadn't grabbed his arm. The scene was comical—barbers and customers rippled with laughter.

"You okay, pops?"

The man barely glanced at Harlan; his eyes were too busy roaming the black-and-white-checkered floor.

"Herbert?" Lucille called. "Herbert Bolden?"

The man squinted at Lucille and frowned. "Where the hell is your hair?"

"Well, hello to you too!"

Herbert gawked.

"It ain't polite to stare," Lucille admonished. "How you been? How's Arlene? I ain't seen y'all in years."

He shuffled over and circled Lucille like an exhibit. "Arlene died last fall," he mumbled, reaching to touch her hair.

"Sorry to hear that. She lived a long life. What was she, fifteen years old?"

"Seventeen," Herbert corrected distractedly.

Lucille looked at Harlan's puzzled face. "We talking 'bout his dog, not his wife. He ain't never married—no woman with any sense would have him," she clucked.

Herbert spun around on well-worn shoe heels. "Who you?"

"See," Lucille shook her head, "he don't have any manners. Never did. He's the man who kept you from falling on your ass, Herbert. It just happened, don't you remember?"

Not taking his eyes off Harlan, he fanned his hand in Lucille's face. "Hush up, woman."

Harlan offered his hand. "My name is Harlan."

Herbert's long face stretched longer. He eyed the younger man's hand with disdain. "I ain't ask your name, I asked who you are."

Harlan moved his hand down to his side. "I don't understand."

"I know you ain't her son, 'cause she don't have no kids. So who are you? Cousin, nephew..." He twisted his neck around to look at Lucille. "Boyfriend?"

"Oh, Herbert, stop being nasty. You know Harlan. He's Emma and Sam's son."

"Emma and Sam who?"

"Elliott."

Herbert brought his face close to Harlan's. "So it is," he said, pulling back. "Heard 'bout your parents. Terrible."

Harlan swallowed.

Lucille climbed from the chair. "I know you don't remember this old fool," Lucille said to Harlan, patting Herbert's back, "but he used to own Club Lola down on 57th Street."

Harlan nodded. "It sounds familiar."

Herbert slipped into the chair Lucille had vacated and pulled one long leg over the other.

The barber drummed Herbert's shoulder with his metal comb. "You trying to start a riot in here? There are three other people ahead of you, Herbert. Get up."

Herbert waved him away. "In a minute. I'm talking." He returned his attention to Harlan. "I used to have a club right here in Harlem, but when the white people stopped coming uptown, I had to move to Midtown where they were spending money."

"Uh-hmm, good times," Lucille moaned.

"Do you still have the club?" Harlan asked.

"Nah, left that life years ago. Now I'm into real estate."

"Slumlord," one of the waiting customers stage-whispered.

Herbert ignored the insult. "I got a few buildings here in Harlem and two in Brooklyn. Almost had the Theresa, but that crooked L.B. Woods swiped it from under me."

Harlan's face glowed. "The Hotel Theresa?"

"The very same," Herbert said before turning to look at the man who had slandered him. "Now, L.B. Woods is the person you should be calling a slumlord. My properties are all well maintained."

Lucille pulled a compact from her purse and flipped it open.

"Hey, ain't it up for sale again?"

Herbert dragged his hand across his mouth. "Sure is, but it don't make no sense to buy it."

"Why's that?" Harlan asked.

"'Cause Harlem ain't the kingdom it once was—all the royalty is dead." Herbert struggled up from the chair. "So what you doing with yourself?"

"Looking for work."

"Looking?" Herbert's eyes rolled over Harlan. "How you been supporting yourself so far? You pushing drugs?"

Harlan shook his head. "No, sir. My parents left me a little insurance money."

"Uh-huh." Herbert sounded doubtful. "Welp, ain't much work to be found 'round here. What can you do?"

"A little bit of everything, I guess."

"Are you good with your hands?"

"Yes, sir, my daddy made sure of that."

"You know about boilers?"

"Some."

"You got any plumbing skills?"

"I can get by."

"Most important thing is taking care of the garbage and keeping the building clean. Sweeping, mopping, and such."

"Important for what?"

"Yeah, important for what?" Lucille echoed.

"Can't you see we mens is talking business?" Herbert snapped.

Lucille threw up her hands.

"I have a friend. Ira. Ira Rubin. He's been on the hunt for a new super... superintendent for his building in Brooklyn. The guy he's got now just ain't working out. It's a pretty sweet deal. You work six days, live rent-free. I don't know what he's paying, but Ira's always been fair. You got a wife? Kids?"

"No."

"Good. The super lives in a kitchenette. Perfect for a bachelor like yourself." Herbert looked Harlan up and down again. "Your father was a good man. Are you a good man?"

Harlan always believed himself to be good, just a little misguided at times. "Yes, sir."

Herbert grunted. "Well, are you interested?"

"Yes, sir, I am."

"You heard the part about Brooklyn, right?"

"Uh-huh. I ain't got no problem with Brooklyn."

Part XI

A Murder in Brooklyn

Chapter 98

There was a man, an old vet, his legs shot dead in some long-ago war, who spent his days rolling his rickety wheelchair up and down the avenues and boulevards of that central Brooklyn neighborhood known as Crown Heights. His place of residence was a mystery, as was his name. He appeared and disappeared like the sun in a winter-torn sky.

He was always attired in army fatigues, highly polished brown shoes, and a dented helmet pushed down low over his eyes. On warm days he unbuttoned his shirt, allowing the panels to flap open, exposing the chain of sparkling dog tags splayed across his clean white undershirt.

He spoke only to himself—spewing long, rambling monologues that went on for hours. When he wasn't blathering, he was belting out Italian operas. The authenticity of the compositions were a hotly debated subject amongst the old European residents who swore to God and country that they had heard a variety of mother tongues minced into the arias. Nevertheless, they forgave the mongering because his voice was so achingly beautiful. He performed these musical wonders all over Crown Heights.

On the morning Harlan moved into 245 Sullivan Place, the former-soldier-turned-troubadour parked his wheelchair in front of 245 and launched into Handel's "Messiah."

On that same morning, another old man sat in his apartment watching the street from his third-floor window; he spent most days doing just that: watching.

At his age, under his circumstances, there was little else to do but sit, watch, and wait for death to find him. He had no family to speak of, nor did he have a significant other. All he had to keep himself company was an ornery, toothless tabby named Meow. On that particular morning, Meow was propped on the windowsill, ignoring the flutter of pigeons on the opposite side of the glass, fascinated for the moment by the rope of smoke curling from the hot tip of the old man's cigarette.

Besides Harlan and the cripple, the only other people on the sidewalk were a roving band of Jehovah's Witnesses clutching briefcases and Bibles, casting pitiful looks at the barflies staggering home from a night of drinking.

The old man stubbed out his cigarette into a nearby ashtray, and glared down at the top of Harlan's head. "Every day there's one more than the day before," he whispered. "Meow, we are so lucky to see another morning, aren't we?"

The cat looked at him passively.

"Yes, yes, of course we are," he said, stroking the tabby's back.

Meow blinked slowly, deliberately, and then yawned.

"Is it breakfast time?"

The skin beneath Meow's fur twitched.

"Yes, I believe it is."

When Meow was done eating, she licked her whiskers and paws clean, jumped to the floor, and sauntered off, leaving the man alone with his thoughts and his saltine crackers. Outside his window, Harlan was gone, as was the cripple, replaced now by an elderly couple seated in matching mint-and-white-striped lawn chairs in the shade of a pin oak.

Just as the old man was about to retire to the cool darkness of his bedroom, his neighbor Eudora Penny marched into view. Tall and robust, sporting a pageboy wig the color of coffee grounds, she strode along with her battered navy-blue purse slung over her shoulder. That purse was as much a weapon as it was a receptacle for house keys, chewing gum, and compact face-powder.

He knew this because one late winter night back in 1962, when the streets were silent and empty, and the sky cloaked in a spooky deep blue, a would-be thief lunged at Eudora from the shadowy entrance of the playground. The two scuffled, falling against parked cars, until Eudora gained an upper hand and caught the goon by the throat. She shoved him against a tree and used her purse as a mallet, whacking it repeatedly across the mugger's face until he fell to his knees, pleading for mercy. Not once did Eudora Penny cry out for help. When she was done beating him, she calmly turned and walked away.

The old man had witnessed the entire assault from the window of his darkened bedroom. The savagery of it conjured memories, stoked a fire deep in the pit of his stomach. He'd returned to bed and spent the remainder of that night reliving the assault in a lucid dream. At daybreak, the old man had thrown his wool coat over his bathrobe and hastened outside in his slippers to check the sidewalk for blood. He was rewarded with a trail of burgundy droplets that led all the way to the gas station.

He suspected Eudora Penny wasn't who she claimed to be, and that excited him because neither was he.

Chapter 99

Brooklyn had been good for Harlan. The air there was different from Harlem. Less polluted. Fresh. Or maybe he just imagined it that way.

The work was even better for him. And there was plenty of it—more than enough to keep his mind from lingering on the past or lamenting the future. His days were consumed with fixing leaky faucets, unclogging toilets and drains, tightening doorknobs, replacing lightbulbs, mopping, polishing, and repainting. Every few days he fired up the incinerator and fed trash into the flames. Later, he shoveled the cool ashes into metal trash cans and set them out on the sidewalk for the sanitation trucks.

Most of the tenants had been welcoming and pleasant toward Harlan, although there were the odd few who couldn't seem to spare a kind word or smile. Within nine months, Harlan had been summoned to all of the apartments for one broken thing or another—all except 3C and 2E.

According to the talk swirling amongst the tenants, the occupant in 2E, Rose Talbot, was an old recluse who hadn't been out of her apartment in twenty years. She had a son who brought a week's worth of groceries over on Friday evenings.

The loon—their word, not Harlan's—in 3C was one Andrew Mailer.

"He only comes out in the evening."

"Or early in the morning. Very early."

"His clothes are too big."

"Baggy, like a clown."

"And he don't talk."

"Oh, he talks plenty! I can hear him through the wall."

"You can? He lives alone, doesn't he?"

"On the phone, maybe?"

"Never heard a phone ringing in that apartment."

"He has a cat. Orange and white, I think."

"How do you know that?"

"It got out into the hall once."

"So he's talking to the gosh darn cat?"

"May I never get that lonely."

On his days off, Harlan explored the Botanic Garden, read at the library, or strolled through echoing rooms at the Brooklyn Museum. Sometimes he'd go to Prospect Park, sit on a bench, and strum his guitar or watch the children go round and round on the colorful carousel horses.

Once a month he went uptown to spend the day with Lucille. Occasionally she'd prepare a meal, but mostly they went out to eat. Herbert often joined them.

"Aww, he ain't all bad," Lucille huffed when Harlan questioned their relationship. "He's alone, I'm alone, we both old as dirt—it just make sense. Don't you worry about me, what about yourself? You still a young man and easy on the eyes. You can get you a woman willing to give you some babies. Make me a god-grandmother. I'd like that."

"I'm sure you would." Harlan planted a kiss on her forehead. "Perhaps in my next life."

Chapter 100

One Tuesday morning, as Harlan fed garbage into the incinerator, the store manager of the neighborhood A&P was patrolling the grocery aisles—straightening boxes of cereal, fluffing loaves of bread, and thumping cantaloupes—in preparation for the onslaught of the day's shoppers.

Andrew Mailer arrived at the store just as the manager unlocked the door. He shuffled in, head bowed, black cap low over his flabby face, grunting at the manager's cheery greeting. Usually, he strode swiftly down the aisles, filled his cart with a week's worth of necessities, paid for the items without meeting the gentle smile of the cashier, and then hurried straight back to the safety and solace of his apartment.

That had been his routine week after week for two decades. But on Tuesday, June 19, 1973, things unfolded a bit differently.

At the door of his apartment, Harlan slipped out of his boots, dropped his work gloves on the floor, and went into his kitchen to prepare a breakfast of scrambled eggs and toast. He was standing over the sink, gulping down a tall glass of orange juice, when his doorbell rang.

Wrapped in a bathrobe and trembling with anger was Gabe Flores, the tenant in 2C. From the look of his bloodshot eyes and scattered hair, Gabe had probably just rolled out of bed.

"Mr. Flores, how can I help you this morning?"

Gabe was barely five feet tall. He took two backward steps so he didn't have to crane his neck up to meet Harlan's questioning gaze. "Look, I got Niagara Falls happening up in my apartment. Christ, my wife is having a fit. The crazy above us must have left the sink running or something! Christ, Harlan, the goddamn ceiling looks like it's gonna fall in... What are you waiting for, an invitation? Let's go already." Gabe sped off with his bathrobe flapping behind him.

With a sigh, Harlan shoved his feet back into his boots, picked up his gloves, and followed the man to his apartment.

When they entered, Gabe jabbed his finger at the kitchen ceiling. "Do you see this, Harlan? It's a fucking mess. What are you going to do about it?"

"Let me go upstairs and see what the problem is."

Gabe threw his hands into the air. "*Bastardo negro estúpido. Él va a ver cuál es el problema. Puedo ver cuál es el problema.*"

"Mr. Flores—"

"Are you kidding me? You don't have to go see what the problem is. I can see what the problem is and so can you. I don't need you to see what the problem is, I need you to *fix* the fucking problem!"

Harlan rang Andrew Mailer's doorbell several times and knocked as loudly as he dared at that time of the morning until he was left with no other choice but to use his master key.

"Hello? Mr. Mailer? Are you here? It's the super, Harlan Elliott. Hello?"

The air in the apartment reeked of cigarette smoke and a putrid litter box. Closing the door behind him, Harlan surveyed the cluttered living room with its matching sofas covered in aged plastic. On each of the two side tables stood lamps capped with embroidered shades, the stitching nearly invisible beneath years of dust.

"Mr. Mailer? It's Harlan Elliott, the super. Are you here?" He gingerly navigated the narrow artery that wound through the molehills and drifts of periodicals. In the kitchen, he sloshed through three inches of water, knelt down in the pool, and investigated the goings-on beneath the kitchen sink.

On the crumbling floor beneath the corroded pipes bandaged in moldy strips of cloth sat a quartet of mismatched bowls, placed there to catch the leaking water.

"Why didn't he just report this to me or the previous super?" Harlan grumbled to himself as he wrenched the valve until it stopped the flow of water.

Back in the living room, the legs of his overalls dripping wet, Harlan called out again, just to make sure: "Mr. Mailer!" Some of the old tenants were hard of hearing. He wouldn't want to startle the man to death. "I'm going to get the mop and bucket!" he continued to shout. "I'll be right back!"

Harlan's finger brushed the doorknob and he froze.

What if the man was dead?

Two tenants had passed away in the nine months he'd been on the job. One went in his sleep, another as he sat slurping Campbell's tomato soup. Both men were well into their eighties.

Harlan had no idea how old this Andrew Mailer fellow was because he had never seen him. He did know that whenever the other tenants talked about the guy, the operative word was always old.

Old coot.

Crazy old nut.

Harlan pulled his hand back and started toward the bedroom. "Mr. Mailer? Mr. Mailer?"

He was halfway through the living room when he spotted an object that nearly sent him screaming from the apartment.

Chapter 101

In hindsight, it was easy for Andrew to identify his misstep—a blunder so garishly bright, it glistened like fool's gold.

That morning at the A&P, as he'd stood considering packages of ground beef, a long, freckled arm reached across him.

"'Scuse me," the woman had said, plucking a package of lamb chops from the shelf.

Startled, Andrew scampered away, tugging viciously at the flat cap until it nearly covered his eyes. In the cereal aisle, he waited and waited for the finger-pointing, shouting, and sirens. Minutes passed, and when nothing in the store changed, he unstuck himself and hurried toward the registers.

He realized too late that he was standing behind the woman with the freckled arm. He tried to back out of the lane but was blocked by a young black mother pushing a cart stacked high with canned goods and soap powder. Heart knocking against his rib cage, Andrew closed his eyes and took three deep breaths.

The freckle-armed lady set her purse on the counter. Andrew chanced a glance at the well-worn navy-blue handbag flecked with tiny lacerations and stains. It looked familiar.

Andrew raised his eyes and saw that he was standing next to his hero, his warrior queen: Eudora Penny. His anxiety was replaced with giddy delight. Feigning interest in a rack of *TV Guides*, he inched closer to her six-foot frame.

Eudora Penny collected her change from the cashier, looped

the purse handles over her shoulder, and started away. Andrew, as if hypnotized, abandoned his shopping cart and followed her out of the store. When she stopped at Henry's Vegetable and Flower Stand, Andrew remained outside, hovering over the buckets of fresh flowers like a pollinating honeybee.

Had Andrew abandoned his pursuit of Eudora, he would have made it back home in time to thwart the watery catastrophe, so that the black superintendent wouldn't have entered his apartment to fix the leak and then stayed when he saw the thing he could never forget.

But Andrew continued to shadow Eudora on her morning rounds, debating how and if he should strike up a conversation with her. It had been years since he'd engaged in small talk of any kind. His interaction with people had been limited to his monthly sojourn into Manhattan to conduct business with a decrepit old man known as Abraham the Jeweler.

Once a month Andrew took the train to visit Abraham in his tiny office at the back of his jewelry shop on West 47th Street. Before they got down to business, the two would exchange observations about current events and the weather, but little else, as Abraham fixed the loupe into his right eye to begin examining the pieces Andrew had brought him.

When he was done, Abraham would grunt, remove the loupe, scribble an amount on a piece of paper, and slide it across the desk to Andrew. If Andrew was pleased with the figure, Abraham would place the money into an envelope, hand it over, and send him off with a "Shalom."

245 fell into view, and Andrew realized that his window of opportunity was closing, so he hastened to catch up to Eudora.

Up ahead, the singing cripple rolled toward them. Eudora bounced her head in greeting; Andrew turned his face away, but out of the corner of his eye he saw the old vet make the sign of the cross over his heart and then aim his finger at him.

Now, Eudora was at the door of the building, silver key poised over the lock. Desperate, Andrew called out to her in German. Eudora's head jerked mechanically around as if her mind and body were at odds with the decision to respond.

"Um, yes?"

He saw her eyes then. They weren't a disappointment; in fact, they looked exactly as he had imagined—deep, ocean blue like his own. Andrew panted out a few more words of German.

"I'm sorry," Eudora said, raising her voice, "I don't under-stand. I. Speak. English." She tapped her chest with every word.

Andrew raised a palm. "*Kein problem, tut mir leid, Ihnen die Mühe gemacht zu haben.*"

Her mouth a thin line, Eudora pushed the door open and stepped aside. "After you."

Andrew scuttled past. "*Danke.*"

"Have. A. Good. Day," she squalled, heels clicking on the floor as she hurried to her apartment.

Andrew's feet did not touch the steps; elated as he was, he floated to the second floor. The door to his apartment was as he had left it and so he entered without any misgivings.

When he saw Harlan sitting in the darkness with the riding crop resting in his lap, Andrew didn't try to run or scream for help because he had suspected for some time that his stolen life was steadily inching to a close. Perhaps that's why he'd finally had his up-close-and-personal with Eudora Penny? God wanted him to know that He was as benevolent as the religions claimed.

The years pressed down on Andrew's shoulders, and his spine bent with the weight. He swiped the cap from his head, clumsily rounded the side table, and sat down on the couch across from the black man. The plastic covering crackled faintly beneath his thighs. Outside on the sidewalk, the singing veteran rolled his wheelchair to the building, leaned over, tightened the laces of his brown shoes, then stood up and walked away.

Part XII

Emancipation Day

Chapter 102

For the first time since his mother died, Harlan was glad she was gone. Had she been alive, saved and reborn in Christ's holy blood, what he'd done would have stopped her heart cold.

His father, also deceased, would not have fallen so quickly out of this life; instead, he would have bestowed upon his son a look so thoroughly soaked with disappointment and shame, Harlan would have been smothered to death beneath his gaze.

Either way, death would have been an inevitable outcome.

Harlan supposed it still loomed, even though capital punishment in New York State went out of style with the electrocution of Eddie Lee Mays in '63. But he was more than sure that the state wouldn't hesitate to resurrect old sparky for a black miscreant like himself.

Even with that possibility, Harlan still chose not to run.

He exited 245 Sullivan Place and glanced at the empty wheelchair. He might have wondered about the whereabouts of its owner if he hadn't had his own pressing issues. But he did, and so Harlan set off to enjoy his last hours of freedom.

He stopped first at the playground next door to 245. Sitting on a wooden bench, he removed a flask from his pocket and turned it up to his lips. The expensive Scotch, a Christmas gift from his employer, slipped down his throat as smooth and silky as sin.

Sun warming his face, Harlan remained in the park for an hour observing young mothers pushing their children in the metal swings and coaxing them down the slides.

With the liquor pulsing through his veins, he eventually left the playground and walked the block to Henry's Vegetable and Flower Stand. There, he fingered the talcum-soft petals of black-eyed Susans which Andrew had lingered over earlier that morning.

"Hey, what you doing?"

Harlan looked up to see Henry standing in the doorway of the store.

Henry waved a meaty pink hand at him. "You gonna buy or you gonna sniff the scent away?"

By the time Harlan reached the busy intersection of Empire Boulevard and Nostrand Avenue, he felt as light as a balloon. He stood on the corner near the Chemical Bank and for fifteen full minutes he admired the sky.

A few pedestrians stopped to look, and those motorists waiting for the stoplight to turn green hung their heads out of their windows, straining to catch a glimpse of what Harlan found so wondrous in that summer sky. But they couldn't find anything exceptional about the peach-colored sun or the smattering of white clouds. So they dismissed the man with a shake of their heads and hurried on to their destinations.

Harlan moved along, strolling leisurely down the remaining few blocks that separated the now from what was to come. At the Carvel Ice Cream stand, located just feet away from the police station, he purchased a cup of vanilla ice cream with a double portion of rainbow sprinkles and sat down on a nearby bench to enjoy it.

As Harlan ate, a band of Hasidic boys came running up the street. One kid, a length ahead of the others, bumped against Harlan's knee as he streaked past. Harlan closed his hand protectively over his cup of ice cream and monitored the horseplay until the group—tzitzit and payot fluttering—rounded the corner and vanished.

Chapter 103

Having finished the last of the melted ice cream, Harlan smacked his lips and tossed the pink plastic spoon and paper cup into a nearby garbage can.

He had in his vision the 71st Precinct—a handsome three-story, sand-colored building that straddled the corner of the residential New York Avenue and the commercial thoroughfare of Empire Boulevard.

The building had not always been a police station; in its former life it had once been the grand residence of some wealthy banker, and then later a private school for boys. Now it was more often than not the first checkpoint on a short journey to the penitentiary.

Harlan climbed the marble steps, and pulled back the heavy door. Inside, ceiling fans whirled and creaked. The clickety-click of type-writer keys, the hushed conversations, and the inter-mittent static blasts of walkie-talkie exchanges bounced off the cream-colored walls and echoed in Harlan's ears.

He made his way toward the officer seated behind the receiving desk. Harlan could feel curious eyes crawling over him, picking him apart, attempting to detect if he was friend or foe. Reaching the desk, he reverently removed the tattered gray cap from his head and offered a soft "Good afternoon, sir."

Twenty-six-year-old Daniel McCollum had rolled his eyes when he spotted Harlan coming through the door. He was not fond of Negroes. So it was to his great dismay that upon graduating from the police academy he was promptly assigned to the 71st Precinct in the Crown Heights section of Brooklyn—a neighborhood teeming with Negroes and, almost as bad, Jews.

McCollum was a proud Irish Catholic boy, a third-generation American who wore a gold crucifix around his neck and sported a tattoo of a four-leaf clover on his right bicep and the American flag on his left.

He surveyed Harlan's faded denim overalls stained with blotches of paint and oil that no amount of soap and water would ever clean away. Beneath the overalls, Harlan wore a blue-and-white-striped collared dress shirt, the front of which was speckled with rainbow sprinkles. His shirtsleeves were rolled to the elbows revealing dark, sinewy arms. Harlan was slim-framed and of average height. His woolly hair was cut close to his skull, calling attention to the triangle of gray extending out in a widow's peak. His bushy mustache was streaked silver as were his eyebrows and eyelashes. His face was deeply lined.

"Yeah?" McCollum grunted disinterestedly.

"I'm here to turn myself in."

A stinking cloud of liquor wafted from Harlan's mouth. McCollum frowned, waved the pungent odor away, and asked, "For what?"

"Murder."

Eyebrows arched, McCollum leaned forward. "Murder? Is that so."

"Yes, sir."

McCollum closed the newspaper he'd been reading and folded his arms. "And when did this murder take place?"

"'Round nine thirty or ten."

"Last night?"

"No. This morning."

McCollum glanced at his watch; it was nearly eleven thirty a.m.

"Uh-huh. And where did this murder take place?"

"245 Sullivan Place. Apartment 3C."

Old drunk, McCollum thought. The old, the drunkards, or a combination of both were always wandering into the police station making ludicrous claims about murders, alien abductions, and government conspiracies. McCollum had seen and heard it all. He smirked. "So, um, who exactly was killed?"

"Andrew Mailer."

"And who killed this Andrew Mailer?"

"I did," Harlan stated calmly.

A few days earlier, McCollum had been out on foot patrol when an old woman—a black old woman—walked up to him and declared that she had murdered her husband of forty years.

"How'd you kill him?" McCollum had asked.

"I stabbed him with my knitting needle," she said.

He had accompanied her back to her apartment where the old woman's fifteen-year-old granddaughter—LaCoconut, LaBanana, La-something, McCollum couldn't quite remember—was sprawled on the couch watching television. McCollum had hastily scanned the small apartment before turning to the wide-eyed teenager and asking, "Where's your grandfather?"

The girl frowned, pointed to a framed photograph hanging on the wall, and said, "Him? He's dead. Died before I was born. I think he's buried at Cypress Hills Cemetery."

McCollum shook his head at the memory and gave Harlan a stern look. "You say you did it, huh?"

"Yes, sir."

"How?"

Harlan presented his hands. "With these."

"I see," McCollum said. "And why did you kill him?"

Harlan thought for a moment. "I suppose because it needed to be done," he said sullenly.

McCollum rolled his eyes. "It needed to be done?"

"Yes, sir."

McCollum dropped his hands onto the desk. "What's your name?"

"Harlan. Harlan Elliott, sir."

"How many drinks have you had today, Harlan?"

Harlan shrugged his shoulders. "One or two, I guess."

"Or five of six?" McCollum said.

Harlan remained quiet.

"Yeah, well, Harlan, the New York City Police Department does not have time for jokes."

"But sir, I ain't joking. Andrew Mailer is dead, and I killed—" He stopped short and gave his head a hard shake. "Wait," he stammered, "the thing is, sir, Andrew Mailer ain't his real name. It's a long story." Harlan's eyes glazed over. "It's a very long story. You see, back in Germany—"

McCollum raised his hand. "Germany?"

"Yes, sir."

"What were you doing in Germany?"

Harlan swallowed. "Well, during the war—"

Again McCollum raised his hand, halting the black man's words. The cop thought he understood now. He had two uncles who'd served during World War II. One drink too many and they started to hallucinate that their living rooms were the front lines. "You having a flashback of some kind? You have them often?" McCollum asked, and then answered, "I suppose you do. Do you got any pills for that sorta thing?"

"Sir, I am not having a flashback. If you just let me explain—"

"Can I call someone to come and get you?" McCollum reached for the black phone on his desk. "A wife, kid—"

"No sir, I'm not married. If you just let me—"

"You live alone? Who comes to check on you? A neighbor, nephew—"

"Sir, please!" Harlan bellowed.

The police station fell silent, and Harlan became supremely aware of the rotating ceiling fans slicing through the June heat.

The color drained from McCollum's face; his warm green eyes turned to ice. "You watch your tone, you hear me, old-timer?"

"I-I'm sorry, sir," Harlan whispered.

McCollum glanced over at the two detectives who had abandoned their paperwork in favor of what was happening at the receiving desk. He nodded assuredly at them before turning his attention back to Harlan. "You *better* be sorry," he growled under his breath.

The sound of hurried footsteps echoed from the corridor behind the receiving desk. Within seconds, a tall, stately looking man with a handlebar mustache appeared. He glanced briefly at Harlan before fixing questioning eyes on McCollum. "Is there a problem, officer?"

McCollum straightened his spine. "No, sergeant. No problem. It's just that this man is claiming he killed someone."

The sergeant's eyes darted between McCollum and Harlan. "Have you confirmed his claim, Officer McCollum?"

"Well, um, no, sir. I figured he was lying," he said, and then lowered his voice and leaned toward the sergeant. "For God's sake, he smells like a distillery."

The sergeant remained unflappable. "He give you an address?"

"Yes, sir."

"Well then, dispatch a cruiser over there to check it out."

"Yes, sir," McCollum said, reaching for his walkie-talkie.

The sergeant stepped toward Harlan. "What's your name?"

"Harlan Elliott."

The sergeant pointed at a chair alongside a desk piled high with folders. "You sit there until we confirm your claim," he said, and walked away.

Eyeing Harlan ominously, McCollum barked the address into his walkie-talkie.

Twenty minutes later, a black-and-white police cruiser stopped in front of 245 Sullivan Place. They pressed six of the thirty bells. A woman's voice blared through the intercom system, "Yes?"

"It's the police, buzz us in."

"Who?"

"The police!"

There was a long silence and then the door buzzed open.

The two police officers climbed the stairway to the third floor.

Their sudden appearance startled an old man dressed in a blue bathrobe who was shuffling from the incinerator back to his apartment. He stood staring at them with his mouth agape until one of the officers snapped, "This has nothing to do with you, pops. Go on back into your apartment."

The door leading into apartment 3C at 245 Sullivan Place

was indeed unlocked. Guns drawn, the officers moved cautiously into the apartment. Meow hissed at them from the shadows.

On the couch was a man in repose. Tan slacks and white shirt buttoned clear to the neck. Black leather shoes. His hands were folded majestically across his chest.

One of the officers banged loudly on the wall and yelled, "Hello!"

At the sound, Meow scurried into view, jumped onto Andrew's stomach as if confirming the obvious, and leveled her yellow eyes with those of the officers.

One cop pressed his fingers against Andrew's neck, checking for a pulse. He looked at his partner and shook his head.

The second officer nodded his understanding of the situation and brought his walkie-talkie to his lips. "McCollum?"

"Yeah, what you got?"

"Um, deceased male, approximately seventy years old. I'm no coroner, but from the impressions on his neck, it looks like he was strangled to death."

Chapter 104

McCollum ushered Harlan into one of the three brightly lit interrogation rooms located at the back of the station. He sat him in a black folding chair behind a silver aluminum table which held two ink pens, one lined writing pad, a glass ashtray, and a box-shaped reel-to-reel tape deck.

McCollum exited the room without a word, leaving Harlan alone with his thoughts. Thirty minutes later, Detective Arthur Graham entered carrying two Styrofoam cups filled with steaming coffee. There was a crisp manila folder tucked securely beneath his arm.

The detective was tall, with a gargantuan belly that sagged over the waistband of his trousers. The wide brown-and-red-striped tie he wore was speckled with lint as was his cream-colored shirt, and he stank of Hai Karate cologne and menthol cigarettes.

"Hey, how you doing?" Graham said, setting the cups and folder on the table.

Harlan looked up into the man's unbelievably blue eyes. "Good, I guess, considering the circumstances."

The detective brushed his hand across his trouser leg and presented it to Harlan. "I'm Arthur Graham," he announced with the eagerness of a salesman.

"Harlan Elliott."

Graham's handshake was firm and confident. "Nice to meet

you, Harlan Elliott." He pointed at the Styrofoam cups as he eased his bulk into the empty chair opposite Harlan. "The coffee is black. Sorry, but we're out of cream and sugar."

Harlan reached for the cup, "Black is fine with me. Thank you."

"You're welcome."

Graham took a few sips of coffee. "So, it seems you've got yourself into a bit of a mess, huh, Harlan?"

"Yes, sir, it looks that way."

Graham wagged his hand at Harlan. "My father is sir," he laughed. "Me, I'm just Arthur or Art. You can call me Art. My friends call me Art. We're not friends... well, not yet. But I feel like we could be. So call me Art, okay?"

"Okay, Art."

"Good. Now Harlan... You don't mind if I call you Harlan, do you?"

"Harlan is fine."

"Good! Now, Harlan, murder is a problem. It's not a problem for the dead man, of course. His problems are all over. It's probably gonna be a problem for his family, and it's most certainly gonna be a problem for you. That is, if you are indeed the murderer..." He trailed off, reached for the manila folder, flipped it open, and scanned the pages. Harlan's rap sheet was short. Mostly moving violations and his arrest and conviction in '67. Since then, Harlan hadn't even received a jaywalking citation.

"You have a bit of a history. But nothing violent," Graham muttered. He raised his head and looked Harlan directly in the eye. "It says here you were born in 1917. Is that correct?"

"Yes, sir, it is."

"Art."

"Sorry. Yes, Art. I was born in Macon, Georgia on December 24, 1917."

"Well lookee here," Art clapped his hands against the table, "I was born in 1917 too!"

Harlan nodded.

"We already have something in common," Graham grinned. "I'm fifty-six years old, and you're, well, gonna be fifty-six come December." Again, Harlan nodded.

Graham closed the folder and pushed it aside. His mood turned serious. "Harlan, you understand that if you are responsible for the death of Andrew Mailer—"

"Sir... I mean Art," Harlan interrupted, "there are no ifs, ands, or buts about it, I murdered the bitch."

Graham's eyes stretched. He couldn't remember ever having heard a man refer to another man as a bitch. But this was 1973 and America had put a man on the moon, so it seemed everything and anything were possible these days. He removed the soft pack of Kool cigarettes from the breast pocket of his shirt, shook one free, and offered it to Harlan.

"No thank you."

"Good for you." Graham slipped the cigarette between his lips and lit it. "I've been trying to quit since I started." Eyes squinting against the white smoke, he said, "I want to make sure you understand the consequences of your actions."

"Yes, I do."

"You got any medical problems?"

"None that I know of," Harlan said. "Knees ache some when it rains, that's about it."

"Wife? Kids?"

"Nope."

"Anybody we should call?"

"There's only me."

"Okay. Let's move on, then," Graham said in a relaxed, friendly tone. "Harlan, I'd like you tell me exactly why you killed Andrew Mailer. Can you do that for me?"

"Yes, I can."

The detective leaned back in his chair and scratched his gut. Arthur Graham was a thirty-year veteran of the force. In fact, at the end of that particular June week, he was to be officially retired. As he sat in the precinct interrogating Harlan Elliott, his wife Maggie was at home putting the final touches on his retirement party, which was scheduled to take place that Saturday evening.

The Grahams had recently placed their beautiful split-level Corona, Queens home on the market, and sold or not, in a month Arthur and his wife of twenty-eight years were moving into a two-bedroom beachfront condo in sunny Ft. Myers, Florida.

If Arthur could've had his way, he'd have stayed on the job for another ten years. He loved it. Police work was the one thing he was exceptional at. But he'd promised his wife that 1973 would be it, and Arthur Graham was a man of his word.

He had seen a lot of things in his three decades in law enforcement. He wished he could say that this thing that was currently unfolding before him was the most ludicrous of all, but it wasn't, at least not yet. Technically, he should have been spending his last week filling out paperwork, tying up loose ends, and shooting the breeze with his coworkers. But the paperwork was all done and the loose ends had been tied up weeks ago.

Goodbyes had been said and would be said again at the party.

What Arthur wanted was one last hurrah before handing over his gold badge and revolver. So when Detective Ellis had dropped the file on his desk and said with a wink, "One more for the road?" Arthur figured his prayers had been answered. "Open and shut?" he had asked.

"Yep. The guy is here to confess," Ellis assured him.

It seemed simple enough. *Easy-peezy*, as Arthur's wife would have said.

"I'm ready when you are," the detective prompted when Harlan just sat there staring into his empty Styrofoam cup.

"May I have some more coffee, please?"

Art pressed his palms together. "I think we could both use some more coffee." He left the room and returned with two fresh cups of coffee and a small box of donuts.

"It's cliché, I know."

"What is?" Harlan asked.

"Donuts and cops."

"Oh."

"I got a sweet tooth," Art said as he plucked a powder-covered donut from the box. "Go on," he pressed, jutting his chin at the donuts, "have some."

"No thanks."

"Watching your figure, Harlan?" The detective chuckled before biting into the donut, sending a flurry of white powder onto his chin and tie. He devoured the first donut, then reached for a second and did away with it in two bites. "Okay," he announced, brushing crumbs and powdered sugar from his face and clothing, "that should hold me for a while. Let's get back to business, shall we?"

Harlan nodded.

Art raised a finger. "Wait a minute, I don't want to forget to record this." He reached over and pressed the red lever on the reel-to-reel and cleared his throat. "This is Detective First Class Arthur P. Graham interviewing Harlan Samuel Elliott of Brooklyn, New York, concerning the murder of one Andrew Mailer. Today is June 19, 1973; it is approximately one twenty p.m." He looked at Harlan and smiled. "Do you want to start by telling me how you knew the deceased?"

Harlan stared at the recorder but said nothing.

"Harlan?"

Harlan blinked. "Um, yes. But I want to tell you the whole story so that you'll understand why I did it; why I had no choice."

The smile remained glued to Art's lips. "That's exactly what I want to hear, Harlan—the entire story, from beginning to end."

Chapter 105

The clock on the wall read nine twenty. They'd been at it for eight hours.

Arthur Graham eyed Harlan intensely and then reached over and pressed the lever on the reel-to-reel, halting the whirling spools of tape.

Harlan bowed his head, awaiting his Miranda rights.

Groaning, Art fell back into his chair, scratching the fresh growth of hair sprouting on his cheeks. He'd heard some outlandish stories in his time—tales so tall, they cast shadows. Fiction, fables, rambling yarns that grew more fantastical with each retelling. Yes, Art had heard it all. But as ludicrous as Harlan's story seemed to be, there wasn't a doubt in Art's mind that he was telling the truth. He knew Harlan's story was true because his own precious Maggie, the love of his life, wife and mother of their children, had also been in Buchenwald.

"What was the concentration camp called?"

Harlan repeated the name and Art's spine went rigid. Their stories were identical—the Singing Forest, the beatings, murder by bullet, by hanging... the Bitch of Buchenwald. His wife had a scrapbook containing newspaper clippings of captured Nazi war criminals, all of whom had been living comfortable lives in foreign lands under assumed identities. After being spirited out of Europe by organizations such as the Red Cross and the Vatican, the criminals went on to fund their new lives with art, jewelry, and money they'd stolen from the very people they'd incarcerated and then murdered. Art remembered reading that in the home of one Nazi criminal, they'd found a velvet bag of gold-filled molars, no doubt removed from mouths of Holocaust victims.

Why Ilse Koch had chosen to live her life in America, as a man, as Andrew Mailer, was anyone's guess. Perhaps she thought disguising herself in such a way would ensure she'd never be discovered. But as Harlan said, "You don't forget people who've done bad things to you. She could have worn a monkey suit, and I still would have known it was her."

Art had never thought of Negroes as Holocaust victims or survivors, and while Maggie had never mentioned black prisoners at the camp, it didn't mean that it wasn't so. Art figured the color of a person's skin became insignificant when people were clawing to survive.

Whenever another Nazi war criminal was captured, Art would come home from work to find Maggie standing out on the porch, waiting for him. "We got another one."

Now that Harlan had finished his statement, Art knew there was only one way this thing should go. Sitting forward again, he removed the reels from the machine and unwound the tape until it lay in ribbons between them on the table. After sweeping the tape into his battered attaché case, he said, "Let's go, Harlan."

Unclear as to what was happening, Harlan rose slowly from the chair.

The detective walked to the door, swung it open, and poked his head into the hallway. Without looking at Harlan, he gestured with his hand that he should follow.

Detective and suspect moved casually down the corridor,

past the bathroom and four empty interrogation rooms. At the end of the long hallway was a steel door. Above it, a sign marked Exit.

Harlan's breath caught in his throat.

In the alley behind the police station, beneath the glow of the new moon, Harlan and Art faced each other for the last time.

"I don't know how much time you'll have, maybe an hour, a day, or eternity." The detective pumped his shoulders. "You just never know with these things."

Harlan opened his mouth to speak, but Art shook his head and removed a battered wallet from his back pocket. "I'm not saying you need it, but I am saying you can't go back to your apartment, not for anything—money, clothes, whatever." He pulled a wad of bills from the wallet. "Go on, take it," he said, pushing the money into Harlan's hesitant hand. "It's not much, but it's enough to get a bus ticket out of town and a night or two in a motel."

Harlan closed his fingers around the bills.

The night hummed.

Art thought to shake Harlan's hand; instead, he clutched his shoulder and squeezed. "The world is round, Harlan."

Harlan wasn't sure what the detective meant by that, but he nodded anyway.

"I wish you the best of luck," Art said, and then did offer Harlan his hand.

"Th-thank you, sir."

"Art. My friends call me Art."

"Thank you, Art."

The detective watched Harlan walk away. He watched until the slate-colored night closed its arms around the black man and he was no more. Art removed the crumpled pack of Kools from his shirt pocket, shook out the last cigarette, and lit it. He hadn't considered how he would explain this to his commanding officer, but he was confident that he would come up with a plausible explanation. He'd been doing this job for a very, very long time. He could pull out loopholes and lies as deftly as a magician pulled a rabbit from a top hat. And if that didn't work, he'd call in favors. He had decades' worth of favors.

He had put a lot of bad guys in prison; it felt good to know that his last hurrah was keeping a good guy out. He dropped the cigarette to the ground and crushed it under the sole of his shoe. He couldn't wait to get home to tell Maggie that they'd gotten another one.

Chapter 106

Under a sky clean of stars, Harlan fought not to run, not to turn back or sit down and throw his hands up in surrender. June heat chomping at his neck, heart slamming, eyes stinging with perspiration, he hastened past hand-holding lovers, old people escaping the fever of their apartments, hoodlums hawking nickel bags, tall trees with limbs flung wide like comforting arms.

This freedom felt unreal to Harlan.

Providence?

Yes. Not earned, but inherited, bound to his DNA and passed down the line like his brown eyes. Even though it had cloaked him his entire life, Harlan was hesitant to utter the word. *God...*

The world was open, so where to now?

Back to the city Emma said was the only place she had roots, back to Macon, where he could finally plant himself and flower.

Afterword

Black Victims of the Nazis by Stephen Bourne

Holocaust Memorial Day, held every year on 27 January, was primarily set up to remember the six million Jewish men, women and children who had been murdered by Hitler's Nazi regime in the 1930s and throughout the Second World War. While a great deal of information has been documented and made public about Jewish victims, the Nazi's persecution and killing of other groups is still to be fully researched and documented. It has been estimated that at least another five million 'others' could have perished in Nazi concentration camps and these would have included communists, lesbians, gay men, Jehovah's Witness, gypsies, and people with physical or mental disabilities. According to the United States Holocaust Memorial Museum in Washington D.C., "The fate of black people from 1933 to 1945 in Nazi Germany and in German-occupied territories ranged from isolation to persecution, sterilization, medical experimentation, incarceration, brutality and murder. However, there was no systematic program for their elimination as there was for Jews and other groups."

When Hitler was the ruler of Germany from 1933 to 1945, many Germans of African descent were rounded up by the Gestapo (the German "secret police") and made to "disappear." In 1937 all local authorities in Germany were asked to submit lists of children of African descent. These children were

433

taken from their homes or schools without the consent of their parents and taken to hospitals where they were sterilized. At least four hundred mixed-race children were forcibly sterilized in the Rhineland area alone by the end of 1937.

Some black Germans avoided imprisonment by working as extras in Nazi propaganda films. After America entered the war on 7 December 1941, African American GI's who were captured and made prisoners of war found that they could also avoid internment.

Doris Reiprich, a mixed-race German, has provided a first-hand account of what it was like to be black and living in Nazi Germany. It was a difficult, terrifying time, but Doris remembered the fun they had during the making of the propaganda films: "On our breaks the Africans would get their drums and we'd sing in front of the studios. People would come running from all the productions. They loved to listen. We earned good money, had fun." She adds: "One time about two hundred and fifty black prisoners of war from the United States were brought in because they needed film extras. Those poor fellows were glad to be with us, since they got to eat and play football. We also put money together to buy things for them."

African American jazz musicians who failed, for one reason or another, to escape the Nazi invasion and occupation of Europe, were also imprisoned. Their stories are not well known, neither is the story of John Welch who was born in New York. He was the younger brother of the singer Elisabeth Welch who made London her home in 1933. In 1932, John had travelled to Berlin to study piano. John remained in Germany for twelve years and, at first, studied music and earned a living as a pianist without any trouble. Just before he was arrested by the Nazis shortly after the outbreak of the Second World War, he had nothing but praise for Germany: "Before Hitler came into power, the Negro was treated exceptionally well." It is likely that Welch was 'shielded' in 1930s Germany by his American status, but soon after the outbreak of war he was arrested by the Nazis, accused of being an enemy agent, and incarcerated in a concentration camp. He spent several years in the camp, during which time his health suffered, and the cold weather he was exposed to caused arthritis in his hands which ruined his ability to play the piano. In 1944, John survived his imprisonment by the Nazis when he was repatriated on board the Swedish ship SS *Gripsholm* along with 661 American passengers who had been interned in France and Germany and had been traded by the American government for German prisoners of war. Among them were twelve other African Americans, including one woman.

Bibliography

Stephen Bourne, *Mother Country - Britain's Black Community on the Home Front 1939-45* (The History Press, 2010) (includes a Postscript entitled 'If Hitler Had Invaded Britain')

Clarence Lusane, *Hitler's Black Victims* (Routledge, 2002)

Hans J. Massaquoi, *Destined to Witness - Growing Up Black in Nazi Germany* (Fusion Press, 2001)

May Opitz, Katharina Oguntoye and Dagmar Schultz (editors), *Showing Our Colours - Afro-German Women Speak Out* (Open Letters, 1992)

About the Author

Stephen Bourne is an award-winning historian of black Britain. He has been interviewed in several documentaries, including *Black Divas* (1996) and *Paul Robeson: Here I Stand* (1999). He is the author of *Black in the British Frame: The Black Experience in British Film and Television* (2001), *Elisabeth Welch: Soft Lights and Sweet Music* (Scarecrow, 2005), and *Ethel Waters: Stormy Weather* (Scarecrow, 2007). For *Black Poppies: Britain's Black Community and the Great War* (The History Press, 2014) he received the Southwark Arts Forum Award for Literature.

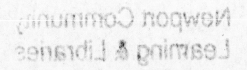

There is no life that does not contribute to history.
　　　　　　—Dorothy West

Abbreviated List of Historical Characters

Louis Armstrong (1901–1971), nicknamed **Satchmo** and **Pops**, was one of the most influential artists in the history of jazz. His career as a trumpeter, composer, and singer spanned the 1920s through the 1960s.

Amiri Baraka (1934–2014), born **LeRoi Jones**, was an African American writer well-known for his political activism and social criticism, displayed through his poetry, drama, fiction, and essays.

Mary Bruce (1900–1995), originally from Chicago, taught dance in New York City for over fifty years. Over the span of her career, Bruce taught students such as Josephine Premice, Ruby Dee, Martina Arroyo, and Marlon Brando; she also offered free lessons to students who couldn't afford them.

Eugene Jacques Bullard (1895–1961) became the first African American military pilot during World War I after working as a boxer in Paris. Bullard eventually became the owner of his own nightclub, L'Escadrille.

Leonard Harper (1899–1943) was a dancer, producer, and choreographer with his own studio in New York City during the Harlem Renaissance. Harper's work spanned a variety of genres, from burlesque to Broadway musicals.

Lucille Nelson Hegamin (1894–1970) was born in Macon, Georgia, and became the second African American blues singer to record. She retired from music in 1934 to pursue a career in nursing.

Ilse Koch (1906–1967), nicknamed the "Bitch of Buchenwald," was one of the first Nazis tried by the US military. She was the wife of Nazi commandant Karl Otto Koch, and was known and feared for her especially sadistic practices toward prisoners.

Milton Mesirow, better known as Mezz Mezzrow (1899–1972), was a Jewish American jazz clarinetist and saxophonist. Over the course of his career, he played with and recorded many African American musicians, including Louis Armstrong.

Bessie Smith (1894–1937), known as the "Empress of the Blues," was the most popular and influential female blues singer of her era.

Mike Todd (1909–1958) was an American theater and film producer best known for his Academy Award–winning movie, *Around the World in 80 Days*. He was married to Elizabeth Taylor before his death in a plane crash.

Ancestral Cast of Characters

Aubrey Gill (1885–1966)

Ethel Louise Gill (1884–1951)

Gwendolyn Dorothy Gill (1922–1997)

Irene Mae Gill (1908–1940)

Aubrey I. McFadden (1941–1992; depicted in this novel as **Bre**)

Harold Isaac McFadden (1917–1958; depicted in this novel as **Harlan Elliott**)

Robert L. McFadden (1942–2005; depicted in this novel as **Bobby**)

Chappo Robinson (1887–1951; depicted in this novel as **Emma Robinson**)

Louisa Anne Robinson (1845–?)

Reverend Tenant M. Robinson (1844–1895), pastor of the First Baptist Church of Macon, Georgia, was born into slavery near Charleston, South Carolina.

Sons of Reverend and Mrs. Robinson: **Seth H. Adams, James Henry Robinson, and John Edward Robinson**.

Darlene Smith (unknown)

John Smith (1927–2002) was an African American musician and a driver for the Safety Cab Company. His arrest on July 12, 1967, sparked a five-day riot in Newark, New Jersey.

Mary Emma "Mayremma" Smith (1911–1976)

I thank you all for blessing this book with your spirits.

Gratitude

I am indebted to my cousins Cherrol Bernard, Lionel Crichlow, and family for providing me a room of my own to live, recharge, figure out my life, and finish this book. Thanks also to cousins Carlo and Quovardis Lawrence; aunt Laura Taylor and cousin Kathleen Taylor; longtime sister-friends Cicely Peace, Andrea Knight, Cecilia Brown, Dawn Nedd, Marsha Cooper, Darlene Harden, Alicia McMillan; and brothers from other mothers Walter Fuller, Derek Rice, Dwight Brown, and Kenneth Wallace—without whom I would have certainly come undone.

I am grateful to Anita Abbott, Gloria Hardy, and Davette P. Reid for loving and caring for me like a daughter.

Vanessa Pettiford and B.J. Bernstein—y'all are some phenomenal women, amazing inspirations, and I'm happy to call you my friends! I am particularly blessed to call these writer-warrior-women not just my friends, but also my family: Terry McMillan, Elizabeth Nunez, Donna Hill, and Margaret Johnson-Hodge.

I'd like to acknowledge the support and generosity of Jackson Taylor, director of the Writer's Foundry MFA Program in Creative Writing at St. Joseph's College in Brooklyn, of which I am a proud alum.

I would also like to thank the El Gouna Writer's Residency Program, the Serenbe Artist in Residence Program, and the Kalani Artist in Residence Program for providing me with the gift of time, space, and quiet.

I remain eternally grateful for Johnny Temple, Johanna Ingalls, and Ibrahim Ahmad of Akashic Books, who came together to rescue me from obscurity. I extend that gratitude to Aaron Petrovich, Susannah Lawrence, and Katie Martinez, who round out the Akashic Books family.

The research for this novel consisted primarily of these published works:

Germany's Black Holocaust: 1890–1945 by Firpo W. Carr
The Buchenwald Report, translated by David A Hackett
Harlem in Montmartre: A Paris Jazz Story between the Great Wars by William A. Shack
Near Black by Baz Dreisinger
Americans in Paris: Life and Death under the Nazi Occupation by Charles Glass
Really the Blues by Mezz Mezzrow and Bernard Wolfe
No Cause for Indictment by Ronald Porambo

While writing this novel I tried to respect history and geography, except when I chose not to.

Back in 2011 I was invited to spend one month at a writers-in- residence program in El Gouna, Egypt. I had a book idea, but no money to get there. A friend suggested that I launch a fundraising campaign, and "Eat, Sleep, Write: El Gouna" was born.

Over a three-month period I received donations from writers, readers, and people who didn't know me from Adam— but wanted to help. Eventually, I met my fundraising goals and set out on a life- changing adventure. Four years later, that journey came to a close when I typed the final word of this novel.

I'm so appreciative of everyone who contributed to my campaign. No amount was too small—I received every cent with the utmost gratitude.

I did, however, want to acknowledge those individuals (friends, family, and strangers) who gave amounts that increased the pot exponentially: Vanessa Pettiford, Chava Frias, Laura Taylor, Tracy Jackson, Tananarive Due, Beverly Jenkins, Donna Woodard, Marcia Wilson, Tuesday L. Cooper, Edward May, Alice Fay Duncan, Ernessa T. Carter, Pascalle Goddard, Melanie McKie, Amy Moore, Kola Boof, Persia Walker, Brigette Major, Gayle Lin, Linda Duggins, Marie Brown, Pamela Walker-Williams, Juan Gaddis, Maria Jackson, Victoria Christopher Murray, Crystal Bobb-Semple, Marsha Cooper, Pricilla C. Johnson, Rebekkah Mulholland, and Trice Hickman.

I would also like to express my deep appreciation and gratitude to my family, friends, all of the book clubs, book bloggers, and readers who have supported me all of these years!

Valerie Beaudrault, without your kindness and guidance, *The Book of Harlan* might not have come to fruition. You have my whole heart!

Finally, I want to acknowledge the tremendous debt I owe in this and everything else I have written to the lives of my ancestors.

Light,

About the Author

Raya

BERNICE L. McFADDEN is the author of nine critically acclaimed novels including Sugar, Loving Donovan, Nowhere Is a Place, The Warmest December, Gathering of Waters (a New York Times Editors' Choice and one of the 100 Notable Books of 2012), Glorious, and The Book of Harlan (winner of a 2017 American Book Award and the NAACP Image Award for Outstanding Literary Work, Fiction). She is a four-time Hurston/Wright Legacy Award finalist, as well as the recipient of three awards from the BCALA.